The Price of Fame

Tales from Grace Chapel Inn®

The Price of Fame

CAROLYNE AARSEN

New York, New York

The Price of Fame

ISBN-13: 978-0-8249-4730-9

Published by Guideposts
16 East 34ᵗʰ Street
New York, New York 10016
www.guidepostsbooks.com

Distributed by Ideals Publications, a Guideposts company
535 Metroplex Drive, Suite 250
Nashville, Tennessee 37211

Guideposts, *Ideals*, and *Tales from Grace Chapel Inn* are registered trademarks of Guideposts.

The characters and events in this book are fictional, and any resemblance to actual persons or events is coincidental.

Library of Congress Cataloging-in-Publication Data

Aarsen, Carolyne.
  The price of fame / Carolyne Aarsen.
    p. cm. — (Tales from Grace Chapel Inn)
  ISBN 978-0-8249-4730-9
  1. Bed and breakfast accommodations—Fiction. 2. City and town life—Fiction. 3. Pennsylvania—Fiction. 4. Sisters—Fiction. 5. Motion picture industry—Fiction. I. Title.
  PR9199.3.A14P75 2008
  813'.54—dc22

                                        2007039193

Cover and interior design by Marisa Jackson
Cover art by Deborah Chabrian
Typeset by Sue Murray

Printed and bound in the United States of America

10   9   8   7   6   5   4   3   2   1

GRACE CHAPEL INN

A place where one can be
refreshed and encouraged,
a place of hope and healing,
a place where God is at home.

Chapter One

"Evening red and morning gray are sure signs of a fine day." Vera Humbert looked up at the clouds that obscured the morning sun. "At least that's what Fred told me when you called about going for our walk."

Alice Howard tucked her shoulders up against a chill wind as she and Vera came around the corner from Village Road, turning onto Hill Street. A few cars passed them, their occupants waving at the familiar figures of Alice and her friend, the town's beloved fifth-grade teacher. Though they didn't go out as often as she would like, Alice appreciated the exercise when she and Vera could squeeze a walk into their schedules. As a nurse, Alice needed to keep fit. She delegated much of the heavier work, but she wanted to be an example to the younger nurses who seemed to think that anyone over sixty, as Alice was by two years, was only capable of charting and consulting with the doctors.

"It's still early. So there's time for your husband's prediction to come true." Alice shivered as she skirted a pile of hard snow that encroached on the sidewalk in front of the

Methodist Church. "I hope he's right about that. Sunshine on a winter day always makes Acorn Hill look like a Christmas card, even at the end of January."

"Fred prefers to use hard evidence when he's predicting the weather, but that little piece of folklore he does agree with. At least that's what he told Carlene Moss when she interviewed him a couple of days ago for the *Acorn Nutshell*."

"She's doing an article on him for the paper? He must be pleased."

Vera nodded, her cheeks dimpling as she grinned. "He was really quite flattered. Though he used all the weather talk to tease me about not having predicted the tornado that must have gone through our house." She shrugged. "It wasn't that bad, but he does like to rib me about my house-keeping. I say clean enough is clean enough."

"You don't have time for much more. Teaching keeps you too busy to be concerned with housework," Alice said. "I'm very thankful that we bring in help now and again at the inn to stay on top of cleaning, though we are okay now. We don't have any reservations for the next few weeks."

After their father, Rev. Daniel Howard, passed away, Alice and her sisters, Louise and Jane, renovated their childhood home and started Grace Chapel Inn. They named it after the church where their father had preached most of his life.

"Anyhow, I hope Fred is wrong about his other prediction."

"And what's that?"

"He said we're in for more snow and colder weather." Vera tucked her yellow and red woolen scarf more snugly around her neck.

Alice shivered again. "I hope not. I was hoping to do something outdoors in the next couple of weeks with my ANGELs. Those girls always get a bit restless in January and February. The excitement of Christmas is over for them and it seems there's not much to look forward to. I am trying to come up with an activity that I can use to reward them for the food baskets they made up at Christmastime." Alice smiled at the memory. "They got such a kick out of keeping it a secret so the recipients wouldn't know." Alice was the leader of a group of girls, ages ten to fourteen, known as the ANGELs. The meaning of the acronym was as much of a secret as were their good deeds.

"If you come up with an idea, let me know," Vera said. "I could use something to distract my students as well."

"Good morning, ladies," a voice called out behind them. "A bit cool for an early morning walk, isn't it?"

Alice glanced back to see Viola Reed marching down the sidewalk toward them, her arms wrapped tightly around her waist as if anchoring her calf-length coat. Over her ample shoulders was draped a bright turquoise and gold scarf, a cheery touch on a dreary morning.

"Good morning Viola," Alice said with a smile. "You're up bright and early."

"I have a lot of work to do at the bookstore this morning. Inventory and restocking." Viola gave a shudder that made her bifocals flash. Viola owned and operated Nine Lives Bookstore, and though she seemed to complain about how busy it kept her, the truth was that she lived and breathed her work. "Could you tell Louise that I can't have her over this evening after all? I simply won't have time."

Alice's older sister Louise and Viola were good friends, though, or perhaps because, they were both strong-minded. "I will let her know. By the way, I really enjoyed that last book you recommended to me."

"I'm so glad you did. I was hoping you could be lured away from the mysteries you seem to enjoy so much. If only I could convince a few more people in this town to pick up other books . . ." Viola pulled her mouth tight as a drawstring purse and let the sentence hang, giving a you-know-what-I-mean shrug.

Alice stifled her chuckle, turning it into a gentle smile. "There are so many other ways to be entertained."

"Like movies for instance. I'm not sure I entirely approve of Nia Komonos carrying all those DVDs and videos in the library." She sniffed her disfavor. "I thought as a librarian she would have more respect for the written word and would not be seduced by the empty-minded twaddle that Hollywood is force-feeding this generation. Movies and television. The death of reading and intelligence." She gave another shudder and was about to say more when the bells of the Methodist Church rang the half hour. She glanced at her own watch as if to verify the accuracy of the church's timekeeping. "Gracious, I better get going. Lovely to see you ladies. Enjoy your walk." And she was gone in a swirl of coat and scarf.

Vera laughed as they crossed Acorn Avenue in Viola's wake. "Does the word opinionated ever come to mind when you think of Viola Reed?"

"Frequently. Though she has a good heart," Alice said with a smile. She inhaled slowly as she passed the Good Apple Bakery, catching a teasing scent of baking bread. Luckily her younger sister Jane had served breakfast before Alice left for her walk. Otherwise Alice would have been even more tempted by the mouthwatering smells wafting from the bakery.

Jane had been up very early that morning, trying out new recipes to serve at their bed and breakfast. During the quiet time that January and February usually brought to the inn, Jane tried her baking experiments on her willing subjects: Alice, Louise and their dear aunt Ethel. Ethel lived in the carriage house behind the inn and was usually available as a taster.

Alice welcomed the slower season when many people seemed content to stay at home. In addition to running the inn, she worked part-time at the hospital, Louise taught piano and Jane continued to develop her chocolate and her jewelry-crafting businesses, do her painting, plan her garden, and involve herself in whatever new project she got excited about.

Sometimes Alice got tired thinking of all the extra things Jane took on. It seemed that her sister was always up for a new challenge, a new idea.

"I love this time of day," Vera said. "It's as if we have the town all to ourselves. I have to confess that at this time of the year I sometimes suffer from the January blahs."

The rattling roar of a diesel motor caught Alice's attention, and she looked down the quiet street in time to see a large black pickup truck park across from the Coffee Shop. The truck stood high off the ground and had four doors on an extended cab.

The doors opened and four people stepped out. One of them stayed by the truck, stamping his feet and shivering. A tall, thin woman with spiky red hair and a pale complexion, carrying a clipboard in her gloved hands, followed the other two men down the street.

"Well-maintained Victorian architecture, with some

vague Furness leanings," the shorter, plumper man said loudly, as if the people with him were ten feet away instead of two. "Pictures, Randall." He snapped his fingers at the tall young man beside him without even looking at him.

A car slowed as it passed the group; the driver looked puzzled at the people gathered in the middle of the street, then drove on.

Alice could understand the driver's staring. Though the streets of Acorn Hill were quiet this early in the morning, residents didn't generally stroll down the middle of them.

The man by the truck got back in and followed the other three as they walked farther down Hill Street. He parked in front of Craig Tracy's florist shop, Wild Things, where the others got in. The driver left the engine of the truck running, and the clattering noise overpowered the quiet of the morning.

"What a noisy vehicle." Vera frowned as she looked back at the truck. "It looks like the kind construction crews use. Though these people don't look anything like the construction workers who come into our hardware store."

"And speaking of your hardware store, here we are," Alice said as they came to the corner of Chapel Road and Hill Street. Fred and Vera Humbert's store was right across from them. The lights were on inside. It looked like José, Fred's helper, was there early getting the store ready to open.

"I enjoyed our walk as usual, Vera," Alice said. "I hope you have a good day with your students."

"I hope so too. Say hello to your sisters." Vera crossed the street and Alice continued up Chapel Road to the inn. She hurried her steps around to the back of the house, eager to get home to a cup of hot tea before she went to work.

Her footsteps echoed hollowly on the wooden steps. She smiled in anticipation, and opened the kitchen door to see her two favorite people frowning at each other.

"But we serve the public." Jane tucked a wayward strand of dark hair behind her ear. She pushed aside a gardening catalog and leaned her elbows on the butcher-block counter separating her from her sister. "That's what it means to be an innkeeper." Her long ponytail bobbed as she nodded her head.

"I don't think that we must make ourselves busier this time of the year." Louise folded the napkin that she had finished ironing and laid it on the neat pile beside her. The lights of the kitchen burnished the silver of her hair and enhanced the blue of her eyes. "I'm looking forward to the quiet of this season." Louise looked up as Alice closed the door behind her. "Hello, my dear. How was your walk?"

"Cold, but lovely," Alice said, glancing from Louise to Jane as she took off her coat. The sisters generally got along very well, but there was the occasional moment when Louise and Jane bumped heads. Louise tended to mother Jane, a holdover from their youth. Madeleine Howard, their mother, had died giving birth to Jane, so Louise at age fifteen and Alice at twelve had taken the responsibility of Jane's care from babyhood on. Because of that, there were times when Louise forgot that Jane was a mature woman whose life had taught her hard lessons.

Jane turned around and leaned back against the counter, her arms crossed over her brightly colored apron in a defensive gesture.

"Am I sensing tension in our happy home?" Alice asked. She rubbed her chilled hands together, then poured herself a cup of tea from the pot sitting to one side of the stove.

"Not tension." Jane's dark eyes flicked to Louise. "Louie and I are simply encountering a divergence of opinions. I was throwing out some ideas for a project that could keep us a little busier during the winter and bring in some extra income. I was talking with Craig Tracy, and he said that he's learned that a steady cash flow is the way to steady profits."

"One would think that you are kept busy enough with all your own pet projects." Louise shook her head as she laid another napkin on the ironing board. "It's not necessary to fill every minute of every day. You have come up with a new idea almost every day this week. "

"But Louise, if I may quote your favorite author, C. S. Lewis says, 'Aim at heaven and you will get earth thrown in. Aim at earth and you get neither.' It's good to try new things. Don't you think we could set our sights a little higher?"

"I sincerely doubt that Lewis was referring to the operation of bed and breakfasts when he wrote that," Louise said dryly. "And if we set our sights any higher, I will need a new optical prescription."

"If we don't move, we stagnate."

"What is the idea of the day?" Alice asked, hoping to distract the sisters and at the same time give Jane a listening ear.

Jane turned to Alice. "I was thinking that Grace Chapel Inn could sponsor a traveling food festival."

"In winter," Louise said, "it's far too cold to have an outdoor festival."

Alice felt a momentary shiver at the thought. She sat down at the kitchen table, and Wendell, their gray tabby cat, jumped onto her lap and curled up with the easy assumption that cats have of a welcoming host. Alice held her teacup with one hand and stroked Wendell's soft fur with the other. The cat's purr gave her the assurance that at least one of the residents of Grace Chapel Inn was completely content.

"It doesn't have to be outside." Jane's hands danced in the air as she spoke. "I was thinking of calling it 'A Taste of the County.' If we got all the eating establishments in Acorn

Hill, Potterston and the surrounding towns to get together, we could have people travel from here to various restaurants in the area. We could add some advertising for local businesses, maybe work in a craft show. What do you think?"

Alice waited before she spoke. Like Louise, she enjoyed the slower pace of this time of year, yet she sensed that Jane was very excited about the prospect of starting something new. "It sounds interesting, but I agree with Louise. It would be a lot of work."

Jane wrinkled her nose, then with a shrug, turned back to her catalogues.

"We certainly can use the rest, Jane," Louise said softly, her voice taking on a gentler tone. "You were saying the other day how much you enjoyed having the time to try new recipes before serving them to our guests."

Jane nodded and closed the catalog. "You're right. It was just an idea, an expanding of my culinary horizons." She gave Alice and Louise a quick smile, as if to show them that there were no hard feelings.

Yet as Alice went upstairs to change into her nurse's uniform, she wondered if Jane wasn't feeling stifled by her older sisters.

A few moments later, Louise had the baby grand piano open

and the parlor ready for her newest student, Tabitha Harke. She did not like taking students in the morning before school. She and her sisters were usually busy with guests at that time, but Jane and Alice assured her that it wouldn't be a problem once a week, particularly now when rooms were not booked. The twelve-year-old had called herself and begged Louise to take her on the one morning a week that school started a half an hour later.

When the girl and her mother arrived, Louise felt her heart sink. Tabitha slouched into the room, looking at neither Louise nor her mother. She wore her long brown hair pulled back in a tight ponytail. Her pale face held no expression. Donita Harke, tall and thin with obviously dyed blonde hair, did not look any more enthusiastic than her daughter did.

Louise smiled and welcomed them both, wondering if she had misjudged Tabitha's enthusiasm.

She gestured to the piano. "We should start with what you know."

"Do you mind if I wait outside?" Mrs. Harke said, gesturing with her thumb over her shoulder. "I don't want to distract you."

"That's fine. There are some magazines on the table in the living room."

Mrs. Harke shook her head. "I'll just go for a walk. Be back in a half an hour."

Louise watched her go, puzzled by her attitude. Most parents were quite involved in their children's lessons. Turning to Tabitha, Louise said, "Your mother tells me that you're at a grade-six level in your piano lessons."

Tabitha shook her head. "Grade seven."

"I see." Louise shuffled through her books and laid out what she thought Tabitha should be doing. "I would like to start with these, just so that I know how much your previous teacher has done and what I can do for you. If you want to warm up, you can play a few scales."

Tabitha nodded, curled her fingers a few times, then frowned at the music. "These are way too easy," she said with a note of disdain in her voice.

"Could you try this then?" Louise put another book in front of her. Tabitha deliberately turned to the *Toccata in D Minor* by Paradies, a grade-seven piece.

Tabitha quickly ran through a few scales, and then started playing.

Tabitha's fingers effortlessly flew over the keys, translating the notes into pure and clear music that made Louise think of her deceased husband. Eliot would have been pleased to hear the piano that he had given Louise played so well.

She gave Tabitha another piece, a very technical one by Haydn, to check the girl's range. Into the tenth bar, Tabitha's fingers faltered and she hit a few wrong notes.

The girl stopped, clenched her fists in anger and started again. After a few more false notes, Tabitha was about to soldier on when Louise gently put her hands over Tabitha's.

"That's all right, my dear. This is not a test. It's just as important for me to know what you cannot play as what you can. You've done very, very well." She smiled at Tabitha who was staring down at her fingers as if they had betrayed her.

"I can do better than this, you know." Tabitha looked up and Louise was surprised to see the fire in the girl's dark brown eyes. "I haven't had lessons for six months. I can do way better."

"I'm sure you can," Louise said gently.

"When we lived in New York, I had a really good music teacher. Then my dad lost his job and we had to move to this little place because my dad's friend found him a job here. Only my mom said it's just for a few months." Tabitha blinked, then looked away. "I can't take that much time away from my lessons or I won't be able to do what I want."

"And what do you want?" Louise asked softly.

"I want to be a concert pianist." Tabitha looked up at Louise and the fire was back in her eyes. "It's what I want more than anything. My teacher in New York took me to a concert at Carnegie Hall once, and I knew from that moment that's what I wanted to do." She sighed. "My mom didn't think we could find a very good teacher in this town. . . ." Her voice trailed off as if she realized what she was saying.

"I'm sorry. I bet you're a good teacher. I mean, I was told you were."

Louise rested her hand lightly on Tabitha's shoulder. "I'm not offended." She sat down beside the girl. "If it gives you any consolation, I have a degree from a music conservatory in Philadelphia and have taught piano most of my adult life. A number of my students have gone on to great things."

Tabitha's expression brightened. "Did any of them become concert pianists?"

"One, Maggie Landau, is now touring Europe. Another is playing for the Philadelphia Philharmonic. I wasn't the one that brought them to that point in their careers, but I was one of the steps along the way."

"My mom says I'm wasting my time. My dad thinks I'm going to be disappointed."

Louise smiled, intrigued by the reversal of situations. Usually it was the parents who pushed the children.

"As C. S. Lewis says, 'We are what we believe we are.' If you believe you can do something and you are willing to make the sacrifices necessary, it can happen."

"So how does that happen?"

"First we concentrate on the next thirty minutes,"

Louise gave Tabitha a quick smile and opened the lesson book she had taken out, "and we go from there."

Jane flipped through the seed catalog, occasionally glancing up at the television sitting on a shelf close to the table. She stopped at the gourds section in the catalog and marked a couple of interesting-looking varieties. They always made unusual decorations in the fall.

Jane had to smile at her own plans. It was January and she was making plans for the summer and fall at the same time. No wonder people said that time flew. It was so often helped along.

She looked out the window and shivered at the sight of the gray clouds and wind-blown leafless trees.

"Next up, an addition to our winter line-up, our new cooking show hosted by Debbie Mandrusiak, live from New York City."

The words of the television announcer caught Jane's attention and, reaching for the remote, she turned up the volume. A few minutes later she saw the familiar face of an old friend beaming out at her from the TV screen. Debbie had lost weight, she had added tasteful highlights to her blonde hair, but it was definitely the same Debbie.

Well, well, Jane thought sitting back as she watched

Debbie introduce herself and explain what she would
be doing.

Debbie was an old friend and, at one time, a fellow waitress. They worked together while they were in art school in
California. Back then, Debbie had often spoken of going to
cooking school and learning to do things right. It looked as
if she had done more than that.

A sharp knock on the kitchen door heralded the arrival
of Jane's aunt Ethel, who bustled into the kitchen without
waiting for a response. Ethel's short red hair provided an
interesting contrast to the pink and orange coat that she
held closed with one hand.

"Hello, Jane. Where are your sisters?" She glanced up at
the television just as Jane reached for the remote to mute
the sound. "What are you watching?"

"Alice had to work an early shift at the hospital, and
Louise is busy with one of her music students. I was watching an old friend on television."

Ethel's eyes popped. "You know someone on television?"

"I guess I do," Jane said.

"Well, I can't wait to pass that on to Florence," Ethel
said, referring to her sometimes friend Florence Simpson,
whose contrary personality made for a rocky relationship.
"Just the other day she was bragging about a niece of hers
who was on some soap opera. Only a walk-on part, but to

hear her talk you would think she was a famous movie star."
Ethel brightened. "Is this woman very famous?"

"I don't think so. Apparently this is a pilot program for
a new cooking show from New York." Jane glanced at the
television, watching Debbie smiling, chopping and display-
ing her work while chatting about what she was doing. "I
still can't believe it. Debbie has her own television show."
Jane couldn't keep the wistful note out of her voice.

"You could have your own show too, you know," Ethel
said, her tone defensive. "You could do an even better job
than that Debbie."

Dear Aunt Ethel, Jane thought. *Always quick to defend her nieces.*

Ethel was their late father's half sister, and she often
stopped by to see what was going on, what guests were staying, and to pass on information or glean some that she could
spread elsewhere.

"Well, I have to confess I'm a bit jealous," Jane said as she
noticed the variety of appliances that Debbie had to work
with and the small army of helpers she had to get things
ready, prepare sauces, and clean up behind her. What a treat
to just be able to create without the tedium of all the prep
work or the tidying afterward.

"I bet she doesn't bake as well as you do," Ethel said.

Her aunt loved sweets and no one was more appreciative
of Jane's January experiments than Ethel was. Jane pulled out

a covered container full of her latest experiment. As she arranged the squares on a clear glass platter, her artist's eye tried to see what they might look like under the lights in a television studio or on the pages of a cookbook. On what color plate would they look best? What garnish could she use to bring out the subtle swirl of cream cheese and chocolate that she had spread over the top of the chocolate pecan squares? White chocolate swirls and halved strawberries still connected by the leaves at the top? Maybe raspberries?

She set a plate and a dessert fork on the table in front of her enthusiastic aunt.

"And what are you up to, Aunt Ethel?"

"I've just finished repotting a plant and decided that I needed another one for the smaller pot." Ethel put two bars on her plate. "I thought I could try an African violet. I don't usually have much luck with them, but Craig Tracy over at Wild Things told me that he just got a shipment of some new plants that were virtually indestructible. Though I don't know about that. Plants are very fragile things." Ethel quickly finished off one square and started on the next one.

"All they need is a little bit of regular care," Jane said. "Just like cats."

"I suppose. Though cats let you know loud and clear if they're hungry. Plants just sit there and wilt, and by the time you find out, it's too late. If I could get a talking plant, I might have a bit better luck." Ethel placed her fork on her plate with a satisfied sigh. "You've outdone yourself, Jane. I'm sure your guests will gobble these down. When you get some guests. You don't have any right now, do you? You know you won't make any money if the inn is empty."

Jane just nodded, glancing once more at the television. A commercial was on. "That's okay. Alice and Louise don't mind the rest."

"Well, I better get going," Ethel said, getting up slowly. "I want to catch Craig as soon as he opens his shop. Though I'm going to have to be mighty careful about bringing home any plant I buy. It's very cold outside today. Maybe I'll ask Lloyd to come and pick me up." Ethel was referring to Lloyd Tynan, the mayor of Acorn Hill and her steady beau.

Ethel glanced up at the television once more. "So you know that woman. My goodness, Jane, a television personality. You'll have to get in touch with her. Who knows what she could do for you? Maybe you could be on her show and then I really would have something to tell Florence."

"Maybe I could." Jane said, smiling at her aunt as she left.

Chapter Two

*J*ane looked around her tidy kitchen and sighed. Alice was at work and Louise, finished with the music lesson, was in the parlor choosing songs for Sunday's church service. Jane was bored. She had energy to burn and ideas aplenty, but for now no outlet for either.

She decided to walk to the Coffee Shop. The exercise would do her good, and the restaurant was always a cozy place for conversation.

When she arrived there, however, the only customers were four unfamiliar people in one corner. A woman and two of the three men were huddled over the cups of coffee, making notes. The fourth, a young man whose long hair was pulled back in a ponytail, sat back, his arms folded over his chest, looking uninterested.

"Good morning Jane." Hope Collins poured Jane a cup of coffee and flashed a smile. "Will you have something with your coffee?"

"A cranberry orange muffin would be just right," Jane said, rubbing her chilled hands together.

"Could I tempt Madame with a latté? Or a cappuccino?" Hope said with an arch smile.

"You have a cappuccino machine?"

Hope's smile turned into a grimace. "I wish we did. Maybe we'll get one when June figures the Coffee Shop is making enough money." June Carter was the owner of the Coffee Shop and a smart businesswoman.

"A couple of those city people in the corner were asking for one of those fancy coffee drinks," Hope added.

Jane frowned. "City people?"

Hope leaned forward, her eyes gleaming as she played with a strand of blonde hair. Hope's hair color changed with her mood. The previous week she had been a flirty redhead, three weeks before a reserved brunette. "I've heard from our other customers that they were in town early this morning, taking pictures and walking around. They said that they were from Los Angeles." Hope leaned a little closer. "They act so mysterious, like they are up to something." She straightened and glanced at the group again. "I better see if they want anything else, then I'll be back with your muffin."

The people in the corner sat back when Hope approached. The oldest-looking man in the group turned over his notepad. They didn't look at her, but allowed Hope to fill their cups. As soon as she left, they went back to their huddle, talking quietly.

Hope returned with Jane's muffin and gave her a discreet wink.

Shortly thereafter, the strangers got up and walked past Jane. As they did, the young man with the ponytail glanced over and gave her a quick smile, but the other three simply ignored her.

Mysterious indeed.

⌒

"I'm sure you and your sisters appreciate this respite from guests at the inn." Rev. Kenneth Thompson took from Louise the list of songs she had chosen and leaned back in his office chair. He scanned the selection, nodding at the choices. "Looks fine, Louise. I'm always thankful that you can find the time to do this for me." His hazel eyes, set off by his dark hair, were warm in the late afternoon light. His smile softened his patrician features, which, when his expression was serious, could make him look austere.

"I appreciate the fact that we can work together. God has given us each our talents, and I would like to think that mine can be used to beautify the service."

"And they do."

Louise fiddled with the neck chain holding her glasses. She opened her mouth to speak, then changed her mind.

She wondered if she should confide in Kenneth. She still

didn't feel right about her offhand dismissal of Jane's idea. Maybe she shouldn't involve him. It wasn't a large problem.

Kenneth looked up at her, a faint smile curving his lips. "If I may be so bold, Louise, I get the feeling that something else is on your mind."

"You're not being bold, Kenneth, you are being a friend." Louise frowned a moment, smoothing a faint wrinkle out of her dark brown wool skirt, as she tried to decide what to tell him. "It's nothing serious, merely sisters trying to reconcile being business partners and seeking different directions for our enterprise."

"Let me guess. You and Jane are having a difference of opinion." Kenneth steepled his fingers and smiled at Louise over the top of them, the signet ring on his finger catching the light.

"You are astute and you are right. This morning Jane was speaking of putting on some type of food festival to bring in new clientele during the off months. Both Alice and I were less than enthusiastic about the idea. Jane seemed resigned to our reaction, but at the same time . . ."

"At the same time . . ." Kenneth encouraged her to go on.

"I wonder if there are moments when she feels professionally stifled here. She's always coming up with new ideas. I wonder if she misses her work at the Blue Fish Grille in San Francisco. She was well known there.

Here she's simply a baker and cook in a small inn in a small town."

"Yes, but Louise, you were very successful in your field. You moved in vastly different circles than you do now, yet I know you are content here."

"I am. But Jane is only fifty and I wonder if she regrets moving here. It seems that every day this week she has come up with yet another idea for doing more work at the inn. I have dismissed each one, but then this morning she made a comment that I can't put out of my head. She said something about expanding her culinary horizons."

"Do you think she's feeling resentful?"

"No, I don't think so." Louise shook her head, buttoning up her soft wool cardigan. "Though one would think that she would appreciate a break from cooking and baking for a while." Louise frowned, still unable to understand Jane's love of cooking. Eliot, her deceased husband, used to say that Louise was made for other pursuits than frying and boiling. As a result, though he was a college professor, Eliot did a lot of the cooking for them and their only child, Cynthia. When he passed on, Cynthia was already pursuing a publishing career in Boston, and so Louise had to cook only for herself. Jane and Alice had always teased her, saying that this was how she maintained her slim figure. Cooking was not Louise's favorite chore, nor one of her talents.

A light rap at the door announced a visitor. "Yoo-hoo," Ethel called out just as the pastor said, "Come in."

"Oh, Louise. I was hoping I might find you here." Ethel flashed Kenneth a smile as she adjusted the tilt of her pink knit hat. "Sorry to disturb you, but Louise needs to come to the inn right now. I met some people on my way back from Wild Things. Craig told me he had some plants that I couldn't kill. That tease. They were fake plants, but they sure did look real. Made of silk, but I don't know if I could have fake plants in my house. Wouldn't seem right somehow."

"And why do I need to come to the inn?" Louise gently encouraged her talkative aunt.

"Oh yes. I'm sorry. I do tend to go on sometimes, but I'm a bit flustered about Craig's little trick. I'm not that bad with plants. At least I'm better with plants than Louise is with cooking." Ethel flashed Louise a guileless smile. "No offense, Louise, but we know that's true."

"The inn?"

Ethel blinked, then nodded. "Oh yes, well, there is a group of people there who want to book rooms. I met them in town after I was at Craig's. They were coming out of the Coffee Shop, and I overheard them say that they needed a place to stay, and I said that the inn was empty."

Louise held her smile but she felt a touch of regret. They had no reservations for the next two weeks and secretly she had hoped that it would stay that way. She knew her aunt meant well, but there were times that she wished Ethel would mind her own business. Of course that would be expecting too much from her dear aunt. Ethel thrived on involving herself in other people's doings. As far as Ethel was concerned, there was no business in Acorn Hill that couldn't use a little minding from her.

"I will be there directly," she said to her aunt. She turned back to Kenneth, who got up from his desk. "If you need anything else, please call. Oh yes, Jane asked me to invite you to supper tonight."

"If you have guests, I don't want to intrude."

Louise waved away his objections. "Your presence is never an intrusion. As you know, we generally only offer our guests breakfast, and I have no reason to believe that we will do anything differently for this group. Please, come. We would enjoy your company."

Kenneth's smile as he ushered them out of his office told her that he would enjoy their company as well.

"I should tell you something, though," Ethel said to Louise as they strode briskly down the walk to the inn. "I didn't realize it at the moment, but after I invited those people to stay and they got into their huge truck . . ." Ethel shook her head. "It was a monster. Loud and noisy. I think I should talk to Lloyd about allowing vehicles like that in town. Surely as mayor he could put a stop to that. But as they got into it, I noticed that one of the men had a ponytail. A ponytail, Louise."

"Well, we shall just have to tolerate that," Louise reminded her aunt.

"I'm sorry if I caused a problem. I knew that you didn't have guests and that you want the inn to be profitable. Goodness knows Daniel would be very proud of what his daughters have done with the family home." Ethel paused to nod a quick hello to a young mother walking her two rosy-cheeked children down the sidewalk in front of Grace Chapel. "But all the same, I think I might have been a bit rash in this case."

"We will deal with things as they come, then." Louise held the door open for her aunt and followed her in.

A young man leaned against the wall of the front hall, his arms crossed over his coat. Louise could see a ponytail hanging over his shoulder. The ponytail bothered her almost as much as the fact that he was leaning against the lovely cream and gold wallpaper. She hoped that his coat was not wet and that his hair was clean.

A thin, angular woman with short, spiky red hair was examining the beech coatrack with interest. Two men, one short and heavyset, the other tall and slender, stood in the living room whispering.

"Good afternoon and welcome to Grace Chapel

Inn," Louise said, hoping she sounded friendly. "How may I help you?"

The woman looked up at Louise with a quick nod. "We'd like some rooms." She angled her chin at Ethel, who stood fidgeting beside Louise. "She recommended this place, and so here we are."

"We have four rooms available," Louise said flipping open the reservation book on the reception desk and stifling a sigh of regret at the empty page that would now be filled. "How long will you be with us?"

The woman glanced back at the two men in the living room. "Trey? How long do you want to stay here?"

"About four, maybe five days." The short heavyset man named Trey bustled over to the desk, frowning as he spoke. "The reception is lousy here."

Louise frowned at him, surprised at his rudeness. "I am sorry. I was not aware that you were here. We weren't expecting guests this week."

"No. No." Trey held up his cellular phone. "Reception. Cell phone. Not great."

"Ah, I understand. I have heard that complaint from others of our guests. Though I have to say that most of them come to appreciate the quiet."

Trey shuddered at that. "Can't imagine. You have Internet here?"

"Yes. Though we are unable to supply a connection to our guests." Louise uncapped the fountain pen that Jane had set out for them to use. Jane had taken a notion to use their father's fountain pens at the reception desk. Each time she used one, Louise thought of Daniel and how, as a little girl, she loved to watch him in his study writing his sermons with one of the pens.

"Is that a Parker 51?" The young man pushed himself away from the wall, shedding his bored look.

Louise looked at the pen she held. It was a lovely fawn color, burnished to a sheen from being held in her father's capable fingers. "I'm not sure. It belonged to my late father."

"Vacumatic or Aerometric?"

For all Louise knew, the boy was speaking French. "I'm sorry?" she said, shrugging her shoulders.

"My brother wrote all his sermons by hand, using a fountain pen," Ethel put in, pleased to be a part of the discussion. "He took very good care of them. We still have the one I gave him for a wedding gift."

"There is more than one?" the young man asked.

Trey cleared his throat as if in warning, and with a shrug the young man returned to the wall.

"Sorry about that. Randall gets a bit carried away," the older man, Trey, said with a wry grin directed at the young man. "Has all kinds of strange hobbies and interests. Fountain pens. Snowboarding. Hockey. He's Canadian."

Trey said the last word as if Randall's nationality explained away his eclectic interests.

Just then the third man started coughing, covering his mouth with his hand.

"You okay, Dan?" Trey asked, frowning at his assistant.

"Do you have a tissue?" he asked between coughs.

"Aunt Ethel, can you please get Dan something to drink?" Louise asked. She took a box of tissues from behind the reception desk and offered it to the man.

Dan gave Louise a grateful look, his dark eyes watering. When Ethel returned with a glass of water, his coughing was under control.

"It's nothing, I'm sure," he said, taking the glass from Ethel. He took a quick drink. "Thank you," he said gratefully.

In a few minutes Louise had checked in Trey Atkinson, Dan Foremost, Randall Marquette and Lynette Teskey. "So you come from California," she said as she led them up the stairs to the second floor. "Our weather must be a bit of an adjustment for you."

"Shocker more like," Trey said as he led the entourage. "You aren't that far from the Mason-Dixon Line. I figured on warmer weather."

"This is an unusually cold winter, and if our local weather forecaster is correct, we're not out of this cold snap yet." Louise stopped in front of the Sunset Room. "I thought you could stay here," she said to Trey, opening the door for him.

"Nice." Trey walked into the room, stopped in the center and turned in a full circle. "Good lighting. Warm colors." He motioned to Randall. "Photos, sonny."

Randall obediently stepped into the room and pulled out what looked like a digital camera and snapped a few pictures.

"My sister Jane would be pleased to see your appreciation," Louise said. "She developed the concept for this room." Louise had to smile as she glanced around the terra-cotta-colored room with its impressionist prints on the walls. Each of the sisters had decided how one of the rooms was decorated and named. She escorted Lynette to the Sunrise Room, the room Alice had planned. The walls of this room were pale blue with cream and yellow accent colors that gave the room a fresh, early-morning feel. Lynette ran her hand over the blue, yellow and white patchwork quilt on the bed. "This is lovely," she said.

Louise brought Dan to the Garden Room, also planned by Jane, with its varying shades of green, which left the Symphony Room for Randall, who was still snapping pictures for his boss. Louise wondered what the young man would think of the room, her creation, with its climbing rose pattern wallpaper. He didn't seem the flowery type.

Louise left the guests to unpack and returned to the first floor, where Ethel waited at the bottom of the stairs. "Well, I better go," Ethel said. "Lloyd promised to treat me to a late lunch and I have to get ready." She pulled on her hat and was off.

Chapter Three

*C*ongratulations on your cooking show. I wish you every success and God's blessing on your endeavor." Jane stopped, read over on the computer screen what she had written and wondered what her friend Debbie would think of the last comment. Though they had never discussed anything more than a shared interest in cooking and baking, Jane was sure Debbie was not religious.

She gave a little sigh, wondering if she would get the chance to tell Debbie what had happened in her faith life since returning to Acorn Hill. This e-mail might be a beginning.

It hadn't taken her very long to find out how to reach Debbie, once she found the television show's Web site. She had wanted to send a card, but the only contact she was given was an e-mail address.

Jane hit send, waited for the message to go through, then logged off. She left the office and walked into her father's study. She had other correspondence to deal with, letters to former inn guests and to old friends that she preferred to write by hand.

She pulled out her stationery and spent the next half hour at her father's desk. Working here gave her a connection to Daniel Howard that she had missed the last few years of his life while she was living and working in California.

Though Jane had written to her father often, she hadn't come home as often as she might have. When she discovered that her father had kept all the letters she had ever written him, she realized that he had understood her absence, and she found peace.

Now, sitting in Daniel's study and using his pen made her feel closer to him. Sometimes she would spend her devotional time in here, feeling that her prayers were mingling with the many her father had raised in this very room.

When she finished the last letter, she slipped it in an envelope and addressed it. Just as she put the pen down, she saw a figure hovering in the doorway. It was one of their guests, the man who had smiled at her in the Coffee Shop.

"Hello, I'm Jane Howard. What can I do for you?" she asked, setting aside the envelope.

"I'm Randall Marquette. Just waiting for my boss Trey to finish talking on the phone before we head out." He glanced at the pen in her hand. "Your sister Louise said that your father has a collection of fountain pens. That must be one of them."

"Father was more of a gatherer than collector," Jane said with a melancholy smile as she thought of Daniel Howard. "And he gathered a number of pens over the years. I think the rest of them are all in this box." Jane got up from the desk and opened a small mahogany display box that sat on one corner of the desk. "Our Aunt Ethel bought this box for him to store his pens."

"Ethel. That's the old lady with the funny hat who told us about this place?"

Jane tried not to bristle at the way he spoke of her aunt. There was no denying that Ethel was a character, but she did not like his tone.

"Sorry," Randall said, obviously sensing her annoyance. "I didn't mean to be insulting." The smile that accompanied his apology was charming and Jane forgave him. "Can I have a look at the pens?"

Jane opened the box and turned it toward him.

Randall bent over the box. "Neat, another Parker 51. Hey, and an older Waterman." Randall lifted a questioning brow toward Jane. "Mind if I have a closer look?"

"Please. Go ahead." Jane sat back, surprised. The inn had many antique pieces of furniture in which guests had expressed interest, but never before had anyone asked about her father's fountain pens.

He picked up one and turned it over in his hand.

"Wow. I haven't seen one of these in ages. A coin-filler Waterman."

"Pardon me?"

Randall looked up at her and grinned. "Sorry. They called it that because they used a coin to fill it. See this little slot in the barrel of the pen?" He held it up so Jane could see it better. "You had to put a coin in there to put pressure on a plate that depressed the ink sac inside. You put the pen in the ink and when you let go, the release of pressure would draw ink into the pen."

Jane looked closer at the pen, trying to imagine her father pressing a coin in the slot, dipping it in his inkpot and filling it up. The thought made her smile.

"Have you had these looked over recently?" Randall asked.

Jane shook her head. "We don't use these. On occasion I use the one Alice bought him just before he died. It's the only one that takes cartridges. Most of the rest are unusable. The one at the main desk is the best one. I like to use it from time to time for sentimental reasons. Just to remind me of Father, I guess."

"It sounds as if he was a special guy."

"Yes, he was. He was a loving father, a dedicated servant of the Lord and a respected man in the community."

Randall popped the cap off the pen and twisted the

barrel open. "These are a nice memory of your father and if you want to keep them, I would suggest a good overhaul. There's dried ink on the nib and I bet the rubber parts are starting to rot."

"That doesn't sound good," Jane said.

Randall smiled as he put the pen back together again. "The pens have rubber diaphragms that help control ink flow. When they fail, the ink comes out irregularly or in sudden spurts." He gently laid the pen back in the case.

"I'm surprised that a young man like you would be interested in fountain pens."

"I have a number of them at home. They're great to write with. I feel more involved with my writing when I'm using a fountain pen."

"You are a writer?" She shouldn't have been surprised. In spite of his blasé attitude, she sensed a watchfulness about him, as if he was taking mental notes.

He nodded, picking up another pen and twisting off the cap. "When I have the time. Unfortunately, my work gives me inspiration but not much time."

Jane was tempted to ask him what business he had in town, but because he hadn't volunteered, she felt it would be rude to inquire.

"My father was a minister. He wrote a lot of sermons sitting at this desk," Jane said, running her fingers lightly over the worn top. "I remember his saying that you don't find time to write. You make time."

"I've heard that one too." Randall tipped her a crooked smile. "If I didn't need to make payments on a candy-apple-red Ford Mustang, work wouldn't be such a priority and I might be able to make time." He glanced at his watch. "And if I don't get ready to leave, I'm going to lose that work."

"And, by extension, your candy-apple-red Ford Mustang," Jane added.

"And my Mustang. Thanks for letting me look at the pens."

"You're welcome."

He shoved his hands in his pockets and slouched out of the office.

Jane closed the box of pens and made her own mental note to ask Fred Humbert if he knew anything about fixing fountain pens. As Randall said, it would be a shame to neglect them.

As she dug through the desk for stamps, Randall's associates came down the stairs, stopping in the hallway.

"So far, we're on schedule," she heard one of them say. "This is what we need to do today."

One of them started coughing again.

"You okay, Dan?" a man asked.

"I don't feel too great. Lousy cold weather."

"You want to stay behind?"

"No. Let's go."

"Okay." The man who spoke first, lowered his voice, talking in a subdued murmur as they left. Jane held back until she heard the front door close and then left the study.

Jane watched through the window as they walked to their truck and drove away. *What business did they have in Acorn Hill?*

⌒

"Just take a sip of water for now." Alice urged her young patient. She held the little girl's head up so that she could drink. Her fever had not broken in spite of the medication the doctor had prescribed. All they could do now was keep her hydrated by way of her intravenous tube and keep her comfortable.

"I'm cold," she said, shivering though her skin was hot and clammy to the touch. "And my throat is sore and my head hurts."

"Drink this water and that will help." Alice smiled her encouragement and thankfully the little girl managed a few sips before she groaned in pain and turned to her side, still shivering.

Alice stroked her blonde hair back from her face,

then straightened as one of the other nurses bustled into the room.

"Thanks so much." The nurse clipped a new cover on the thermometer and inserted it into the little girl's ear. "I've about run my feet off here."

"I have to warn you," Alice said, "I just got a call from admitting. We're getting another patient."

"What's the diagnosis?"

"Another severe case of the flu. Older man. Dehydrated and weak. High temperature and elevated blood pressure. We'll put him across the hall."

"I thought we were done with flu season," the nurse said, marking the girl's temperature on the chart. She threw the cover in the trash. "I don't know why it had to make one last stand here."

"This too will pass." Alice gave her a quick smile, but before she left, she paused and prayed for the little girl's healing. In her job as a nurse, she knew that this was as much a part of her calling as the skills she had learned and acquired over her career.

She stepped into the hallway just in time to meet an orderly pushing a gurney with an older man lying on it. "Newest patient up from Admitting," he said, handing Alice the chart.

"We'll put him in this room." Alice led the way, glancing

at the clock above the nurse's station as she passed. The next shift was due to arrive in ten minutes and she was behind on her charting. Looked like she was going to have to stay late to catch up. She had better phone Jane to let her know.

⌒

"Mystery Supper," Jane announced as she flailed at a chicken breast with a meat mallet. "How about that?"

"I sincerely hope you are not discussing the evening's menu." Louise replied, setting the plates out on the table in the kitchen.

Jane had been surprisingly upbeat since this morning. Louise had been worried that she would be upset with her sisters for vetoing her plans for a winter food festival.

Jane stopped and looked up at Louise, her expression puzzled, then she laughed. "No. Tonight, in honor of our cold weather, we are eating food from the south of France. Chicken with bell peppers and olives, Provençal salad and asparagus with roasted red pepper velvet."

"It definitely sounds warm." Louise folded the soft red and gold paisley napkins and laid them beside the plates. This evening she decided to use plain white china to contrast with the red cloth that Jane had selected.

"A Mystery Supper is something we could try here in Acorn Hill. It's an idea I had this afternoon as I was surfing the Net." Jane slid the chicken breasts into a hot pan coated with olive oil and waited for the initial sizzling to die down. The heavenly scent of herbs wafted through the kitchen as Jane continued with her suggestion. "The guests could guess the ingredients of the dish I was serving. Whoever was closest would win a prize."

"I don't think eating something called a 'Mystery Supper' sounds too appealing to our guests."

"Maybe you're right," Jane conceded.

A quick rap at the door preceded Ethel's "Yoo-hoo," and Louise was thankful that the conversation was interrupted.

Ethel stepped inside and paused, sniffing the air expectantly. "You haven't had dinner yet?"

"Alice got held up at the hospital," Louise said. "Pastor Ken is coming for dinner. We had to call him about the delay." She waited a moment to see what Ethel would do, but her aunt's bright eyes flitted from the already set table to the bowls arranged around Jane on the counter.

Jane caught Louise's dry look and winked. "Would you like to join us, Aunt Ethel?"

"Well, now, if Kenneth is coming for dinner, I don't want to impose."

"You won't be," Jane said. "As you can see, this is a casual, eat-in-the-kitchen evening."

"Then I'll stay. I had planned to skip dinner after having had a big lunch with Lloyd, but I am a bit hungry."

With a wry smile, Louise went to the cupboard to pull out another place setting. Ethel generally needed very little encouragement to stay for supper and they were glad to have her.

"I brought along the *Acorn Nutshell*. Have you had a chance to look at it? Carlene did a piece on Fred Humbert and how he's our local weather prognosticator." Ethel pulled the paper out of her bag and laid it out on the countertop. "No matter what Punxsutawney Phil predicts, Fred says that we are going to have more than six more weeks of winter and that it's going to be colder than usual for the next two."

Louise repressed a shiver as she rearranged the plates she had laid out. "This weather is entirely too cold for my liking as it is."

"Fred is going to Punxsutawney himself, he says. Though I think that could be a waste of time. I doubt Fred would even be able to see Phil. My goodness, all you would have to do is check your own shadow." Ethel stopped and sniffed, following her nose to the stove where Jane was busy. "What is that wonderful smell? I'm sure whatever it is, it will be delicious. You are such a good cook, Jane. I wish I had half your talent. I bet that lady on television isn't as good as you."

"I'm sure she is better. That's why she has a television show in New York and I'm cooking in Acorn Hill," Jane said with a smile as she removed the chicken from the skillet and added the peppers, sending another wave of delicious smells flowing through the kitchen.

Louise thought that she heard a note of regret in Jane's voice, but she pushed her concerns aside, telling herself that she was being overly sensitive.

Twenty minutes later, Alice arrived, and shortly after her, Pastor Ken. After they had gathered around the table Louise asked, "Ken, will you say grace?"

"Gladly." His eyes met each of theirs before he lowered his head in prayer. "Dear Lord, we want to thank You for friends and neighbors and food we can share that You have blessed us with. For our community, may we always seek to build each other up and help each other in our service to You. Help us to use our talents to Your edification and in the service of others. Help us to encourage others to use their talents to the best of their ability. Bless this food unto our bodies. May we be nourished and strengthened by it. Amen."

Louise kept her head down a moment, reviewing Kenneth's words. She thought of Jane and her talents. Were she and Alice holding back their sister?

"Louie, don't tell me you need to pray a little longer for

your food than the rest of us," Jane said, nudging her sister. "It's not that exotic."

Louise smiled at her sister's teasing use of her nickname. "It smells delicious and looks even more wonderful." Indeed, the salad with its black olives, red onions, white mushrooms and butter lettuce looked festive against the red and black bowl that Jane had bought from a potter this summer. The matching platter was also perfect for the chicken and red peppers.

"Well, I must say, Jane, you can make even a simple meal look beautiful," Ethel said. "As I said this morning, I think you could do a cooking show as easily as your friend Debbie." Ethel turned to Kenneth. "Did you know that Jane has a friend who has her own television show? A celebrity." She looked around the table, beaming. "Isn't that interesting? I think it would be so interesting to know someone famous. Or to be famous. As if that will ever happen in a town like Acorn Hill. Though to listen to Florence go on, you'd think her niece was going to be nominated for an Oscar."

"I think it's the Emmys for television," Jane said.

"I can't see anything famous happening here. As Lloyd always says, 'Acorn Hill has a life of its own away from the outside world' . . ."

"'And that's the way we like it,'" Jane joined in on the last portion of the mayor's now well-known slogan.

Ethel frowned at the sisters. "Well I have to say, there has been some talk about the people who are staying here, Louise." Ethel helped herself to salad and passed the bowl on. "It seems your guests from California did an awful lot of driving around today and asked a lot of questions. They were down at Sylvia's Buttons. Sylvia Songer said they were looking around, taking pictures—after they asked, of course. They stopped at the Acorn Hill Antiques and asked the Holzmanns a bunch of questions. I even saw them walking around the chapel," Ethel said with a frown toward Kenneth as though he should have stopped them.

"Those people are our guests, Aunt Ethel," Alice put in gently.

"Yes, I know, but I sure wonder what they are up to and so do a lot of other people in town."

"I don't think that we need to concern ourselves with their activities. They are entitled to their privacy." Louise tempered her comment with a smile, and the conversation moved on to other topics.

"How is work going at the hospital?" Kenneth asked Alice. "I understand you were delayed coming home this evening."

"I'm concerned. This lingering influenza season is similar to last year's." She spoke of how busy they were and how it didn't look as though things were going to slow down for a while. "I don't know how much help I'm going to be around here," she said. "I might have to cover a few extra shifts at the hospital if any of the nurses get sick."

Louise assured her that they would manage. "After all, Jane seems to have enough energy for the both of us," she said.

Jane shook her finger at her sister. "Laugh now. Remember what happened when we started our afternoon teas. We don't do them often, but when we do, they are very popular. I thought we could maybe work something into January and February that would make people want to come out here during those months."

"What kind of things?" Ethel asked. "You don't want to compete with the Coffee Shop or Zachary's. What could you offer that they don't?"

"Actually it doesn't have to be a food thing," Jane replied. "We could offer some kind of craft retreat. I could give a class in jewelry-making. The students could work in the dining room during the day."

"You are certainly artistic enough," Ethel said, "but wouldn't that make a mess to clean up?"

Jane just shrugged away the comment. "Even better, how about we add a hot tub and sauna and we could offer relaxation retreats during the winter? A sort of post-Christmas-blahs treatment."

"And where would we put these accoutrements?" Louise asked.

"Accoutrements." Jane laughed and shook her finger at Louise. "Have you been reading your thesaurus again?"

"A hot tub sounds lovely," Ethel said with a sigh, "though I can't imagine sitting in one when it's this cold outside."

"That's precisely when they are the nicest," Jane said.

The conversation moved to other topics. Louise talked about Tabitha and the drive the girl had. Alice mentioned her plans for the ANGELs group, and Kenneth talked about an outreach project he wanted to start at the church.

When supper was finished, Kenneth offered to help Jane with the dishes, and Jane shooed everyone else off to the living room with their tea and decaf.

As they were sitting and chatting, the front door opened, announcing the return of their guests. Louise got up to welcome them and to offer them some coffee.

Randall merely shrugged his narrow shoulders and slouched upstairs. Louise guessed that was a rather rude way of saying no. Dan declined politely and retreated upstairs, coughing as he went. The poor man did not sound healthy at all. Louise wondered if he was coming down with the flu. She hoped not. Sick guests were generally not happy guests, and the illness could spread.

Lynette took off her long black woolen cape. Underneath that, she had on a bright blue-and-gold-patterned knit sweater that looked as if it had come from South America. She stabbed her fingers through her hair. "I'd love a cup of coffee," Lynette said. "How about you, Trey?"

Trey was looking around, squinting up at the lights, turning in a half circle, his pudgy arms crossed over his chest. "This entryway has some intriguing lighting," he said, nodding. "Interesting how the shadows fall in the evening as opposed to the morning." He snapped his fingers, then frowned. "Where is that boy when I need him?"

"Randall is upstairs," Lynette said with a touch of asperity in her voice. "I think he's a little tired of you bossing him around."

"I'm his boss. Bossing is what I'm paid to do," snapped Trey. He glowered at Louise as if it was all her fault that there was dissension in his ranks. "I'm going to bed."

Louise raised her eyebrows in mock surprise and said to Lynette, "I will get your coffee."

"That's okay," Lynette said, following her toward the kitchen. "I can get it myself."

They arrived in the room just as Kenneth was rolling down the sleeves of his white shirt. He glanced up, nodding politely at Lynette.

"Thanks for dinner, Jane. It was, as usual, delicious," he said with a smile for Jane. "You make sure you get some rest, now. Louise, thanks again. Tell Alice I said good-bye. I should get back to the chapel. I have a few things to go over on my sermon for Sunday."

"You're a minister?" Lynette asked, staring at him.

Kenneth nodded, a half-smile teasing his mouth. "For a number of years now."

Lynette shook her head, her eyes still on Kenneth.

The mother in her made Louise want to nudge Lynette and remind her that staring was impolite.

As Kenneth left the kitchen, Lynette turned to Louise. "Is he married?" Lynette asked. "Or is that not allowed?"

"He's a widower," Louise said.

"Oh, poor fellow. That's too bad," Lynette said distractedly. A thought seemed to come to her. "He should probably remarry. That man is way too good-looking to be unmarried and a minister," Lynette said with a lingering sigh. She sat down at the kitchen table and took a sip of coffee. "He could be a leading man in a movie."

Louise bit her lip, avoiding looking at Jane. Though both were aware of Kenneth's good looks, they had never heard anyone sighing over him.

"Does he preach at that church by the inn here?"

"Every Sunday," Louise assured her.

"I'll be there," Lynette said with another sigh. "In the front row."

"I hope there are other reasons to attend our worship

service," Louise said, unable to keep the slightly ironic tone out of her voice.

Lynette glanced sidelong at her, frowning. "Why do you go?"

"It's pretty simple actually. To worship God with His people, to recognize our need for grace and forgiveness." Louise knew that she was preaching, but for this woman to go to church only to see a man was one of the saddest things she had ever heard.

Lynette shrugged. "And what's wrong with wanting to look at the preacher?"

"He's a minister, a servant of the Lord," Jane put in, and though her sister was smiling, Louise knew from the tone of her voice that Jane wasn't happy with the way Lynette was talking about her friend. "He's not a movie star."

"He sure could be." Lynette flashed Louise a smile, seemingly oblivious to what the sisters were trying to say.

"Not Kenneth," Louise said with conviction. "He is very dedicated to his calling. The lure of fame would not entice him."

Lynette laughed. "You might be surprised what people will do for fame and fortune. Wave the right amount of money in front of their faces and things change really quick." She looked down at her coffee, the steam wreathing around her face as her expression became serious. She bit her lip and then, without looking at either Louise or Jane, excused herself and walked rapidly out of the kitchen.

"The plot thickens," Jane said. "She doesn't seem like a happy person and neither does Trey."

"That is the impression I have as well." Louise thought of Trey and Dan. "More than ever we will need to remember the message of the plaque on our front door."

A PLACE WHERE ONE CAN BE REFRESHED AND ENCOURAGED. A PLACE OF HOPE AND HEALING. A PLACE WHERE GOD IS AT HOME. Jane recited the words softly, then smiled at her sister. "We will have to pray that we can find a way to give these guests more than just beds and physical nourishment."

Chapter Four

*M*iss Howard, did you come up with an idea for our fun activity?" Sissy Matthews asked Alice as the girl carefully pasted another picture on her box.

Alice and her ANGELs were working on their newest charitable project, craft boxes for hospitalized children. Each girl had brought an appropriate box from home and a supply of old magazines. Using magazine photos and paste, they were decorating the boxes that they would later fill with crayons, stickers and a pad of paper. The girls were excited about the project, and as they worked, a friendly rivalry developed as each girl tried to make her box the prettiest.

"I had hoped that we could do something outside, but it is too cold for any of my ideas."

Sarah Roberts shivered. "My mom says this is one of the coldest winters she can remember."

"Mrs. Humbert told her class that her husband said we're going to have a cold February too," Ashley Moore put in. "And we're going to get more snow."

"We could make snowmen," Sissy said.

"Too bad we can't do a hayride," Ashley said with a grin. "I love horses."

"Big surprise," teased one of the girls. "I saw your bedroom. It's full of horse posters."

"Not completely full of horse pictures," said Sissy. "I saw one wall had a poster of Josh Kerrigen."

"Who is Josh Kerrigen?" Alice asked.

Seven pairs of eyes turned to her, wide with surprise.

"Miss Howard, you don't know Josh Kerrigen?" Sarah sounded shocked. "He was on *A Better Place* and now is the star of *Why Not?* He is so cute. Haven't you seen those shows?"

"I'm sorry, I haven't," Alice said with a grin. "I don't watch much television."

"When I go for my music lessons from Mrs. Smith," Sissy said, "I noticed that they only have a small television in the kitchen and it's never on."

"How old is this Josh Kerrigen?" Alice asked.

"I read that he'll be seventeen in July. He doesn't live with his mom and dad but already has his own apartment and owns three cars," Sarah said shaking her head. "The magazine said he's a millionaire."

"That poor boy," Alice said. "That's far too young to have so much money."

"I wish I could have that much money," Ashley said with a long-suffering sigh. "Then I could buy my own horse."

"Money doesn't make a person happy," Alice said. "Jesus told us not to lay up treasures on earth because they will disappear and rot. Our treasure should be in heaven. Jesus told us that because we can spend too much time trying to grab what we can here on earth, we neglect the true treasure He gave us when He took our punishment for our sins. Anything else is just shadows and dust."

Although the girls nodded to indicate that they knew what she was saying, Alice could see that they had their reservations about how unhappy rich and famous Josh Kerrigen was.

♰

Alice sniffed appreciatively as she came down the stairs, the wonderful fragrance wafting from the kitchen telling her that Jane was busy preparing breakfast for their guests. Louise was at the reception desk, frowning at a piece of paper.

"Good morning, Louise. You're at the books early."

Louise looked over the lenses of her wire-rimmed glasses. "Good morning, Alice." She held the paper out to her sister. "Did Jane say anything about this to you?"

Alice skimmed the paper, which was an e-mail to Jane from someone named Debbie Mandrusiak offering Jane a position on a cooking show. "I don't understand."

"Jane was reading it when I came downstairs this morning. She looked troubled, so I asked her what was wrong. She asked me to read this letter when I had time, then she went directly to the kitchen." Louise lowered her glasses, letting them hang from the fine gold chain anchored to the earpieces.

Alice put the letter back on the desk, an uneasy feeling curling around her stomach. "You seem concerned. Did you get the impression she's considering it?"

"If she's not, why did she give me the letter to read?" Louise picked up a pen and fiddled with it, then laid it down, her movements distracted.

"Maybe she wants some advice?"

Louise shook her head, then looked around the corner. Water was running in the kitchen. Jane was still busy. "What advice can I give her? This is an offer to be on a nationally syndicated cooking show. Jane is such a talented cook. I sometimes wonder if her talents are not being wasted here in Acorn Hill."

Alice didn't want to believe that Jane would even consider the opportunity. She was so thankful the three sisters were together again after their long separation.

Louise and Jane had both left Acorn Hill to follow their various dreams. Louise went off to college, married, had a daughter and pursued a career in music in Philadelphia. When Jane won a scholarship to art school in

San Francisco, she moved to the West Coast. There she discovered a passion for cooking and, through hard work and innovation, had become head chef at a well-known restaurant. She had married a fellow chef, but his jealousy of her success eventually led to the breakup of their marriage. After graduating from a Philadelphia nursing school, Alice returned to Acorn Hill and lived with their father. Alice loved running the inn as a joint effort with her sisters and had assumed that both Louise and Jane felt the same.

Louise turned back to Alice and sighed. "We shall just have to wait and see what she decides. I don't want to get in her way if this is what she wants to do. This sounds like an excellent opportunity and I want to make sure she doesn't feel that we are holding her back."

"She seems happy here," Alice said.

"I think that she is, and yet, when I think of her busyness, her restless desire to fill her time, some of the comments she has been dropping into conversations . . ."

Louise let the sentence trail off in a most unLouise-like way, which showed Alice how troubled Louise was.

"I wonder if she feels constrained by us. She is younger and has more energy. Some of the ideas she has come up with. . . ." Louise shook her head, yet smiled. "I want the best for her. I want her to be happy and fulfilled."

Alice reached over and gave her sister a quick hug. "I know you do, Louise. We will just have to wait and see what Jane decides, and pray for her and for her decision."

Louise returned the hug, though somewhat awkwardly. She adjusted her glasses and straightened her dove-gray sweater. "I have a few more minutes of work here, then I will come and help get ready for our guests."

"I'll be in the kitchen," Alice said to Louise, who only nodded.

"Good morning, Jane," Alice said, bustling into the kitchen as if everything was just fine, determined not to jump to conclusions.

Jane looked up from the croissants she was setting out on a wire rack to cool. "Good morning yourself." Jane spoke quietly and did not give Alice her usual smile.

Alice took out the cutlery, trying not to look as if she was watching Jane, which she was.

Jane usually moved through the kitchen full of energy and vigor doing two or three things at one time, but this morning she seemed listless. She pulled out a basket from the cupboard and carefully laid a napkin in it.

"Breakfast is just about ready, Alice," Jane said, sounding a bit hoarse. "Could you set the table?"

"You look tired," Alice said, concerned.

"I think I may be coming down with a cold. I have a

headache and my throat is a bit sore. It will go away." She gave Alice an apologetic smile. "I may have stayed up too late last night surfing the Net."

And reading e-mail from friends, Alice thought.

Alice heard footsteps on the stairs and quickly set the cutlery on a tray and added the plates and cups. For now, they had guests to feed.

"C'mon, Randall. Get a move on. Light's changing already," Alice heard Trey call up the stairs. She felt sorry for the young man. Trey was quite short with him.

She quickly finished setting the table, taking a moment to make sure that the cutlery was aligned properly with the plates. Jane always maintained that the table setting was almost as important as the food.

Trey strode into the dining room and looked impatiently around, his beefy hands on his hips. "I'm the first one here?"

"Yes. We'll be ready in a moment," Alice said with a smile. "I hope you had a good sleep."

"It's as quiet as the grave in this town." He shrugged. "But then a sleepy town is what we're looking for." He stopped, as if he had said too much. He pulled out his cell phone and started punching in numbers.

"I'll be right back," Alice said, feeling dismissed. She returned to the kitchen with the empty tray just in time to see Jane holding her head between her hands.

"Jane, what's wrong?"

Jane forced a smile. "I'm fine. Just that headache." She drew in a long breath and walked to the sink to run some cold water. "It's making me feel a little dizzy."

Alice came to her sister's side and put a hand on her forehead. She felt warm, but not enough to be concerned. "Maybe it's the heat of the kitchen."

"Then maybe I should get out."

Alice's heart skipped a beat. "What are you talking about?"

"You know the saying, 'If you can't stand the heat, get out of the kitchen'?" Jane gave her a weak smile, then before Alice could reply, said, "The croissants and the apple dumplings are ready. I made up a fruit plate and put out some muffins. I have a raspberry and chocolate sauce that goes with the croissants that I have to put in a bowl yet." Jane stopped, put her hand to her head again.

"You don't look well," Alice said, concerned at the pallor she suddenly noticed on Jane's face.

Jane waved her hand in dismissal. "I'm sure it's just a cold. It will pass. Now get this food out there. I heard Trey in the dining room."

"He's here but not the rest of our guests, much to his dismay."

When Alice came back for the remaining food, Jane was standing right where Alice left her, shivering.

"You are going to bed right now," Alice commanded, just as Louise came into the kitchen.

"What's wrong?" Louise asked.

"Jane is not well. I want her to lie down for a while."

"I need to get breakfast for our guests," Jane protested.

"My goodness, you are as pale as a ghost," Louise said. "Alice is right. We can take care of things here."

Jane seemed to wilt, then shivered again. "Are you sure?"

"Everything looks as if it is ready. I think Alice and I are capable of putting the food out," Louise said with a quick lift of one eyebrow.

"Okay then. I'll be back down in a bit. You don't have to walk up with me," Jane said as Alice went to help her. "Just see to it that our guests get fed." She gave Alice a limp smile. "And don't let Louise near the food."

"I see you haven't lost your sense of humor," Louise said primly even as Alice laughed.

They watched her leave, then Alice turned to Louise. "I'm concerned about Jane. She looks like some of the flu patients who have come into the hospital lately. I'll look in on her later, but right now we have guests to feed."

By the time they had laid out everything, Trey, Lynette and Randall were standing in the living room, talking. Or rather Trey was talking, and Randall and Lynette were listening.

"Excuse me," Alice said. "Breakfast is served."

Trey frowned and shook his head. "We don't have time for breakfast." He looked at Randall and Lynette. "If Dan isn't coming, we'll get going."

He turned to Alice. "Dan is still in bed. Says he's not feeling well, so he'll stay here for the day." He nodded at Lynette and Randall. "Long day ahead of us. Let's get at it."

"What must we do about Dan?" Louise asked, her voice crisp.

"Just poke your nose in his room once in a while. Make sure he's still breathing." Trey waved away Louise's concern with a brisk motion of his hand. "He said he's not hungry, so you don't have to feed him."

"We can stop here in the middle of the day and check on him ourselves," Lynette said to Louise.

"That would be fine," Louise said.

"Okay, crew," Trey said. "Let's motor."

Randall glanced back at the table and Alice could see a trace of longing in his eyes.

"Just a moment," she said, holding up her hand. She got some plastic disposable containers, some paper napkins and plastic cutlery from the kitchen and brought them to the sideboard where the food lay, waiting for their guests. She put a few steaming croissants in one and some fruit in the other, then brought them to Randall. "Why don't you take this along?"

"You're a doll," Randall said, as he took them from Alice. "It smells and looks so good in here, I hate to leave." He glanced over his shoulder at Trey, who was putting on his coat and cap. "But duty calls and I must obey if I want to keep my job." He gave Alice a quick smile, then walked past Trey and Lynette, his coat open, no hat on his head, while they bundled up as if they were leaving for the North Pole.

Louise toyed with her glasses as she shook her head after they left. "What an odd group of people."

"They are a puzzle, that's for sure."

Alice and Louise were returning to the kitchen when they heard a knock at the back door and then a cheery "Yoo-hoo."

"Thank goodness for Aunt Ethel," Alice said. "This breakfast won't go to waste after all."

$\backsim$

"Good morning, Louise," Viola looked up from the stack of books on her desk at Nine Lives Bookstore, her eyes magnified behind her bifocals. "How did you enjoy that book I recommended to you?"

"Actually, I haven't had time to read it. I just took on a new pupil and have been busy the past week doing the inn's accounts, and now we have four guests." Louise pulled up a chair beside her friend's desk and picked up one of the books, weighing it in her hand. "*War and Peace?*"

Viola beamed. "I had a number of requests for Russian classics since one of those TV book clubs featured *Anna Karenina.*" She picked up another book, and held it at arm's length, her fingers trailing over the dust jacket almost lovingly. "Such a beautiful cover, who could resist it?"

Louise shared her friend's love of books, but Viola's passion ran deeper. "It's appealing, though I don't know if all your customers would share C. S. Lewis' sentiment that you cannot have a cup of tea or a book big enough." She put down the large book, glancing around the shop. Portraits of Viola's favorite authors graced the walls. "You shall have to find a portrait of Tolstoy for your gallery if his books sell."

"That is an excellent idea." Viola put down her book, her eyes sparkling. "Actually, that gives me another idea. I could have a Russian theme. Spotlight some other Russian authors. Dostoevsky as well as Tolstoy. You would be interested to know that they were both Christians."

"Struggling ones, I might add."

"I thought Christians weren't supposed to have struggles," Viola noted, sorting the books into piles on her desk. Viola's faith was a patchwork of religions, depending on which author she was enamored of at that moment, but she enjoyed discussing her beliefs with anyone who would listen.

"Christians are always struggling. We work through the tension of God's grace being offered and our inability to accept it."

Louise picked up another book to head off the discussion. Though she usually enjoyed sparring with Viola, today she just didn't have the energy. She was too preoccupied with the offer Jane had received. She couldn't get it off her mind. After breakfast, she had gone upstairs to talk to Jane, but found her sister asleep.

"You are frowning, Louise. Surely I didn't say anything to offend you?"

Louise shook her head. "No, my dear friend, you didn't. I'm just a little concerned about Jane." Louise bit her lip, wondering what to tell Viola. "Jane received an e-mail from an old friend of hers," Louise said. "She has a televised cooking show and has asked Jane to join her on it."

"What an opportunity!" Viola exclaimed, pushing her glasses up her nose and leaning forward, as if to hear better. "Is she going to do it?"

"I haven't had a chance to ask her about it, but Alice and I both agree that it is a wonderful opportunity for Jane. She has been restless of late. She has made comments that make me wonder if she's looking for something more challenging to do." Louise couldn't stop the sigh that slipped out.

Viola shook her head. "It definitely sounds interesting, though it would be difficult for you."

"We're hoping she will choose not to go." Louise picked up *War and Peace* again. "If she does go, I won't have time to read this."

Suddenly Ethel appeared from the back of the shop and set a stack of books on the cash desk, her movements awkward in her haste. "Hello again, Louise." She nodded at her niece. "I was going to buy these, Viola, but I changed my mind. Lloyd is waiting for me so I don't have time to reshelve them. Sorry." She shot Louise a furtive glance, then scurried out of the shop.

"Well, I wonder what that was about?" Viola said, as she got up to reshelve the books.

Louise stood and walked to the door, watching as her aunt stopped on the sidewalk. She could see Ethel glance back at the store in a most mysterious way. Then she turned the corner toward the Coffee Shop and disappeared from view. Louise wondered what had so excited her aunt.

⌒

"I think going to Zachary's is a great idea," Jane said, slipping on her winter coat.

"It was just a suggestion," Louise said, still holding her hat and gloves in her hand. "We don't have to go if you aren't feeling well." Zachary's was the nicest restaurant in town, and though it was only open for dinner, owner Zachary Colwin always served good food in an elegant setting. The Howard sisters considered it a treat to dine there.

"I think I'm feeling better now," Jane said.

When her sisters made the suggestion, Jane's first impulse was to say no. All she wanted to do was crawl back into bed and sleep. But Alice was getting a hovering-nurse look on her face and even Louise, who never met a germ she couldn't overcome, was starting to look concerned.

She was fine. It was just a cold and the best way to get over it was with a positive attitude and action. At least that was what Louise always said.

"If you say so," Alice put in, tugging her hat over her hair. "Though I'm still not sure this is a good idea."

"It is a great idea," Jane said, then sneezed. She was so tired that she didn't feel like cooking and this way she knew Alice and Louise would get a good dinner.

"You seem to enjoy rising to challenges," Alice said.

Going to Zachary's was hardly a challenge, but her sisters seemed determined to make her sicker than she was. "Of course I do," she said briskly. "Who doesn't love a new challenge? A new opportunity."

"Of course," Alice said, exchanging a quick look with Louise.

"Let's go," Jane said, stepping out the door and making the decision for them.

"I was hoping we would be getting some warmer weather coming in," Alice said, shivering as they stepped out the door into the dark night. "Should we drive?"

"I think that we should walk," said Louise, pulling on her gloves. "This brisk air is just the thing we need to clear our heads after being indoors all afternoon."

"And that's the end of that," Jane said with a teasing grin. She linked arms with Louise, then caught Alice by the other arm, pulling them close to her. The glow from the street lamps lent a dreamlike quality to the evening, sending spangles of light bouncing off the snow. "Now, isn't this cozy?"

Louise frowned down at her, looking so much like an elderly sister in the half-light that Jane had to laugh.

"C'mon, Louie," Jane said, giving her sister's arm a shake. "You're the one that wanted to walk. I'm so frail and weak that I need your support."

Louise gave her a quick smile, then patted her mitten-covered hand with her own. "I think we need to support each other."

Jane laughed, tucking her arms closer against her sisters. She thought of Debbie's letter, which made her think of some of the plans she had wanted to instigate. "An e-mail from a friend made me think about the inn and the future . . ." she stopped talking and started coughing. She couldn't seem to stop.

"Jane, are you okay?" Alice asked.

Jane felt a flush of heat followed by a chill. She blinked as the streetlights grew fuzzy. Louise was leaning toward her on one side and Alice on the other, but they just would not keep their heads still. "Stop swaying," she said, blinking as she tried to clear her eyes.

"You are going back to bed," Louise said firmly.

Fifteen minutes later, Jane was tucked in bed.

"We're going to stay here with you," Alice announced, laying a cool hand on Jane's forehead.

"No. Please. I want you to go," Jane mumbled, closing her eyes against the swimming motion of her room.

Though they didn't say a word, she could feel their objections. She forced her eyes open and smiled at the two concerned faces hovering over her. "I'll rest a lot better knowing that my sisters are getting a good meal and that you're not rattling around in my kitchen."

They looked at each other, still hesitating. *My goodness,* Jane thought, *they could be stubborn.* "Go," she said, waving them away. "I want it quiet in here while I rest."

"Before we go, I'll bring you some hot soup," Alice said.

"I'm not hungry," Jane replied. "I'll be fine."

Alice sighed, then nodded. "Okay. But we won't be

staying long. Just long enough to eat and then we'll be back."

Jane nodded, rolled over and drifted off into blessed sleep.

$\backsim$

Alice breathed deeply, then coughed as the cold air stabbed her lungs. "Goodness, it's cold out," she said with a shiver. "We'll have to walk faster just to keep warm."

"I don't like leaving Jane behind," Louise said. "The idea of going out was to give her a break."

"Which we're still doing," Alice said. "She was right. If we stay, she'll know we are at the inn and she will feel guilty about being in bed." In spite of Jane's objections, she and Louise still made up a thermos of soup and a pot of tea and put a bowl of cherry gelatin at Jane's bedside in case she changed her mind. They had done the same for Dan previously.

"I had also hoped that we could talk to her about her friend's offer," Louise added.

"We'll have lots of time to talk about it later. For now we'll have to pick up the pace if we don't want to stumble into Zachary's on frozen feet."

Zachary's was almost full by the time they arrived. Nancy Colwin greeted them at the door, her thick black hair swept up in a fashionable twist, her smile wide.

"Welcome," she said ushering them into the dining room.

In a few moments they were settled and had ordered. In one corner of the club, they could see Trey, Randall and Lynette.

"Good evening, Louise, Alice. Where's Jane?" Hope Collins stopped by their table, her coat folded over her arm.

"She's a bit under the weather."

"Aren't we all these days? My goodness, I hope it warms up," Hope said, sighing. "I'm so sick of being cooped up. I just had to get out tonight so I came here."

Alice studied Hope's hair. She was sure that the last time she saw Hope, her hair had been medium blonde.

Hope noticed Alice's puzzlement and combed her fingers through her curls. "What do you think? I just got Betty Dunkle at the Clip 'n' Curl to lighten this up for me. The older man, Trey? The chubby one who is staying at the inn? He said I would look like a young Betty Grable if I dyed my hair a little lighter." She glanced back at the corner where the inn's guests sat, then stepped closer to the table, her eyes shining brightly in the subdued lighting. She lowered her voice. "I found out what they are doing in town."

She paused, looking eagerly from Louise to Alice. "They are a film crew and they are thinking of doing a movie in Acorn Hill. That's why they've been snooping around here taking pictures." She sighed dramatically, her hand on her chest.

"And how do you know this?" Alice asked.

Hope leaned closer and continued in a stage whisper. "I overhead them talking about it in the Coffee Shop. Trey is in charge. He's the director. The two others are his assistants and the tall boy with the ponytail is a location scout. They were writing all kinds of things on napkins, just like they do in the movies."

"So life imitates art," Louise said dryly.

"Just think. We could be in a movie. We could become famous."

"The famous have famous problems," Louise said, "and no privacy whatsoever."

Alice stifled her laughter. Trust her sister to bring dear Hope's soaring ambitions firmly down to earth. Now, with Hope's information, she understood their guests' behavior a little better, but she didn't know if she liked the idea of Acorn Hill being used as the site of a movie.

"Don't you think the idea's exciting? Acorn Hill is such a pretty town, people would come from all over to see it once it's featured in a movie."

"Most assuredly they would change the name," Louise said.

"They always put a note in the ending credits of movies that tells you where the film was shot. I've wanted to see Canmore, Alberta, ever since I saw that movie *Mystery, Alaska*.

They filmed it there." Hope held out her hand in a stop motion, her mouth forming an O. "What if they want to use the inn? Wouldn't that be fantastic advertising for you?"

Louise glanced at Alice as if enlisting her help.

"For now this is all just speculation, isn't it?" Alice put in.

"They would have to get permission from the town," Louise added. "The town council may not want Acorn Hill to be the setting for a movie. What if the filming disrupted the community too much?"

"I used to dream of being a movie star," Hope said wistfully. She sighed, then brightened. "Who knows, it might happen yet. Maybe people would like the idea if they were convinced." With a quick smile at the sisters, she turned and left.

Louise folded her hands on the table. "Well, that mystery is solved," she said. "Though I'm quite sure I don't like the idea of a movie being made here. I know what Mayor Tynan would have to say about this."

"He's not the only one to make that decision," Alice said, "but I agree with you."

"There would be repercussions, as Hope was saying. We could easily have more tourists coming," Louise said. "I think making a movie in our town could throw off the balance of life here."

Chapter Five

*J*ane rolled over in bed and blinked at the alarm clock, trying to get the numbers in focus. The time suddenly registered on her fuzzy brain and she bolted out of bed, then promptly sat down. The room tilted and twisted in time with the pounding in her head. Her throat felt thick and raw and she couldn't get her hands to cooperate as she picked up her clock to get a better look. How could she have slept through the alarm?

Her heart slowed down when she discovered she had read the digital numbers incorrectly. It was only six-thirty.

She stumbled to the bathroom. As she washed, she caught a glimpse of her face in the mirror. She pinched her pale cheeks and blinked her watery eyes. She knew she would feel better when she dressed and started moving around. A fit of coughing seized her and she took a drink of water to stop it.

Once she made it to the kitchen, however, she caught hold of one of the chairs and dropped onto it. While she waited for the room to stop spinning, she tried to decide what to make for breakfast.

A hazy memory pierced her muddled thoughts. She had made crepe batter yesterday in preparation for this morning. *Three cheers for being organized*, she thought.

She was sure that there were some peaches left from yesterday's breakfast. She could cut them up. That shouldn't be too hard.

Wendell sauntered into the kitchen and jumped onto Jane's lap, curling up contentedly. Jane stroked his soft fur, trying to remember what it was she had to do.

Fifteen minutes later Louise came into the kitchen, then stopped when she saw Jane, still petting Wendell. "What are you doing out of bed?"

Jane tried to focus on her sister standing in the doorway. "I'm going to make breakfast."

"No, you're not. You are ill. You should be in bed."

"No. I've rested enough." Jane nudged Wendell off her lap and got up. She found her apron and put it on, then washed her hands. Her movements were shaky, but better than before. She just had to focus on the next job.

That job was making crepes. She got the batter out of the refrigerator and set it out on the counter. It needed to be stirred, but first she had to cut up the fruit. Or did she need to whip the cream? She could not seem to sort one job from the other.

"If you won't go to bed then at least let me help you." Louise put on an apron as well. "Give me a job to do."

"Why don't you whip cream for the crepes? You'll need some confectioners' sugar." Jane paused, trying to remember where the sugar was. Louise, however, was already taking out a bowl and the whipping cream. Moments later the mixer was whirring and Jane had one less job to focus on.

When Alice came into the kitchen, Jane set her to cutting up peaches.

She just had to make the crepes and fry up the pork sausages. When she put the crepe pan on the stove, her hands shook and she dropped the flat frying pan with a clatter.

"My goodness, Jane, you scared me half to death." Louise spun around, her hand on her chest. She set the beater on end and strode to Jane's side. She took the pan and set it back on the burner. "Tell me what to do and I will take care of it. I'm a little out of practice with cooking, but I certainly can follow directions."

Jane wanted to protest. Louise could find her way around the kitchen, but cooking for Louise was simply another duty rather than the art Jane believed it to be. Yet Jane's shaky legs were convincing her that aesthetics were not as important as simply getting breakfast on the table.

"You have to do exactly what I tell you," Jane said, trying to be firm with her older sister.

Louise waved down her protests. "I will listen to every word."

"It's not the listening I'm worried about," Jane said, settling back in the chair. She walked her through the first steps of greasing the pan and heating it. "Make sure it's not too hot or they'll cook too fast. You also need to give the batter a stir."

Louise nodded, frowning as she concentrated. Jane tried not to fuss when she noticed that Louise didn't swirl the batter all the way around the pan. She knew this took some practice. When the next one came out oblong, and the third oval, she could not stay quiet.

"Louise, the crepe should be round."

Louise frowned. "This is round."

"If you think that's round, you need to take geometry again, my dear sister. It looks like an egg."

"The shape does not affect the taste." Louise flipped the crepe and shook it down so it settled on the bottom of the pan.

Jane suppressed a sigh and a cough that tickled her throat. She was going to rise above this cold, she decided. She stifled the urge to remind her older sister that food should be presented in a pleasing manner. A series of coughs racked her body and pain stabbed at her temples. *Please, Lord,* she prayed, *let this pass so I can take control of my kitchen again.*

"Should I start the sausages now?" Louise's question filtered through the vise grip of pain holding Jane's head.

She only nodded, closing her eyes. A few moments later she heard the sizzle of the sausages frying. She opened her eyes in time to see Louise frantically stabbing at the crepe pan with the spatula. Smoke rose as Louise dropped a blackened oval on the plate beside the stove.

"I guess we won't be serving that one," she said with a weak smile directed at Jane.

"Jane, you should be in bed," Alice said quietly, giving her a glass of water. "We'll manage here."

Jane took a drink. Then she shot an anguished look at her crepe batter, her once immaculate stove now spattered with grease from the sausages that Louise was ignoring as she poured too much batter in the crepe pan. She pushed herself up from her chair and slowly made her way up the stairs. Breakfast was out of her hands. With a bit of luck their guests would repeat the previous day's pattern and skip breakfast. She hoped for the sake of their stomachs that they would.

$\backsim$

Alice watched Jane slowly make her way out of the kitchen, clinging to whatever solid surface she could grasp.

"I'm sure she has the flu," Alice said as she tipped the peaches into the bowl that Jane had told her to use. "She has all the symptoms. Cough, chills, headache and fever." She found a glass platter and arranged some fruit on it. The grouping of strawberries fell over and the pineapple slices slid from their arrangement. *How does Jane manage to make everything look so easy?* Alice wondered.

Louise poured more batter into the pan, then made a face.

"What's wrong?"

"I forgot to grease the pan." She blew out her breath in a long sigh. "It will probably be okay."

"Shouldn't you rotate the batter like Jane told you?"

"I used the ladle to do that. This one looks a little better."

Alice transferred the whipped cream to a glass bowl and put it in the refrigerator as she tried to think of a tactful way to take over. The ringing of the phone thwarted that plan. It was the hospital asking her if she could come in right away. One of the other ward nurses had called in sick and they were shorthanded.

She glanced back at Louise, who was hovering over the spattering sausages and the plate of odd-shaped crepes beside the stove. Breakfast was going to be a minor disaster. But it was out of her hands now. She was going to look in on Jane and then she had to go to work. Maybe she could get Dr. Bentley to check on Jane and Dan some time today.

$\backsim$

"I am glad you decided not to skip breakfast this morning," Louise said to her guests as she laid out the food on the table. She managed to salvage the best of the crepes. They looked okay. They were not perfectly round and some were a bit dark, but they were still edible.

"Randall convinced us to give your food a try," Lynette said with a grin a she unfolded the napkin and laid it on her lap.

"Well, I'm glad for that," Louise said, smiling Randall's way. "I shall have to tell my sister Jane. She is the main cook."

"Where are your sisters?" Randall asked, wiping his mouth with a napkin.

"Jane is not feeling well and Alice was called in to the hospital where she works as a nurse."

"I wonder if we shouldn't get her to take a look at Dan," Randall said. "He barely ate any of his supper last night."

"He got up for a bit this morning and drank some of the juice I brought him," Lynette said, "but he didn't want any breakfast."

"He has not been very productive this trip," complained Trey. "I might have to call the head office and get them to send someone else down."

"Cut him some slack," Randall said with an exasperated sigh. "He's been putting in long, hard hours. Like the rest of us."

Though the sisters often ate breakfast with their guests, this was one time that Louise felt out of place. She wished Jane or Alice could have joined them. Right now she felt as if she was eavesdropping.

"Alice has been in contact with Dr. Bentley, a local general practitioner. He was nice enough to offer to stop by to check Dan out," Louise said.

"Just add his fee for Dan to our room rate," Trey said with a wave of his hand, as if dismissing that particular problem. "I also need to know who I have to talk to about the chapel," Trey asked, rubbing his hand over his round stomach.

He must mean for the movie they want to film, Louise thought. "Well, Rev. Kenneth Thompson is our pastor. You can begin by talking to him and explaining how you want to use Grace Chapel in your film."

Trey narrowed his eyes. "What do you mean? What do you know about the film?" His gaze flicked from Randall to Lynette. Lynette kept her eyes on her food. Randall ignored him and cut up his blackened sausage into little bits.

"None of your associates told us anything," Louise said, turning to Trey. "My sister and I heard about your plans at Zachary's last night."

"Small towns and small-town gossip," Trey said with a note of disgust edging his voice. "Can't keep anything quiet."

"We are a community," Louise said, trying not to sound prim. "We care about what happens, and the people of this town are quite observant."

Trey shrugged her comment off. "So I need to see this Kenneth Thompson about the church?"

"Rev. Thompson," Louise corrected with a smile.

"He's the good-looking guy, isn't he?" Lynette put in, suddenly interested. She wiped her mouth and pushed her plate away, her breakfast unfinished.

Louise sent up a prayer for patience and understanding. "He was the man you saw here the other night."

"Great. I don't have to go to church to see him again then." Lynette grinned. Today she wore another brightly colored sweater over black pants.

"He's a minister, Lynette." Randall popped the last of the sausage in his mouth and grimaced.

"Is something wrong, Randall?" Louise asked.

He shook his head quickly and covered his mouth with his napkin, then lowered it onto his plate. "No. Thanks for breakfast. We should get going, Trey."

"Do I need to make an appointment to see this Thompson guy?"

"Rev. Thompson," Randall corrected this time.

Louise's opinion of the young man edged up a notch. At least he seemed to understand how to address an ordained servant of the Lord.

"Whatever," Trey dismissed Randall's comment.

"I'm sure that if you call ahead, Rev. Thompson would be more than happy to spend some time with you," Louise said.

"Great. 'Cause if we can't get that church, the movie is dead in the water. What is the number?"

Louise gave it to him as Trey pulled out his cell phone. He got up from the table and started dialing. Then he frowned. "Busy," he grumbled.

"Guess we'll just have to go stop in there then," Lynette said, with a wink at Randall. "Surprise him, so to speak."

Louise drew in a long, slow breath, then let it out again just as slowly. She prayed Rev. Thompson would be able to deal with these people.

As they left, Louise had to think once more of their mission to make Grace Chapel Inn a welcoming place of refreshment and healing. They had had difficult guests before, and with prayer and patience, they had managed to give each of them some memory worth keeping. She wondered if they would be able to do the same with Trey, Lynette, Randall and Dan.

She cleared the table of the dishes and was disappointed to see quite a bit of food left and that only Randall had finished most of his breakfast.

She put together a plate of food for Dan and went upstairs to his room to see how he was doing. He didn't reply to her gentle knock. She quietly opened the door of the Garden Room and found him still lying in his bed, a silent lump under the covers. Louise was suddenly very glad that Dr. Bentley would be coming to look at him.

Jane was sleeping when Louise checked on her, but Louise was gratified to see she had taken some of the apple juice that Alice had brought up earlier.

After she had the kitchen tidy, Louise tackled the bedrooms, wishing she had even a smidgen of Jane's seemingly boundless energy. She could do a lot of the work required, but the thought of running the inn with only Alice to help made her feel distinctly gloomy.

Maybe she shouldn't have dismissed Jane's plans so cavalierly. Just because Louise herself didn't have the energy didn't mean that Jane couldn't be allowed to expand her horizons. While Louise changed the linens in the guest rooms, she prayed for patience and peace, and that they would be able to encourage Jane and keep up with her. And as she worked, she felt God's peace wash over her.

Jane was still sleeping when she checked on her again. As Louise closed Jane's door, she heard the telephone ringing. She quickly made her way down the stairs to answer it.

The person on the other end of the telephone was Donita Harke, Tabitha's mother.

"I need to talk to you, Mrs. Smith," Mrs. Harke was saying. "Do you have some time? I'm in town right now but have to leave in about an hour."

"I have some errands to run in town. Give me a few moments to get ready and I'll meet you at the Coffee Shop."

Ten minutes later Louise sat in a booth across from Mrs. Harke, who was nursing a cup of coffee, her hands curled around it.

"You seem concerned, Mrs. Harke. What was it that you wished to talk about?"

"It's Tabitha. She is so set on the idea that she's going to be famous." Mrs. Harke hunched over her coffee cup, looking defensive. "I'm worried about her. All she does is play that piano. She doesn't get out with other kids. It's like it's her whole life."

"She is very talented," Louise said carefully. Mrs. Harke's concern for her daughter changed Louise's first impression of Tabitha's mother. "Given the right opportunities I can see her achieving her goal."

"I just don't want her to be disappointed," Mrs. Harke said, tunneling her fingers through her blond hair. "Her first teacher didn't think my daughter had it in her, so Tabitha wanted me to find another teacher. She was so determined to prove her first teacher wrong that all she's been doing is practicing." Mrs. Harke shot Louise a pleading look. "I'm thrilled that she's found something she's passionate about, but I also want my daughter to have a normal, happy life. I'd like to see her get involved with friends and do ordinary things."

Louise took a sip of her coffee, thinking. "I could speak to my sister, Alice Howard, about getting Tabitha involved in the church's girls group that Alice leads. The group is called the ANGELs, and the girls are about Tabitha's age."

Mrs. Harke gave Louise a quick smile. "That would be great. Maybe if she spent time with other girls she could see that there are things besides music." Mrs. Harke finished off her coffee, then glanced at her watch. "I'm sorry. I have to run. Thanks for taking the time to talk."

"I will let you know the time of the next meeting for the girls," Louise said as the woman gathered her bags and scooted out of the booth.

As Louise watched her go, she felt a mixture of emotions.

On the one hand, she could understand the mother's concern. Yet at the same time, Tabitha had a real talent that Louise wanted to see nurtured.

"Some more coffee, Louise?" Hope stopped by her table with a coffee pot and a smile.

"Just a little bit more," Louise said, holding out her cup.

"Did you hear about Fred Humbert?" Hope asked, as she filled it up. "He's going to Punxsutawney, where some television program wants to interview him." Hope grinned at Louise. "Isn't that exciting? And your guests were talking to June this morning about using the Coffee Shop as one of their locations. She's thinking very seriously about it."

"Well, that certainly does sound exciting," murmured Louise, though she wasn't sure she liked the idea. She wondered if June understood the implications of having a movie filmed in Acorn Hill.

"Yes, there are all kinds of things happening around here these days. A movie crew wants to film here. Fred is going to be on television and Jane is joining that cooking show."

Louise straightened at Hope's last bit of news. "Excuse me? What cooking show?"

"I heard this morning that Jane was going to be on a cooking show that a friend of hers has. Clara Horn was telling me. She heard it from Florence who heard it from Ethel."

Had Jane been talking to Ethel about Debbie's offer before she spoke to Alice and me? Jane wouldn't do that, would she? Louise's mind raced as she remembered how unsupportive she had been of Jane's various ideas. She recalled that Jane had been on the verge of saying something to them on the way to Zachary's. Maybe she had been about to tell them that she was going to take the job. *No, it couldn't be true*, she assured herself, deciding that this was just the small-town gossip mill grinding at full speed.

"I think it would be neat to see Jane on television," Hope said.

Though Louise had to agree, she didn't want to even think about it.

"These are prescriptions for cough medication," Dr. Bentley said as he handed Louise slips of paper. "There is one for Jane and one for Dan." He took his coat from Louise with an encouraging smile. "Give it to them as needed, but be careful with the dosage. It has codeine in it."

Dr. Bentley, tall with dark hair and kindly brown eyes, had an aura of confidence. Louise felt better about Dan now that the doctor had looked at him.

"Should Dan be in the hospital?" Louise asked.

"If he's not better by tomorrow, I would recommend

that he be taken in. Jane is okay for now. You can do more for her here than we could at the hospital."

"Thank you so much for coming," Louise said. "Would you like a cup of coffee?"

"Thank you. Though I would love a cup, I have a few more calls to make and then I have to make my rounds at the hospital. Try to get plenty of fluids into both of them." He slipped on his coat, picked up his bag and, with a sympathetic smile, left.

Louise glanced down at the incomprehensible prescriptions that he had scribbled. She put on her coat and made her way down the street to the pharmacy. As she walked, she prayed for Dan and for Jane.

And she prayed that she and Alice would be able to deal with whatever decision Jane made about Debbie's offer.

Chapter Six

"Are you sure Jane is taking the television job?" Alice pushed a potato around on her plate, distracted by what Louise had told her. "Wouldn't she talk to us before making such a decision?"

"Maybe she was trying to before she got sick." Louise finished her dinner, then frowned. "Is it my imagination or were those potatoes a little hard?"

More than a little hard, Alice thought. They were undercooked. The chicken was hard too, but that was from overcooking.

"And how was Jane today?" Alice asked, avoiding Louise's question. "When I checked on her before dinner, she was sleeping."

"I brought up some soup to her and to Dan for lunch, but she didn't eat any. She was coughing so badly that I gave her some of the cough medication Dr. Bentley prescribed. I looked in on her a few more times during the day, but she was sleeping each time."

"Did Dan eat his soup?" Alice asked.

"Only a little of it. Before you leave for your meeting, perhaps you could have a look at him."

"I'll do that," Alice agreed, setting her knife and fork across her plate in a futile attempt to hide her unfinished supper.

Louise glanced at Alice's plate and frowned. "You will not be able to keep working if you don't eat properly."

"I had something to eat at the hospital cafeteria," Alice said, avoiding Louise's concerned gaze. She thought it best that she not tell her sister that the something she ate was a doughnut and a chocolate bar. "I don't want to be late for the church board meeting, and we should clean up before I leave."

"No, you better leave. I understand from Trey that he is going to be making a presentation to the board, and from what Hope said this morning at the Coffee Shop, June might not be entirely opposed to the idea of a movie being filmed here."

"June is only one member of the board. I can't imagine that Florence Simpson would be in favor. She so often takes a contrary view, and Ethel will do what she imagines Lloyd will want."

Louise took a bowl of raspberry gelatin and another of yogurt from the refrigerator and set them on a tray with a plate of chicken and potatoes. "I'm going to bring this up to Jane. I am not sure what she will eat so I'll give her a variety."

"She might not want to eat at all, but try to make sure she has some liquids." Alice ran her fingers over the butcher-block counters and glanced around at the paprika-colored cupboards, the colorful tiled backsplash and the black and white tiles on the floor. Jane had decorated this kitchen, and her warm, lively personality came through in the decor. Since starting the inn, the sisters had weathered only a few minor storms, some of them in this very kitchen. For the most part, however, they had been very happy. Jane had never let on that she wanted anything more.

Of course, Jane had never had an offer to do a television program before now.

Alice pulled her sweater closer around herself, a thin barrier against the pervasive chill of the church's Assembly Room. It was as if the weather outside the buildings of Acorn Hill was determined to make itself felt inside too.

"Good evening, Alice," Florence Simpson said, taking her place across the table. She set a purple binder on the table, fussing with the pages, making notes in the margins.

When she noticed Alice's interest, she quickly slapped it shut and folded her ample arms on top.

Alice had to smile, wondering what was so important and so secret.

Ethel bustled into the room, carrying a number of plastic containers. These she set out on a side table in the meeting room. Right behind her came Lloyd carrying decorative paper plates and napkins, which he set beside the containers. Then June entered with a couple of carafes and paper coffee cups. Alice was puzzled; they had never had refreshments at a church board meeting before.

Ethel and June huddled over the table putting squares and tarts onto plates, talking quietly.

Fred Humbert arrived and sat down beside Alice.

"I understand you're going to Punxsutawney as a guest of a television station," Alice said.

Fred nodded, grinning. "It's like dominoes. Someone from the station read the piece by Carlene Moss that was picked up by that Philadelphia paper. They phoned and asked if I would be willing to do an interview."

"I think that's wonderful. Our very own celebrity."

"What celebrity? Here? Today?" Florence spun around, her eyes darting around the room as if hoping to find a movie star suddenly appearing at the church board meeting.

"I was just saying that when Fred gets interviewed by that television station, he's going to be a celebrity," Alice said.

Ethel wiped her hands on a napkin, shaking her head. "No. Our Jane is the one who is going to be the celebrity. She's going to be on a cooking show, a nationally syndicated cooking show." Ethel put heavy emphasis on the last four words, verbally underlining their importance.

"We don't know that yet," Alice said with a warning frown at her aunt. "Jane hasn't said anything."

"To you." Ethel nodded smugly, as if she possessed some secret that Alice knew nothing about.

Henry Ley, the chapel's associate pastor, arrived with his wife Patsy. Patsy took notes at the board meetings though she was not a member of the board. Cyril Overstreet came in immediately after them.

"Good evening," Fred said, glancing around the room, rubbing his hands together. "Though it's a bit chilly in here, I'm sure once we start this meeting, things will warm up," he said with a broad smile, taking in all the members present as they took their places around the table. "Sylvia Songer is not able to attend. She's not feeling well."

Sylvia too? This flu seemed to be sweeping through the county.

"I'd like Pastor Ley to open this meeting with a reading and a word of prayer," Fred said, once everyone was settled in.

Henry Ley adjusted his glasses and ran his hand through his white hair with one motion, then picked up his Bible. "I t-t-took this piece from Psalm 111. I thought it ap-p-propriate." He cleared his throat, held up his worn Bible and started reading. Alice was pleased to note that he got through the entire passage without faltering. He had been working with audio tapes to help his stutter. He finished with "The fear of the Lord is the beginning of wisdom; all who follow his precepts have good understanding. To him belongs eternal praise." He closed the Bible and slowly looked around the group. "Tonight, I p-pray that we may have a good meeting."

He bowed his head and prayed for a blessing on the meeting.

Fred took them through the first items on the agenda fairly quickly. The heating bill was a concern and it was decided to bring this to the attention of the congregation. Henry Ley made mention of a new family, the Harkes, who had moved temporarily into Acorn Hill, and encouraged the church board to welcome them.

Fred suggested that they send the family a welcome basket. Alice instinctively glanced in Florence's direction. If anyone was going to raise an objection about cost, it was Florence. But Florence simply smiled and nodded. Fred worked his way through the agenda item by item. Florence continued to be agreeable. She quietly tolerated Cyril's tendency to wander off the topic and to refer to situations that had taken place years ago when Daniel Howard was the pastor of Grace Chapel. She said nothing when Henry Ley recommended that the church board do some extra work on canvassing members for the outreach committee. June was also unusually quiet.

They worked through the rest of the agenda in record time.

"Our last item is a visit from Mr. Trey Atkinson and his associates. They wish to address us with a request," Fred said, giving Cyril a quick nod.

Cyril went to the door of the meeting room and ushered in Trey, Lynette and Randall. For once, Trey was not talking on his cell phone.

The three of them sat in the chairs reserved for them at one end of the table. Trey set a briefcase on the floor and looked around the room with a wide smile.

Eye contact and smiles from Trey Atkinson? Alice felt immediately suspicious.

"Welcome to Acorn Hill," Fred said, leaning forward, his hands crossed on the papers in front of him. "And welcome to our meeting."

Trey nodded, still smiling. Randall, as usual, simply slouched back in his chair looking uninterested. Lynette wore a brightly colored turtleneck sweater, leather vest and narrow black skirt. Her eyes, enhanced by makeup, looked expectantly around the table. Alice realized she was hoping that the church board included Kenneth Thompson. As Lynette made an inventory of the room, Alice saw her face fall.

Trey cleared his throat, then began to talk with unusual heartiness. "Thank you to the good people of the board for allowing us to address you. This is a privilege and an honor. If you will allow me to hand out some papers, Mr. Humbert?"

Fred nodded, and Trey handed Lynette a bundle of papers stapled together. She passed them around, carefully placing one in front of each member.

"What Lynette is distributing is a simple story treatment and very confidential. I would appreciate it if you would give me the papers back at the end of the evening. You'll notice that each group of pages is numbered so Lynette can keep track." Trey gave everyone another toothy smile, then pulled his chair forward. "What we're hoping to do with this film is re-create a post-World War II town. The first paragraph lays out a short synopsis of the basic story line. The focal point of the story, as you will notice, is the church." Trey waited a moment, giving everyone a chance to read the first page. Alice glanced over it, but what she read only added a little bit of information to what Trey had said. The main character of the story was a minister, and the movie would follow his adventures and misadventures with his faithful flock. It also looked as if there was a possibility for a sequel.

Alice thought of Lynette's fawning over Pastor Thompson a few days ago and wondered if she had pictured Ken in the movie.

Trey spoke about the movie and the implications for the chapel. "We wouldn't interrupt church services. We would film during the week and by Sunday the church would be yours again."

"We wouldn't be making a lot of changes to the decor," Lynette said paging through her notes. "The stained glass windows are especially wonderful and give just the right touch to the chapel's interior. Possibly a new coat of paint on the interior because of lighting concerns. We would like to change the carpet as well because of the color. All of this will be paid for by the production company and when we are finished filming, the church will look even better than it did before."

"But we like the color of the carpet," Pastor Ley said.

"We would keep it red," Lynette hastened to add. "Just a different tone."

"Are those the only changes you would make?" June asked.

Lynette glanced furtively at Trey, who quickly took over. "Inside. On the exterior, we would possibly be looking at some landscaping. Adding a few shrubs and plants and possibly a fence. I have some concerns about the paint and the roof." He languidly waved his hand as if this was all negligible. "All of this is, of course, pending approval."

"How much disruption would this cause?" Cyril asked.

Trey clasped his hands and leaned forward. "We understand how important the church is to you, and we don't want to cause any disruption. We've been touring a number of towns and we have to say that Acorn Hill is the most appropriate, architecturally. We would really like to make the movie and possibly a sequel in this town. All the ingredients that we require are right here."

"What do you hope to accomplish with this movie?" Fred asked quietly. "What is going to be the tone?"

"This is a lighthearted story," Trey said. "We think that there is enough drama and doom and crime these days on television and in the movies."

"Comedy?" Fred pressed.

Trey rubbed his chin lightly, as if trying to draw the right words out. "Humor. A big difference."

"Would you hire local people to be in the movie?" Florence asked.

Trey's glance slid quickly to Lynette, who nodded.

"We would hope to hire locals for walk-ons and crowd scenes," she said.

"What about local businesses? Would you do much purchasing here?" Fred asked.

"As much as we can," Trey countered. "We like the idea of a strong local economy. Many businesses would be featured in the movie. The hardware store, for instance, and the Coffee Shop. That is called product placement. It's great advertising without putting out any money."

"Would the church keep its name?" Cyril asked. "I have watched some movies where everything has a completely different name."

"We could keep it the same, but it might change. The writers and director are the ones who decide which name best sums up the tone of the movie."

Lynette leaned forward to add her comments. "The name Grace Chapel and Acorn Hill are lovely names. It's all about synergy and flow."

This answer told Alice absolutely nothing. Which, she suspected, was exactly what Trey and Lynette intended.

The board asked a few more questions. Trey and Lynette answered them as best as they claimed they could, using the same back and forth technique. Randall stayed slouched in his chair, glancing around the room from time to time. Alice wanted to walk over and give him a nudge to straighten up.

When there were no more questions, Fred thanked the Hollywood group for coming. Lynette gathered up the story summaries and followed Trey and Randall out of the room.

"One moment, Mr. Atkinson," Florence said loudly, pushing her chair back with a screech. "I must talk to you." She grabbed her binder off the table and ambled toward him, looking very self-important.

Alice wondered what Florence could possibly have to talk to Trey about, but she wasn't going to find out because Florence ushered the group out of the room, talking in a low voice to Trey.

"Well," Fred said quietly, tapping his pen on the papers in front of him, "I'm sure we will have things to discuss, though we should probably wait until Florence returns."

"We could have some coffee now, couldn't we?" Ethel asked, her eyes darting about the room. "Florence and I brought some treats for the meeting, though we were hoping that Mr. Atkinson and his group could join us."

"I think that is an excellent idea," Lloyd said, rubbing his portly stomach as if in anticipation.

While they waited for Florence, Ethel scurried about the room, putting napkins in front of everyone, offering a choice of squares and tarts from the plate she had made up. June went around with a coffee pot.

Alice chatted with Fred about his upcoming trip. Then Henry asked about Jane and how things were going at the inn.

"Not as well as when our Jane does the cooking," Ethel piped up, offering Cyril the plate. "No one can cook like Jane can. I don't want to sound unkind, but Louise is a terrible cook."

The door opened and Florence came back, beaming, still clutching her binder.

"I'm sorry to have left the meeting like that," she said, slipping into her chair. "Oh my goodness, Ethel. Look at these lovely tarts. You have outdone yourself."

Ethel just beamed with the unexpected praise.

The board members continued to chat until Fred called the meeting back to order.

Florence sat back, looking around the room. "I want everyone to know that I'm in favor of the crew filming here," she said with the forcefulness of a political candidate throwing his hat into the ring. "It's a good opportunity for our small town, a very good opportunity. I vote in favor."

Alice was taken aback. Florence Simpson? In favor? This was an unanticipated turn of events.

"We are not looking for a vote at this time," Fred

replied. "Mr. Atkinson was merely presenting a proposal. I invited him to come but right now I don't think we have enough solid facts to make a decision."

"They're going to fix up the chapel. We know we need a new roof and paint," Florence said, her frown turning her plucked and penciled eyebrows into one thin line across her forehead. "That would be money that the congregation doesn't have to come up with."

"I agree," Fred replied. "But for now, I think we should pray about this and try to speak to Mr. Atkinson, Ms. Teskey and Mr. Marquette individually to learn more. I would like to table this item until the next meeting."

"But what if they change their minds in the meantime and we miss this opportunity?" Florence turned to June. "Just think of how much business the Coffee Shop would be doing. There would be all kinds of people coming into town. And Fred? They would need supplies from the hardware store. This could help our local economy, couldn't it, Mayor Tynan?"

Alice was dumbfounded by Florence's championing of Trey Atkinson's cause. Alice could only suspect that Florence had something to gain by having a movie shot in Acorn Hill. But what?

Chapter Seven

Alice frowned as she added another item to the grocery list, while Louise made breakfast. It was early morning. She had just checked on Jane, who was asleep.

"I don't suppose you have any creative ideas for an activity I can do with my ANGELs," Alice asked Louise. "I really wanted to do something special for them. Something outdoors, but all my ideas call for warmer weather."

Louise shivered as she sifted flour into a bowl. "I can't think of a thing. It has been so cold." She dropped the sifter and a cloud of flour flew up, causing her to sneeze. Behind her, a pot of oatmeal started bubbling furiously on the stove. She grabbed a wet cloth and turned down the flame, wiping the stove at the same time.

"Here, let me do that," Alice said, taking the cloth out of Louise's hands. She rinsed it out and filled the large sink with warm soapy water. She wiped down the entire stove, which still had some grease spots from Louise's attempts to fry chicken last night.

Alice had volunteered to make breakfast this morning,

but by the time she had awakened, Louise was already busy in the kitchen. Though Alice had her concerns about Louise making breakfast, she was too tired to do anything about it. If the movie crew moved out of the inn because of the bad food, well, right now she didn't care. During last night's meeting, her misgivings about Trey and his sincerity had grown.

"Alice, could my new piano student, Tabitha Harke, join the ANGELs?" Louise asked. "I know she would enjoy the group."

"Of course," Alice said. "Did you want me to contact her mother?"

"If you could, then she would know that you approve." Louise sighed and picked up a can of baking powder. "Now did I put this in already?" She frowned at it as if the can could tell her. "I suppose it wouldn't hurt to add some more. What do you think, Alice?"

"Dip your finger in the flour. If it tastes sharp, you've already added it." Alice had done enough baking to know how easy it was to forget what was added and she had taught herself a few little tricks.

Someone was knocking on the door. Alice put the cloth down and walked to the back door, wondering who was there. Ethel usually gave a quick knock and then came in. But Ethel hadn't come to visit them since Jane became ill.

Not that Alice blamed her. The appeal of their meals had been greatly reduced since Louise took over the kitchen.

The visitor was Florence Simpson.

"Come in," Alice said, standing aside so Florence could enter. "What can we do for you?"

Florence clutched the same purple binder that she had taken to the church board meeting. She glanced around furtively, then leaned closer to Alice, whispering. "I need to talk to Mr. Atkinson. Alone."

"Mr. Atkinson has not come downstairs yet," Alice said.

Florence raised her chin in a haughty manner. "I spoke with him last evening, and he asked that I come to see him at the inn at ten, but I simply can't wait that long. This is very, very important." Florence clutched the binder closer to her and sighed dramatically. "I can't tell you what it's about, I'm afraid. Most confidential."

"I understand," Alice said, trying not to smile. "I shall tell him you are here."

Alice returned a few minutes later. "He said he would meet you in the study."

"Now don't disturb yourself further. I know where the study is. And I thank you for your time," Florence said. She gave Alice a condescending smile and swept through the kitchen on a wave of self-importance.

Louise lifted an eyebrow as the door swung closed behind

her. "And there goes a perfect example of the saying, 'Anything worth doing is worth overdoing.'"

Alice laughed aloud, then picked up her cloth and rinsed it out again. "I don't know what is happening, but since the movie crew came, this town is changing in front of my very eyes," she said as she finished wiping the stove. "I saw Hope Collins the other day with a script tucked into her apron. She told me she and June were practicing a scene. She sounded as if it was certain that a movie was going to be made in Acorn Hill and that she would have a role. Then Bobby Dawson, one of the boys in the youth group, asked me when the movie people were going to do auditions because he wanted to try out. Is it just me or has this town gone movie crazy?"

Another knock at the door interrupted their conversation. Alice opened the door, and Viola Reed hurried into the kitchen.

"Good morning," Viola mumbled in response to Alice's greeting.

Viola was almost unrecognizable. Her head was swathed in a thick, woven scarf and her coat collar was turned up. In her arms she had a stack of large books, which she deposited on the kitchen table.

She shivered as she looked around the kitchen, her glasses turning into twin disks of frost. "My goodness, this is not weather for humans," she said, unwinding her scarf.

Alice took her scarf and coat, and Viola pulled off her fogged-up glasses and wiped them with a paper towel.

"Would you like a cup of tea or coffee?"

"Coffee sounds divine," Viola said. She walked to the counter and peered into the bowl in front of Louise. "What are you making?"

"Cheese biscuits." Louise was still holding the can in one hand, a measuring spoon in the other. "I'm not sure if I put the baking powder in or not. It has been too long since I have done any baking." She put her finger into the bowl and lifted it to her mouth, then shrugged and plunged the measuring spoon into the tin, as if she was afraid she would change her mind.

Alice returned to her cleaning, smiling at the picture of the two older women hunched over a bowl, both frowning as if they were conducting a very important experiment.

"I've come to help you," Viola said. "I heard that Jane is ill, and I know how difficult cooking is for you." She strode to the table and came back with a large binder. "I brought you a cookbook."

Louise peered through her dusty glasses at the cover. "*Baking for Dunces*? I sincerely hope this is not a commentary on my mental skills."

"Now, now, we both know that you are as sharp as a tack, if you'll forgive the cliché," Viola said, dropping the cookbook down on the floury counter. "There are some basic but tasty recipes in here that you could use for your guests."

"Jane has always insisted on gourmet cooking for our guests," Louise grumbled, swiping at her glasses with one corner of her apron.

"You are my friend, Louise, and I hate to be blunt . . ."

Alice smiled at the disclaimer. Viola lived to be blunt.

". . . but I know that you see cooking as a necessity, not an art. Now, if we sit down and make up a basic menu, I can help you."

"You are far too busy for this," Louise said.

"Stop protesting. Friends help each other. Alice, where can I find a pen and paper?"

"There should be some in the far drawer by the telephone," Alice said, returning to the stove to give the oatmeal a stir. She wondered what Louise had done to it. It was a curious gray with brown lumps that she suspected must be apples. In spite of the unappealing stuff in the pot, her stomach growled at the thought of food. Supper last night had not filled her. From the look of it, breakfast might not either. Maybe she would eat at the hospital cafeteria.

"This morning we shall have to go with what I already have," Louise said, mixing up the dough. "After breakfast we can work on a menu."

Alice gave the oatmeal another stir, wishing that she had come down sooner to help Louise.

"Have you seen that show Jane was asked to join?" Viola asked, paging absently through the cookbook.

"I've been so busy lately, I haven't even had time to watch my weight," Alice said.

"Not that you need to." Viola glanced over Alice's uniform. "Your regular walks with Vera Humbert seem to be paying off. By the way, did you hear about Fred going to be interviewed? Isn't that exciting? Acorn Hill is full of celebrities."

"From the sounds of things, there are more to come," Alice said with a sigh, thinking of the church board meeting of last night. She glanced at the clock. "Well, I'm sorry to eat and run . . ."

"What do you mean, eat? You haven't had any breakfast yet," Louise said.

"Sorry. I don't have time. I have to cover for one of the other nurses again this morning. I'll be here for supper tonight, though," Alice said, wondering if Louise would be insulted if she stopped at a pizzeria on the way home and picked up a pizza.

One thing was for sure, she doubted her stomach could take one more of Louise's gourmet meals.

"So what are we supposed to do?" Lynette hissed, glancing over her shoulder at Louise, who tried to look as if she was not listening.

"What people expect," Trey whispered. "And try to keep that Florence woman away from me, okay?"

"Pretty hard to do when she shows up right where we're staying," Lynette said aloud.

Trey, Lynette and Randall sat at the table, their bowls of oatmeal untouched in front of them. Louise had excused herself for a moment to bring in the biscuits and had just pushed through the swinging door, followed by Viola with the coffee pot, when she overheard Lynette's comment. She set the plate of golden brown biscuits on the table.

"These look lovely," Lynette said, taking one and breaking it open. Picture-perfect steam wafted out of the broken halves. Lynette buttered one half, took a bite, then pursed her lips. She swallowed, grabbed her glass of orange juice and gulped it down.

"Are you all right?" Louise asked, concerned.

"Fine. Just fine." Lynette flashed a tight smile, then set the rest of the biscuit down.

Louise waited until Viola was finished pouring and then they joined their guests. Louise had asked Viola to stay for breakfast. Her presence made Louise feel less like a visitor in her own home.

Louise took a taste of the porridge and frowned. It was a mite sticky, but all a person needed to do was add a bit more milk and sugar and it would be fine. As for the biscuits, perhaps she put a bit too much baking powder in them, but enough butter covered up that particular fault.

"Mrs. Smith, I was wondering if you could tell us what time the church service begins at Grace Chapel tomorrow?" Trey was asking her.

"Ten o'clock," Louise said, surprised at his interest.

"Would it be okay if we attended?"

"You would be more than welcome," Louise said.

Trey smiled, his eyes flicking to Randall and Lynette.

"You will find that the people at Grace Chapel are friendly and welcoming," Viola said, taking a biscuit herself.

"Do you attend?" Lynette asked Viola.

Viola shook her head. "I haven't made up my mind concerning religion."

"The opiate of the masses?" Trey said with a quick laugh.

"That title, I feel, should be given to television and movies," Viola said, sprinkling more sugar on her oatmeal.

Louise tried to catch her attention. No matter Viola's opinion of their business, these people were their guests and Louise didn't want them insulted. Viola, however, was frowning at the bowl in front of her. She held another spoon of sugar poised over the top, as if trying to decide whether more sugar would help.

"Why do you say that, Ms. Reed?"

Viola made a decision, poured the sugar on and returned the spoon to the bowl in the center of the table. "I say that, Mr. Atkinson, because it is true." She looked up at him, pushing her glasses farther up her nose.

Louise recognized the gesture as Viola's preparation for argument and once again tried to catch her friend's attention, but Viola's eyes were firmly fixed on Trey.

"Television can be educational," Trey said.

"I agree with that," Viola said.

Louise relaxed. Her friend was going to be agreeable.

"So educational in fact," Viola continued, "that every time someone turns it on, I go off and find a book to read."

Louise stretched her foot out to give Viola a light nudge, but she couldn't reach her.

"Do you know that when you read, you use far more of your brain than when you watch television or movies?" Viola asked, her full attention on Trey. "And that the portion of your mind that makes choices and decisions is far more involved when you read?"

"Movies and television are entertainment," Trey said with a shrug. "You're not supposed to think."

Viola raised one finger. "Precisely. Because no discernment is involved, any information gleaned from movies or television is not given critical thought. People simply absorb it, repeat it. Knowledge and independent thought have been swept aside in the name of entertainment." She sat back, and underlined her statement with a decisive nod of her head.

"Would anyone like another biscuit?" Louise asked, trying to head her friend off at the pass, or impasse, if Trey's stubborn expression was any indication.

"There are a lot of nothing books printed too," Trey said. "At least even a so-so movie gives you something to look at."

"Eye candy," Viola said.

"People are tired. They have too much stress in their lives. They need a break."

"How is Dan?" Louise interjected quickly, hoping to change the subject.

"We're taking him to the hospital in Potterston this morning at Dr. Bentley's suggestion," Trey said. "He's just not getting better. You may as well check him out of the inn."

Louise was taken aback by his cold attitude. "I shall remember him in my prayers," Louise said.

"For what that's worth." Trey dropped his napkin unceremoniously on his plate. "I think we're done here. Crew?" he said, pushing away from the table. "Quick meeting in my room in ten, then we take Dan to Potterston." He turned to Viola. "Ms. Reed, interesting discussion. Maybe we can continue some other time?" He gave her a quick smile and left with Lynette at his heels.

Randall finished off the last of his biscuit, mumbled a quick thank you in Louise's general direction, then followed Trey.

Viola picked up a still-full bowl of porridge and frowned at it. "Look, that poor girl didn't touch her oatmeal. Nor did Mr. Atkinson, but then I'm not surprised. He didn't strike me as the oatmeal type."

"I really appreciate your help," Louise said, trying to find a diplomatic way to chide her friend as they cleaned up, "but arguing with our guests is not good for our business."

"That man needed to be taken down a peg or two. I didn't like what he said about religion." Viola looked up at Louise, smiling. "I didn't think it proper that he make a comment like that."

"But it was my religion he was slighting, not yours."

"And you are my friend, so by extension, he slighted me as well."

Louise patted Viola on her shoulder. "For that I thank you, but if you're going to help me, then you will have to follow the cardinal rule. Whether they are right or wrong, we do not argue with the guests."

"I shall try to keep my opinions to myself in the future," Viola said with a placating smile for her friend. Viola picked up the plate still holding half a dozen biscuits. "What do you want me to do with these?"

"I want to make a plate up for Jane's breakfast," Louise said. "I will give her some biscuits and some porridge."

"Make sure you bring her some orange juice," Viola said, reaching for the half-empty juice pitcher. "That seemed passable."

Louise frowned at her friend's comment. "She doesn't usually drink orange juice in the morning."

"Oh, she might this morning," Viola said. "When you come back we should work out a menu for the next few days. It will make our job easier if we know in advance what we must prepare."

"You don't need to be here every day." While she appreciated her friend's help, Viola had her own business to run. "You are busy enough with your shop."

"I have help. And from the taste, er, I mean, the look of things, you are going to need all the help you can get."

"Well then, thank you. I will bring this up to Jane, then I will be right back."

∾

Jane slipped a loose sweater over her T-shirt and sat at the edge of the bed, trying to find the energy to stand.

An ominous tickle started in her throat and then

another wave of coughing came that just would not stop. Pain jabbed behind her eyes with each cough. In desperation, Jane grabbed the bottle of cough syrup that Louise had left and took a swig, shuddering at the taste.

As Jane set the bottle down, she saw the tray of food from last night. Louise must have forgotten to pick it up. Jane had eaten some of the gelatin and had obediently drunk the water, but dry, hard chicken and undercooked potatoes had held no appeal.

Thank goodness Louise didn't have to cook supper for their guests. If all went as it had before she got sick, maybe they would continue to skip breakfast too.

Our reputation as a bed-and-breakfast is on the line, she thought.

They were going to lose all their business. Lose their coffee cup rating. All her hard work, gone. The inn would have to close down. She would be out of a job. She groaned, and a wave of dizziness washed over her as incoherent thoughts danced through her heated mind. Television program. Debbie. A cooking show. She could work for Debbie. Cooking.

The door opened and Louise breezed in, carrying another tray. She frowned at the tray beside the bed.

"You didn't finish your supper," Louise said. "You won't recuperate if you do not eat."

"Sorry," Jane mumbled, looking up blankly at her sister as she tried to understand her fuzzy thoughts. Debbie. Job. "I need to talk to Debbie," she said. "We're going to lose our coffee cups. Debbie has a job."

Louise blinked quickly, then nodded. "I made you some oatmeal. Try to eat some."

Jane turned to the grayish mass congealing in a bowl beside her bed. Was that glue Louise was trying to feed her? Why would her sister do that? "I'm tired," she mumbled.

Louise handed her a glass of juice. "Drink this."

Jane drank obediently. Then Louise held out a spoon with some cough syrup on it. Jane opened her mouth to tell her that she already took some, but Louise swooped the spoon into her mouth, giving her some more.

"Now some oatmeal," Louise was saying.

Jane took a spoonful and worked the warm lump down her throat. Louise offered her another spoonful and Jane took that too.

When Louise tried for a third, Jane waved her away. "Too tired," she muttered. "My stomach is sticking together." Jane lay back, closed her eyes and pulled up the covers. "Need to call Debbie," she mumbled as she drifted off to sleep.

Louise closed the door to her sister's room and paused a

moment outside. So it was true then. Jane was going to leave.

Louise sighed and walked slowly down the stairs, carrying Jane's dinner tray. She stopped a moment on the second floor to catch her breath. Though generally in good shape, lately she had been feeling a little under the weather herself. Maybe she was also getting a touch of the flu. She straightened her shoulders. That couldn't happen. She would not allow it. It was simply a matter of, well, mind over matter.

". . . I don't care what you think, Randall. Lynette and I have to go Sunday afternoon, but this is where I want to make the movie."

Through Trey's door, Louise heard his voice raised in anger.

"You are going to stick around another week and make sure that the people of this town are on board. This is a list of church board members and people from the town who seem in favor. Convince them that this movie is a great idea and get them to work on the rest of the town."

Louise was chilled by Trey's words. He had a list of people who wanted the movie to be filmed in Acorn Hill? How had he compiled it and who was on it?

Chapter Eight

Kenneth looked up from the Bible that he held in his hands. "Jesus cleansed the temple because it had been turned into a marketplace. It was as if a company were to come into our church and conduct their business right here in the sanctuary."

Louise glanced over to where the film crew sat.

Trey was surreptitiously looking at his electronic date book, while Lynette leaned forward as if listening intently to Kenneth. Her coat was opened to reveal a demure high-necked red knit dress. She had tamed the spikes of her hair. Randall sat back in the wooden pew. His frown gave no indication if he was listening or off somewhere else. His ponytail hung over one shoulder of his sheepskin-lined jean jacket, as if mocking the more conservative attire and shorter hair of the male congregants.

Every time Louise saw that ponytail, she was tempted to take a pair of scissors to it. Men with ponytails seemed, well, unseemly.

Louise closed her eyes a moment, chiding herself for

her unkind thoughts. It still puzzled her that Trey had asked Randall to stay behind and work on the people of the town. Randall seemed so lackadaisical that it was difficult to imagine his striving to win over the townspeople.

You are doing it again, she reminded herself. She took a long, slow breath and concentrated once again on what Pastor Ken had to say.

". . . so people of Grace Chapel, our challenge, given to us by our Lord Himself, is to be that light to the world. To be a reminder of what God has to offer to the wayward and the lost. To draw others by our example and by the love that God has given us."

Louise glanced sidelong at Alice, who was nodding at Ken's words. When Louise thought of someone who personified that light to the world, Alice always came to mind. Louise had a harder time seeing herself in that role.

Now, she saw that as her challenge.

Kenneth announced the final hymn, and as the congregation rose, Trey slipped out of the church, his cell phone plastered to one ear, his free hand pressed over his other.

Oh, Lord, give me strength, Louise prayed silently, walking to the back of the church to take her place in front of the organ. *And please give Jane strength as well*. The sooner Jane was better, the sooner the three of them could sit down and talk about the future of the inn.

Louise sent up another prayer for trust as she played a short introduction to the hymn. She sang along, her mind moving between concern for her sister, concern for herself and trying to recognize that in all things, God was always in control. She had learned that lesson in the hard times after her beloved husband Eliot had died. She had learned it again when she, Jane and Alice had started up the inn with no guarantee of its success.

It seemed that one more time, she needed to put everything in God's hands.

◠

A light rap on the door made Jane roll over in bed. She blinked and then smiled as Louise came into the room. "What day is it?"

"It's Sunday afternoon. How are you feeling?" Louise asked, setting a tray on the table beside Jane's bed.

"My head feels funny."

Louise gently put her hand on Jane's forehead, frowned and then straightened. "You are still running a fever."

"It comes and goes," Jane croaked.

"Well, I wish it would go," Louise said, her hands resting on her hips, as if trying to exert her will over Jane to get better. "Playing Florence Nightingale is not as easy as it looks."

In spite of how she felt, Jane had to smile. Louise was

no Florence Nightingale. Over the course of the day, Louise would whisk into her room, set a tray down, plump up pillows, and straighten blankets, so full of energy that she made Jane feel even weaker.

"I appreciate what you do." She closed her eyes, and once more prayed for strength. "How is Dan?"

"When I called the hospital, they said he was stable." Louise said.

"Hospital?" Jane asked.

"He's doing better," Louise said quickly. "And Trey and Lynette just left, leaving only Randall."

Jane pulled her thoughts together. "How are you managing with him?"

Louise pressed her lips together as if holding back a comment. "He is . . . reserved. I'm not sure of his motives."

"What do you mean by that?"

Louise looked down at Jane, then smiled. "I want you to concentrate on getting better while I concentrate on keeping this inn going. "

"I should get up," Jane said, feeling suddenly guilty. "I can do something."

"Alice and I have everything under control." Louise picked up the cough syrup.

"Open up," she said, holding the spoon out to Jane.

Jane frowned but obediently opened her mouth. She

was fairly sure she had taken some already. "You can stop fussing over me," Jane said with a grimace. The syrup tasted vile.

"Oh, you would miss me if I didn't fuss," Louise said, putting down the spoon.

Jane tried to make a joke so Louise knew she was feeling better. "Will you miss me when I go away?" *Wait a minute. That came out wrong. It was supposed to be "How can I miss you if you won't go away?"*

Louise paused, as if she was about to ask Jane something else, but the ringing of the cordless telephone in her apron pocket stopped her. Louise answered it, then frowned and gave it to Jane. "It's Josie."

Jane smiled and took the handset. Jane had befriended Josie, a young girl who was often dropped off at the inn while her mother, a single parent, was at work. "Hello, Sunflower. How are you?"

"I'm good. My mommy told me you were sick. So that means no tea parties."

"No, honey, not for a bit."

Josie sighed dramatically.

Louise pointed downstairs and whispered, "I will pick up the phone later."

Jane acknowledged her words with a nod that sent a sharp needle of pain lancing through her head. "When I'm better we can have one," Jane said to Josie, trying to focus on the conversation, not the pain.

"My mommy said I couldn't talk to you long because you are sick. I hafta go now. Bye."

Jane smiled and set the phone on the bedside table and let the sleep that was hanging around the edges of her mind claim her.

⌒

What was a woodpecker doing in the house? Jane kept her eyes closed, listening to the light tapping. Slowly she pulled herself awake. She looked around her room and yawned as she recognized the sound.

Someone was knocking on her bedroom door.

"Come in," she whispered.

The door creaked slowly open, and Ethel stuck her head through the opening.

"How are you, Jane? May I come in?"

"Oh, please do." Jane pushed herself up on her pillows, happy to see her dear aunt.

"Wonderful, wonderful." Ethel swept into Jane's room and set a white cardboard box on her end table. "Brought you some tarts," she said. "Louise felt you might not be ready for rich food, but I am pretty sure after eating her cooking, you're ready for anything that resembles real food. Louise means well and tries hard, but oh my, her cooking."

Ethel fairly clucked as she straightened the bedclothes and patted Jane lightly on the cheek. "I wanted to come and visit you sooner, but I've been busy."

"With what?" Jane said, trying to concentrate on what she was saying.

Ethel smiled at her and pulled a chair closer. "I don't know if you heard that Sylvia is sick as well. I stopped by her place and she sent her greetings. Alice was going to bring her chicken soup." Ethel paused a moment, then hurried on. "Craig Tracy said to say hello." Ethel's chatter flitted through the room, bringing Jane up to date on who got a perm at Betty Dunkle's Clip 'n' Curl and what new dishes Zachary was offering on his menu.

Jane wanted to ask her about the movie, but Ethel never gave her a chance to talk. Besides, Jane could not seem to keep her eyes open and the headache that had threatened when Josie had called was now making itself felt.

The ringing of the phone echoed shrilly in her head.

Ethel picked up the receiver, said hello and nodded. "She's right here." Covering the mouthpiece with her hand, she handed the phone to Jane with a conspiratorial smile. "It's Debbie," she said in a stage whisper.

"Hey there, Jane, nice to get your e-mail," Debbie was

saying. "Have you considered my offer? I'd love to have you on board. I know what a great cook you are. Innovative and sharp. Just what I'm looking for. I already ran the idea past . . ." Jane shook her head as she tried to catch up to Debbie's rapid-fire delivery of information, her mind unable to sort out the words that seemed to scatter once they got into her head.

"I haven't been feeling well," she said in the first lull in the conversation. "But I don't . . ."

"Now then, Jane, I don't want to hear 'I don't.' What I want to hear is 'I'll think about it.'"

Jane tried to absorb the words, then said, "I'll think about it."

"That's my girl. I want to come and talk to you. When is a good time?"

"I don't know." She looked at Ethel and then, unable to make another decision, handed her the phone.

She heard Ethel chatting with Debbie. "Why don't you come as soon as possible," Ethel was saying. "We have room here at the inn." Ethel talked a bit more, then hung up.

"What a lovely lady," Ethel said. "I'm looking forward to meeting her. It would be fun to introduce her to Florence."

She chatted on. Jane began to feel increasingly tired and woozy. Her mind drifted away. Ethel's voice faded in and out, her words barely registering with Jane. "Groundhog Day . . . famous people . . . Fred . . . and you too, Jane . . . cooking show . . . Debbie . . ." Jane just smiled and nodded.

"You really are not well," Ethel finally said, seeing Jane's glazed look. "Do you need anything?"

Jane turned her head and the room seemed to continue revolving. She saw a bottle beside the bed and remembered Louise giving her a spoonful. Maybe she needed some more. She pointed to the bottle with the spoon beside it. "I think I need to take that."

Ethel picked up the bottle, measured out some syrup and gave it to Jane, who took it and smiled at her aunt. The last thing Jane remembered before drifting off to sleep was Ethel's light kiss on her forehead.

⌒

"Drink this tea," Louise said to Jane. "Maybe you should get up. You have been sleeping a lot." Louise knew that sleep was good, but this much?

"I don't want to get up," Jane mumbled.

Louise had hoped that Jane might be better this morning, but her glassy eyes and the bright fever spots on her cheeks told Louise that it would be a few more days before Jane was up and about. "I have to do my Monday shopping and then I will come again and check on you."

Jane nodded, finished the tea, obediently swallowed some pudding and then curled back in her bed.

Louise sighed and went downstairs. She would have to ask Alice about how much Jane was sleeping. It didn't seem right.

She put away the tray, put on her coat and hat and headed out to her car. She drove to her first destination and worked her way through her list with her usual brisk efficiency. Her last stop was at Wilhelm Wood's shop, Time for Tea.

"I would also like a packet of that special blend, 'Winding Down,'" Louise said to Wilhelm as she consulted her list.

"For Alice?"

Louise laughed. "I think I might need it for myself."

"Things pretty busy at the inn these days, aren't they?" Wilhelm said as he bagged her purchases.

"We only have one guest at the inn. Randall Marquette." Louise forced a smile as she spoke his name. She was practicing her resolution of yesterday to only think kindly of the young man. It was difficult, knowing what she did about the mandate that he had received from Trey to win over the town.

"What do you think of a movie being made in Acorn Hill?" Wilhelm smoothed his thinning blond hair down in a nervous gesture. "Trey Atkinson told me that I could gain some good exposure in the movie. That Time for Tea could really benefit. But I don't know. I'm not sure that a movie would be right for the town."

Louise gathered up her purchases. "I don't think that Trey is giving us the whole story. Alice feels the same way and she is far more trusting of people than I am."

"What could he be hiding?" Wilhelm asked. "We know they want to make a movie in the town."

"That's true. But what would the repercussions be? What kind of movie do they intend? Will they let us see the script? These are questions they don't seem to be willing to answer."

"I heard that you can get paid quite well if Hollywood decides to use your property for a movie."

"They want to use Grace Chapel for a large portion of the movie."

"How does the church board feel about that?"

Louise shrugged her shoulders. This was not her information to divulge, but from what Alice had told her after the meeting, she felt uneasy about how the church board would vote. And if the church went along, it seemed likely many other people would too.

"Surely if most of the people were against it, the town council couldn't allow it to go through, could they?" Wilhelm asked.

"I'm quite sure they couldn't."

"Then let us hope that common sense prevails. I wouldn't want to see Acorn Hill overrun with tourists."

Coming from Wilhelm, who traveled extensively, this amused Louise.

"Nothing has been decided," Louise said. "Well, I had better get back to the inn." Louise was tired of talking about the movie. All she wanted right now was a cup of coffee in the peace and quiet of her own home.

⌒

"Sissy Matthews said I could take her lesson this afternoon." Tabitha stood in the front entrance, clutching the music books Louise had given her in her mittened hands. "When I called her to talk to her about music, like you suggested, she told me she wasn't going to take her lesson today. I thought maybe I could. That's why she didn't call you to cancel."

Louise pulled her pale peach sweater tighter around herself as she considered this unique situation. Never before had she had a piano student want to come for extra lessons. It appeared that Mrs. Harke was correct about Tabitha's dedication.

"That is fine with me," Louise said, smiling at the girl who looked up at her with such determination, "but what is as important as lessons is the daily practice."

"I practiced twice as hard," Tabitha said, lifting her chin in the air. "Right after my homework, I play for two hours and I also play in the morning before school."

Louise remembered devoting hours of the day to piano practice, but at an age considerably older than Tabitha's. "Then I think we should see how well you have done." Louise gave her a quick smile and led the way to the parlor.

Tabitha set the books on the piano and pulled off her mittens. "My hands are a bit cold yet."

"Please, warm up your hands first. I have to go to the kitchen to check on something that I'm baking." Louise closed the door of the soundproofed parlor and hurried down the hallway. Besides taking over Sissy's lesson, Tabitha was also early. Louise had not counted on starting the lesson for at least ten minutes.

She stopped when she came into the kitchen, sniffing suspiciously. She opened the oven door and stared in dismay at the cake that was now overflowing its pan and spilling onto the bottom of the oven. She pulled a cookie sheet out of a cupboard and set it under the cake pan to catch any more drips. The timer showed precisely thirty-five minutes to go. With a sigh, she closed the oven door and hoped the burning drippings did not trigger the smoke detector.

Tabitha was already running over her scales when Louise

returned. As they went through the lesson, it was apparent that Tabitha indeed did show a tremendous aptitude.

"You have done very, very well," Louise said as she closed the books at the end of the lesson. "You are very talented."

Tabitha ran her fingers up and down the edges of the books, her expression suddenly wistful. "Mrs. Smith, I need to make a confession."

"Go ahead, dear," Louise said, trying not to glance at her watch. She still had three minutes before she had to take the cake out of the oven.

"My mom doesn't know I came here this afternoon, so I can't pay you for the lesson right away." She clutched the books harder. "I got a job shoveling sidewalks after school to help pay. Can I give you the money later and can you please not tell my mom about this? She'll flip when she finds out I did this."

"I don't like the idea of hiding this from your mother, but I also doubt she will 'flip' if she finds out."

Tabitha sighed. "She will. She keeps telling me she doesn't want to see me disappointed." Tabitha looked up at her, her dark eyes intent, and Louise had to smile. "Do you think I will be?"

Louise gave into an urge and stroked the girl's hair. "I think God has given you a tremendous gift. The important thing is to use it for Him."

"If God gave me this gift, does that mean I can only play in church?" she asked with a wary look.

Louise laughed. "No. I think it is very important that you use your gift for God wherever He places you."

"My mom keeps telling me not to practice so much." Tabitha bit her lip. "I'm scared she's going to tell me that she's not going to pay for my lessons anymore. I don't know what I'll do then."

Louise's heart ached for the girl, but at the same time, she could understand her mother's concerns. "I think your mother would support you if you showed that you were willing to do some of the things she wants you to do."

"Like what?"

"Spend time with other girls, do some ordinary middle-school things."

Tabitha caught one corner of her lip and chewed it as if thinking. "I don't know who to hang out with."

The insistent beep of the oven's timer intruded on their conversation.

"You have to go and so do I," Tabitha said as she grabbed her mittens and her books and scooted toward the front door. Before she left, she turned to Louise. "Thanks, Mrs. Smith, for helping me."

"You are welcome. Tabitha, did you know that there is a special meeting this week of the ANGELs, our church girls group? It will be some kind of fun activity. I know that the girls would be happy if you joined them."

Tabitha gave a noncommittal shrug as she slipped on her thick winter jacket.

"It could be enjoyable," Louise said, remembering Mrs. Harke's concern about Tabitha's single-mindedness. In spite of herself, Louise had to agree. The girl needed balance in her life. "Maybe if you went, your mother might be more willing to support your piano lessons."

Tabitha pulled her stocking cap down over her ears. "I'll see. Thanks again for letting me take the lesson. I enjoyed it." She flashed Louise a quick smile, then scooted out the door.

Louise watched her run down the walk, her open jacket flying out behind her and, in spite of her concern for the girl, she had to smile.

Dear Lord, she prayed, *help that girl use her gift for You. Help her not to seek fame, but to seek You first.*

That evening Louise was alone for supper. Alice had to work and Jane was still up in her room. The quiet time gave her a chance to finish the bookkeeping and to confirm a few reservations they had for guests coming in a couple of weeks. She wrote their names in the appointment book and wondered if she was going to have to cook for them.

She sincerely hoped not.

Chapter Nine

"H ello? Anybody home?"

Louise came down the stairs the following day just as Florence closed the front door behind her. "Good afternoon, Florence," Louise said, adjusting her grip on the overflowing laundry basket. "What can I do for you?"

Florence unwrapped a heavy scarf from around her head. "I tried the back door," she said, "but I didn't get an answer, so I thought I would try the front door. I was wondering if I could visit Jane?"

Louise hoped she didn't look as perplexed as she felt. Jane was not fond of the meddlesome woman, and Louise suspected that the feeling was mutual. Jane's quick rejoinders and sarcasm often got her into trouble with Florence.

"Is she awake?" Florence continued. "Able to have visitors?"

"She is sitting up and reading right now." Though Jane seemed much better, her pale face and shaking hands told Louise that she needed a few more days to recuperate. She would have liked to visit with Jane herself and ask her about Debbie, but she did not have time.

"That's wonderful." Florence laid her binder on the reception desk and struggled out of her coat. Underneath she wore a bulky sweater that added to her formidable size. "I really need to talk to her. I mean, visit her," Florence added as Louise took her coat. "I just thought she could use some cheering up."

Somehow, Louise thought, Florence and cheering up do not go together.

"Ethel told me she visited her so I thought I could too," Florence continued. "No need to show me up," she said, bustling past Louise. "Ethel told me that Jane's room is on the third floor. I'll find her."

Before Louise could stop Florence or warn Jane, the woman was huffing up the stairs.

✑

Jane was thankful that she was feeling a bit better than yesterday. If she conserved her strength, by tomorrow she might be able to go downstairs. *If only I didn't feel so sleepy all the time*, she thought.

A knock on her door lifted her spirits. *A visitor!* Maybe it was Sylvia. Jane wanted to find out what was happening in the world outside of her bedroom. She had tried to listen to the radio, but the sound seemed to scrape across her mind like fingernails on a blackboard.

"Come in," she said, sitting up, a smile on her lips.

"Hello, Jane," Florence said as she marched across the room and pulled a chair up close to the bed with one hand. In her other hand she clutched a purple binder. "For someone who is ill, you don't look too bad. Your cheeks have some color and your hair isn't that dull and lank."

Jane's smile strained.

"I knew you could use a visitor," Florence said, her plump hands folded over the binder resting on her lap.

"That's kind of you, Florence," Jane said.

Florence tapped her pudgy fingers against her binder, as she looked around the room, trying to find a topic for discussion.

"And how are things in Acorn Hill these days?" Jane asked. The sooner she got this visit going, the sooner Florence would leave.

"Busy, busy." Florence gave Jane a conspiratorial grin. "Ever since that film crew has come to town, that's all we've been talking about. Well, and that you're not going to be around, and that Fred's going to Punxsutawney, of course. Let me tell you, Jane, with this movie, Acorn Hill is going to be recognized as the wonderful place it is. I'm hoping you can convince Alice to see that as well. I think she is hesitant."

Of the flurry of words that Florence heaped on her, one phrase stood out.

"Not around? I'm not that sick," Jane said.

Florence forged ahead, ignoring Jane's comment. "They want to use the chapel for the movie and if they want to do that, why then, it must be a good movie. We would have a chance to promote family values and many good things. If Acorn Hill is featured in a movie, it could put us on the map."

"We're already on the map," Jane said.

"But more importantly, this could be a chance for local artists, such as you and, well, I almost hesitate to add myself, to be recognized." Florence paused a moment, trying to look humble but failing.

"Yourself?" Jane was truly lost now. Florence? An artist?

Florence leaned forward, tapping her fingers on the binder on her lap. "I have a movie script that I have been working on." She glanced over her shoulder as if making sure no one could overhear and leaned a little closer, almost whispering now. "It's a story about a young woman and how she overcomes various trials."

"A movie script?"

"It was going to be a book, but I read somewhere that movie scripts don't need to be as long and because I'm so busy, I decided to do a movie script instead. They said to write what you know, so I set it here, in Acorn Hill. And if the movie company is already shooting a movie here, why, they could just stay here to do mine."

Florence shifted in her chair, all enthusiasm and excitement now. "I have only shown this to Trey Atkinson and he suggested I get someone else to look at it. I was thinking of our librarian, Nia Komonos, but she told me she didn't know enough about movies to give any advice. Clara Horn is my dear friend and all, but she knows even less about movies. Viola," Florence waved a dismissive hand, "feels the same way about movies as she does about best sellers. So I thought of you. You are also an artist and I know you can keep a secret."

And right now I'm a captive audience, thought Jane, sinking lower into her pillows.

"Do you want me to read some of it to you?"

While Jane was trying to formulate a polite way to say no, Florence opened the binder, taking Jane's silence as acceptance.

"I won't read it all to you," Florence said, glancing over her shoulder. "It's too long and besides ideas get stolen all the time, you know." She waggled a finger at Jane as if warning her. Jane was surprised that Florence didn't check to see if she was wired.

"Maybe you should just read what you think is the best part," Jane suggested, seizing the opportunity to shorten the visit.

"Oh yes. Very good idea." Florence licked one finger and paged through the binder. "I really like this part. What has happened is a young woman named Carlita has stumbled across two bodies in an alley. Of course she is frightened and starts running. This is where things get interesting. 'The young woman pauses midflight . . .' I'm reading the notes to the director now," Florence glanced at Jane. "You have to write these things present tense, you know."

Jane gave her a vaguely encouraging smile and fought another wave of dizziness.

"Okay. Where was I? 'She glances over her shoulder in time to see a dark figure hulking in the alleyway. Her movements are jerky. She pulls her hanky out of her pocket and blows her nose'—I put that in for verisimilitude," Florence explained. "'But that very movement draws the attention of her pursuer and he comes after her. Just as it seems our heroine is in grave danger, out of the shadows steps another man' . . ." Florence read on while Jane looked longingly out the window at the sun glinting off the snow. Louise had told her it had snowed during the night. All morning she had wished she could be outside. Now, more than ever.

"Listen, this is the best part," Florence was saying.

Jane reluctantly dragged her attention back to Florence's screenplay and pretended to look suitably terrified by the actions Florence was describing. The stalking scene went on for about fourteen pages, which, by Jane's estimation, was fifteen pages too long.

"Mr. Atkinson says I need a car chase in here to liven things up, but my story takes place right here in Acorn Hill. I just can't imagine cars and trucks tearing harum scarum down the streets." Florence shook her head, her lips pressed primly together. "It just isn't realistic."

But a grisly murder or two in Acorn Hill was realistic, it seemed. Jane thought she should warn Alice of Florence's tendencies. She might think twice about voting for the woman's proposals to the church board.

"So what do you think?" Florence asked, finally closing her binder.

Jane hesitated, struggling to find suitable words. "I think it's amazing that you managed to write an entire screenplay without telling anyone about it."

Florence nodded solemnly. "You know how we artists are. Sometimes it's best if things are kept quiet. Otherwise, people are always bothering you, asking pesky questions about when it's going to be finished. I didn't want to put myself through that. The muse, you know." She heaved a deep, theatrical sigh.

"I understand." Jane took a sip of water and laid her head back, hoping she looked as weak and tired as she felt.

"I can read you more if you like."

Jane held her hand up in warning. "You must be careful, Florence. You shouldn't reveal too much of your story too soon." She looked past Florence as if checking for spies that might be lurking. Florence glanced suspiciously back in time to see Wendell stroll past the door. "You never know," Jane said ominously.

Florence clutched her binder even closer, as if afraid the words might spill out and reveal themselves. "You are right. Thank you, Jane." She leaned forward. "Now you know why this movie is so important to me. I believe your sister Alice does not want that movie crew to film in Grace Chapel. They need to, Jane." Florence's eyes glowed with a fervor that made Jane thankful she was not on the church board. "You must help me make Alice see. If they don't film here, my script, my hopes . . ." she shook her head, her lips drawn tight, as if the possibility couldn't even bear mentioning. Florence rose from the chair, clutching her binder like a mother would a child. "I need your help, Jane. Think about it." With a dramatic turn, Florence swept out of the room in a manner worthy of a film star.

$\backsim$

"How is Jane feeling?" Randall asked. He had been out most of the day but was now hanging around the kitchen. Alice didn't have the heart to ask him to leave. He seemed to enjoy sitting at the table and chatting while she read the recipes Viola had given them.

"I thought she was getting better but she has been sleeping all afternoon."

"There's a pond a little ways from here. I was wondering if you knew how deep it is?" Randall was winding up some string into a ball.

"Fairy Pond? I have no idea," Alice said with a shrug, trying to read Viola's handwriting. Viola had written out some recipes that she had declared Louise-proof. Alice, however, was determined to pull her share of the inn's workload and had sent Louise upstairs to finish changing the bedding while she made supper. Louise looked tired. Though Louise's strong constitution matched her strong will, Alice knew that her sister needed a break from cooking. And Alice needed a break from eating Louise's cooking. Though Alice was no chef, she could manage in the kitchen. She had cooked for herself and her father for many years.

Potato soup and omelets with cheese and green peppers were on the menu. Simple and nutritious. Just to be on the safe side, Alice was doubling the recipe. Ethel hadn't been coming around since Louise started cooking, but she might make an exception tonight. For Jane, she was heating up some chicken noodle soup. That and a slice of toast might tempt Jane's appetite.

"Could you skate on the pond?" Randall asked.

Randall had gone last night to the Coffee Shop to eat, but tonight seemed disinclined to leave. He now hung around the kitchen teasing Wendell with a ball of string that he'd found in one of the drawers. Though Louise had discouraged serving meals to guests other than breakfast, it appeared that Alice might have to ask him to join them for dinner.

"It hasn't been cold enough in recent winters for it to freeze over properly," Alice said, cutting up the onion she needed for the soup. "I don't think anyone has skated on it in years."

"It's probably cold enough now. This weather reminds me of a good old-fashioned Canadian winter," Randall said with an unexpected grin. "I love it." He seemed much more animated since Trey had left, and Alice wondered if his previously sullen attitude was because of his boss.

She looked outside. The weather had taken a turn for the worse with snowflakes falling from a leaden sky. She had a hard time understanding his enthusiasm. She was, frankly, sick of the cold and the snow.

"How was Dan today?" he asked. "I didn't have a chance to go visit him at the hospital."

"He's better. We had to put him on an IV. There was a danger of dehydration, but otherwise he's doing well, though the flu hit him quite hard."

"Dan's probably exhausted as much as anything," Randall said, leaning back against the counter. He threw the ball of string toward Wendell, still holding one end of it. Wendell twitched his tail as if considering whether to play along. Then he suddenly pounced on it before Randall could pull it back.

"Why was he so exhausted?" Alice asked, curious with Randall's vague disclosure.

"Ever since Dan joined the company, he's been trying too hard. Trey says jump and Dan hands him a measuring stick. Trying to figure out what Trey wants is a time-and-a-half position."

"You sound as if you don't have a lot of respect for your boss."

"I used to, when he was promising me all kinds of things. But I keep waiting."

"Waiting for what?"

"I've written a few things that he has promised to look at and pass on to the studio. I should know better by now, though." Randall laughed without mirth. "Trey is a taker. The trick with working for him is making sure you know exactly how much you're willing to give him."

"And how much is that?"

"As little as possible." Randall did not meet her gaze, but Alice had the impression that he was warning her.

"Is he true to his word?"

"He can be. Just make sure you are very clear what his word is."

Randall bent over and picked up the ball of string, and Alice sensed that it was the end of that conversation. Wendell looked up at him a moment, as if making sure the game was over, then turned and sauntered out of the kitchen in search of other entertainment.

"Thank goodness that job is done." Louise entered the kitchen carrying the last of many basketfuls of laundry. Because of Jane's illness, they had fallen behind on the wash and had four days of linens to launder and put away. "This is the last load."

She stopped in the middle of the kitchen, shifting the basket to her hip, her eyes flicking from Randall to the clock.

"Are you back from dinner already?" she asked.

Alice could see the smile on Louise's face, but she knew her sister well enough to hear the faint chill in her voice. She sensed that Louise was not fond of Randall, in spite of being unfailingly polite and kind to him. Something had happened with Randall since Trey and Lynette had left to put Louise's defenses back up, and Alice wondered what it could be.

"Actually, I thought he could join us," Alice said suddenly. Out of the corner of her eye she saw Randall's head snap up. She looked toward him and as she saw the slow smile crawl across his mouth, she realized that he had been hoping for an invitation. "You don't mind having soup and an omelet with a couple of older women?"

"Sounds great."

"There is one condition," Alice said. "Whoever cooks doesn't have to do the dishes."

"I'll gladly help," he said with a shrug. Alice wondered if he knew that meant he would be assisting Louise.

"Even if I told you the dishwasher is broken?"

"It's not really, is it?" Louise asked.

"Really. I just discovered it. I'll call Fred when he comes back in town and ask if José can fix it for us. I suspect that these industrial dishwashers can be tricky to repair."

The phone rang. Alice turned the flame down under the onions she was sautéing and went to answer it.

"I'm just calling to remind you to turn on your television in an hour or so," Vera said breathlessly. "Fred's interview is going to be on."

"Oh, Vera, how exciting."

"Fred told me he had two interviews, but he only knew when the one is going to air."

"Be sure to tape it, Vera," Alice said. "Just in case we miss the broadcast." Alice glanced over at the stove, keeping an eye on her onions. Louise was stirring them and was about to turn up the heat when Alice stopped her. "Viola had said that they must not get brown or the soup would have a muddy color," she said to Louise, then turned her attention back to the phone. "I should go, Vera. I'm making dinner tonight."

"I thought Louise was cooking."

"She had a busy day today and I took off early. I've been working so much at the hospital that I felt guilty for not helping her. Thanks for reminding me about the program. Bye now." She hung up the phone and took over for her sister.

"You have worked all day," Louise protested. "I can cook supper."

"And you worked hard as well," Alice said, gently escorting her sister away from the stove. It had taken some doing on her part just to get to the kitchen before Louise started dinner. "Sit down and visit with me. You have to help me remember to turn the television on later. Fred is going to be on television in about an hour."

"First, I'll bring Jane's food up to her." Louise gave Randall another puzzled glance, got Jane's tray ready, then left.

"This guy who's going to be on television, is he someone from around here?" Randall asked.

"Yes. Fred Humbert. He was invited to go to Punxsutawney for Groundhog Day because of an interview in our local newspaper."

"Cool." Randall pushed himself away from the counter and came to stand beside Alice, watching her as she started cutting up potatoes. "What are you making?"

"It's supposedly a fool-proof recipe. I guess we'll see."

"Is there anything I can do?"

"No. If you cook, then you're exempt from doing the dishes. While I don't enjoy cooking, I enjoy doing the dishes even less. Besides, Louise would make you wear a hairnet over that ponytail if you started cooking."

Randall held his hands up in a gesture of surrender. "Will I have to wear one to set the table?"

"I think you can manage that. That way you'll know where to put the dishes when you're done."

Louise popped her head in the kitchen door a few moments later to tell Alice that Jane had eaten some of the food and had gone back to sleep. Then she went back down the hall. Alice was about to follow her and find out what was bothering her when a knock at the door stopped her.

"Yoo-hoo." Ethel called out as she stepped inside the kitchen. Her bright red nose matched the twin circles of red on her cheeks. "It's nice and warm in here," she said with a shiver.

"Aunt Ethel, I'm so glad you came. How are you doing?"

"Busy. Busy. I've come to see Jane," Ethel said.

"She's sleeping now."

Ethel sniffed. "What's that I smell cooking?"

"I made supper this evening. Would you like to join us?"

"You cooked? Not Louise?"

Alice stifled a chuckle and shook her head.

"Then I'll stay." Ethel gave Randall a broad smile. "Are you joining us as well?"

"Yes, Alice invited me," Randall said.

"Why don't you sit down and talk to us while we finish up here," Alice said, pulling out a chair for her aunt.

"Louise is practicing, I hear," Ethel said.

Alice paused a moment, listening. Alice's spirits dropped. Louise only played that piece when something was bothering her.

"Can you stir this soup for me, Randall?" she asked, wiping her hands on her apron. "I need to ask Louise something."

Alice went to the open door of the parlor and said softly, "Supper will be ready in a few minutes, Louise." Stepping into the room, Alice closed the door behind her.

Louise sat at her piano, running her hands lightly over the keys, a faintly melancholy look on her face. She glanced up at Alice and smiled.

"What is bothering you, Louise?"

Louise got up from the bench, carefully closing the lid. "I am concerned about Randall hanging around the kitchen."

"Why?"

"Just before Trey left, I overheard him give Randall specific instructions to make sure that the people of the town were agreeable to filming."

"I get the impression that Randall is not particularly fond of Trey."

"He could be saying that," Louise said, "to get on your good side."

"I think he's sincere. Besides, I believe most of the town would not approve of having the movie made here anyway."

"I wish I were as sure. Florence has been bustling around town trying to convince people otherwise." Louise got up from the piano bench. "Make sure that he doesn't try to change your mind. I'm keeping my eye on him."

"Just don't make him feel unwelcome," Alice said with a light tone of reprimand in her voice. "I think he's lonely. Since Trey and the others left, I've been seeing another side of him. Now, I am just going to check on Jane and then I'll be back down to finish making dinner."

Thankfully, as Louise had said, Jane had eaten some of the food, but she was sleeping again, her dark hair fanned out on the pillow. Alice stroked her sister's head, puzzled that she was sleeping so much. She would call Dr. Bentley tomorrow morning to see what could be the problem. Even their patients at the hospital did not sleep as much as Jane had been.

She picked up the tray but left a pitcher of water beside the bottle of cough syrup. When she came downstairs, Louise was already in the kitchen.

Randall looked up as she came in and gave her a quick smile. "Table is all set and I didn't burn the soup."

"Why don't you sit down and I'll serve," Alice said, putting the tray on the counter.

"I think Jane would have put some garnish on this," Ethel said, looking down at the steaming bowl of creamy soup.

"I'm sure Jane would have done a number of wonderful things," Louise said with a gentle smile, folding her hands and resting them on the table. "But for now, I'm thankful that Alice did such a fine job with dinner." Louise looked around the table, her eyes resting on Randall who had already picked up his spoon. "We usually say grace, Randall, before we eat."

Randall looked taken aback for a moment, then put his spoon down. "Good idea."

Louise prayed for a blessing on the food and their work of the day. She prayed for health for Jane and as she prayed, Alice silently added her own prayer for patience with Randall and for them to be able to take this opportunity to show him what family and community were really like.

Because in spite of what Louise had said about him, she sensed that Randall, in his own way, was dissatisfied with his life and was seeking . . . something.

Chapter Ten

*O*kay, I don't mind doing the dishes after supper, but I do have one condition," Randall said after wiping his mouth with the napkin.

"And what is that?" Louise asked. She was surprised that he was willing to help. Of course, if his job was to get people on his side, it would make sense that he make a good impression on Alice. After all, she was one of the church board members who did not approve of what Trey and his crew were proposing.

Ethel was more tractable. During the entire meal, she had peppered Randall with questions about movies that he had helped on and the famous people he had met. She was awed by the list.

Randall swallowed and flashed Louise a quick smile. "My condition is that I get to watch the hockey game while I'm doing them."

"I don't care for watching television after supper," Louise said, trying not to sound petty. "I prefer good conversation. Besides, I don't believe you can find a channel here that will broadcast a hockey game. We don't have cable or satellite."

"That's okay," Randall said. "The games are shown on farmer vision too."

"Farmer vision?" Louise asked.

"Antenna. Local joke," he said with a light grin.

"I don't mind the television being on," Alice said glancing at her watch. "I would like to catch Fred's interview. Vera said he would be on fairly soon. Randall could watch after that."

"Well then, we will watch television while we do the dishes." Louise said, looking across the table at Randall. Though she knew she was right in mistrusting Randall's motives, she was wrong in holding back hospitality from him. Yes, they had boundaries and, yes, they should be maintained, but he was alone. Maybe by showing him the love and forgiveness she had been granted, she could show him a better way to live.

Forgive me, Lord, she prayed as she rose to clear the table.

Alice also rose from her seat. "Aunt Ethel, may I get you a cup of coffee while we watch Fred?" Alice asked, turning on the television.

"Coffee would be lovely." Ethel sat back with a well-satisfied look. "That was a good meal, Alice. Not quite up to Jane's standards, but nourishing and filling."

"It's very difficult to attain Jane's standards," Alice agreed with a smile.

"Has she told you exactly when she's going to do that cooking show?" Ethel asked. "I have to confess I was so excited when I heard. Now I won't have to listen to Florence going on and on about her niece. A five-minute walk-on part in a soap opera is nothing compared to Jane being on a show."

"She hasn't said anything to us about it," Louise reminded her aunt. "Jane has been too ill to discuss it."

"Well, I think it would be exciting for her," Ethel said. "Aren't you excited about it? This would be such an opportunity for her."

"It is entirely up to Jane, Aunt Ethel," Louise said with a warning note in her voice, puzzled that Ethel was so enthusiastic about the possibility of Jane's leaving Acorn Hill. "If Jane wants to do it, we shouldn't try to stop her."

Even as she bravely spoke the words, she hoped that Jane would share her sisters' desire for the status quo.

⌒

"Tonight on the eve of Groundhog Day, our roaming reporter has been doing what she is paid to do, roam. We have a series of interviews from Punxsutawney." A broadly smiling woman holding a large microphone replaced the smiling anchorman on the television screen. She stood facing the camera, a thick red stocking cap pulled over her ears.

"Punxsutawney Phil has many detractors and a few imitators. There are those who believe that Phil has been wrong more often than he has been right. I've managed to find a couple of people on location, and I've asked them if they could beat Phil's prediction and if so, how."

The picture dissolved again and suddenly there was Fred, looking surprisingly calm.

"There he is," said Alice, pointing at the television with the fork she had picked up from the table. "Isn't this exciting?"

"Fred Humbert from Acorn Hill, Pennsylvania," said the woman as the camera came back to her, "claims that Punxsutawney Phil has been wrong over fifty percent of the time." The woman gave the camera a can-you-believe-it smirk. "He believes that with a little bit of information mixed with observation and common sense, anyone can predict the weather better than Phil. Here's what he has to say."

Fred's calm and smiling face was back. It looked and sounded as though they caught him midsentence though.

". . . pigs gather leaves and straw before a storm, or it will be a cold and snowy winter if the breastbone of a fresh-cooked turkey is dark purple . . ."

The woman's face came back with its smirk in place.

"Now this is interesting, and let's face it, far more scientific than a groundhog popping out of a hole and seeing its shadow. Let's see what other pearls of wisdom the Acorn Hill prognosticator has for us."

Fred returned, still smiling. "If a dog pulls his feet up high when walking, a change in the weather is coming. But . . ." and he was cut off and the woman was back. "So, folks, there you have it. With a little bit of observation and information, you too can predict the weather. And now, I'm going to put our local weatherman out of a job by cooking a turkey. Bye." Her grinning face faded out and was replaced by the anchorman again.

Louise frowned. "He was going to say something else, I'm sure of it. She made him look foolish," she said.

"Spin," said Randall, getting up to clear the dishes from the table.

"What do you mean by 'spin'?" asked Louise.

"The reporter decides what kind of story she wants to tell. She talks long enough, asks enough questions until she gets the quotes that will fit in with her story." Randall set the plates on the counter, his eyes still on the television screen. "Happens all the time."

"But Fred is a very intelligent man who knows a lot about weather," Louise sputtered. "Why did she do that?"

Randall shrugged. "She wanted a humorous story." He

gave Louise a sympathetic glance. "Doesn't matter what your friend said. The interviewer had her own agenda. She asked him enough of the right kind of questions to get the answers she wanted. Then the editors simply deleted what didn't fit with the spin they wanted to put on it."

"That's outrageous," Louise said.

"That's entertainment," Randall replied. "Where is the soap for the dishes?"

"Under the sink," Alice said.

Randall turned on the tap and started rinsing the plates, setting them aside.

"I can't believe they could do that to Fred. They made him look like a yokel." Ethel said angrily, almost quivering with indignation. "They made Acorn Hill look like a place where yokels live."

"Don't upset yourself, Aunt Ethel. Most people wouldn't have paid attention to the mention of his hometown," Louise said, clearing away the rest of the meal. "Now you sit down, Alice, and keep Aunt Ethel company."

Louise tied an apron around her brown wool skirt, pushed up the sleeves of her sweater and took a clean, folded tea towel out of the drawer.

While Randall washed the dishes, he kept his eyes on the television. Louise picked up the remote and was about to turn it off when Randall reached out a soapy hand to stop her.

"Hey, the deal was I get to watch the hockey game."

"You are dripping on the counter," she said.

"Sorry." He pulled his hand back. "Alice said I could watch the game if I did the dishes."

Louise looked up at the television, the noise of a series of commercials intruding on the usually quiet kitchen. "All right then," she said, meeting his gaze and remembering her resolution to treat him with respect and consideration. "I'm not one to back out on a deal, so I guess we're watching a hockey game."

Randall's eyes sparkled with fun as he reached past her for the remote control. "Who knows, Mrs. Smith? You might enjoy it."

Louise looked back at the television and the blur of movement and shook her head. "I doubt that," she said.

"Here we go. Hockey game is starting," Randall said, turning up the volume just a notch. He flashed Louise a grin. "So, who are you going to cheer for? It's the New York Islanders against the Vancouver Canucks. Eastern States versus Western Canada. I have to cheer for the Canadian team, which means you have to cheer for the American team. Though it's a moot point. Most of the players on both teams come from Canada anyhow."

"I don't have to cheer for either team. I have never watched hockey before."

"You are now."

The teams were introduced, the national anthems of the two countries were sung and, with a loud cheer, the teams skated off.

"What are they doing now? I thought they were going to play?" Alice asked from her seat at the kitchen table.

"They are. Only eight players are allowed on the ice at a time. The other lines wait their turn." Randall explained the basic rules of the game, which to Louise were basic indeed. Keep the puck moving with the hockey stick and get it into the opposing team's net. It did not seem very interesting.

Randall washed off a plate, but his entire concentration was on the television screen, a grin teasing his mouth. This was the most animated Louise had seen him since he had arrived at the inn.

"Oh yes. Good shot," Randall called out. "Again. Hit it again."

"What is going on?" Louise asked, trying to figure out which team had the puck.

"Scramble in front of the net. C'mon. Get it in." He held his hand up as if urging them on, then lowered it again when a whistle sounded and the players stopped what they were doing and skated away.

"Why are they stopping?" Alice asked.

"Whistle on the play. The goalie has the puck under his glove and that means they have to have a face-off."

"Face-off?" Ethel sounded puzzled.

"They stop the game, and the referee and the players go to one of those painted circles on the ice where they drop the puck to start the game again." Randall explained a few more things whenever the referee's whistle blew and the game was stopped for one infraction or another. Then New York scored a goal.

Louise felt her heart skip a beat before she caught herself. *This is ridiculous*, she thought as she watched grown men cavorting around the rink, hitting each other on the back.

Alice and Ethel were cheering loudly.

"Oh, good job," Alice called out, clapping her hands.

Louise shot her a frown, but Alice's attention was on the television. *Goodness, she is getting as caught up in this as Randall is.*

A knock on the door was her deliverance. If anyone could balance out this foolishness, it was Viola.

"Come in," Alice called out, getting up from the table, but Louise could see that she could not keep her attention away from the television set. Ethel was leaning forward, also avidly watching the game.

"What is going on here?" Viola asked, stepping into the kitchen.

"We're watching the hockey game," Ethel said. "Come join us. New York is winning."

"Just for now, Mrs. Buckley," Randall said, setting the last pot on the rack for Louise to dry. He dried his hands, sauntered over to the table and pulled out a chair. He turned it around and straddled it, his arms resting on the backrest as he tipped it forward.

Louise was about to tell him to put the chair down, but then remembered that she had resolved to be kind to him. The chair could handle the abuse.

Viola gave Louise a puzzled look. "We are going to have to work around them," Louise said. "We promised Randall that if he helped with the dishes he could watch his hockey game, and Alice and Ethel seem to be entertained by it as well."

"I brought over a few recipes for snacks that can easily be frozen," Viola said, brandishing a sheaf of papers. "If you have enough containers, we will do as much as we can this evening."

They read over the ingredient list and Louise set out on the counter what they needed.

"Do you need any help?" Alice called out. "Oh my goodness! Randall, is that allowed?"

"That was nasty," said Ethel.

She was not going to look, Louise promised herself, but

the very startled reactions of her sister and aunt irresistibly drew her gaze to the television screen. She winced as the replay showed a New York player checked so hard by a Vancouver player that the jarring noise could be heard on the television.

Barbaric, she thought, turning back to the recipe.

"I thought we could start with this brownie recipe," Viola said. "It is supposed to be no-fail . . ." she let the sentence drift off as she pushed her glasses farther up her nose and glanced sidelong at the television.

Louise sighed, took the recipe from Viola's hand and glanced over the ingredients. "You can start by melting the butter in a saucepan. I'll beat the eggs."

As soon as she started up the mixer, Ethel picked up the remote and turned the volume up on the television.

Louise kept her focus resolutely on the eggs she was beating, then frowned. Was she supposed to beat three or four eggs? She looked back at the eggshells she had set aside, but Viola had already thrown them into the garbage can.

"Do you remember how many eggs I used?" she asked.

"Check the carton," Viola said, stirring while she watched the television.

That was a good idea, but there had been a few eggs missing before she started. Louise took another egg and broke it into the bowl. *Just to be on the safe side*, she thought.

The announcer's voice slowly increased in intensity, then suddenly he shouted out, "Sco-o-o-o-o-re," and Randall was hollering.

"That's not good," Viola called out, then clamped her lips together when Louise sent her an irritated glance.

"We are still winning," Ethel said when the noise died down.

Louise closed her eyes and sent up a prayer for patience. When Viola had first suggested a baking evening, she had imagined a chance to spend some time with her friend talking about literature. Instead they were surrounded by people intent on watching grown men hit each other and chase a piece of rubber up and down the ice.

She looked back up at the television just in time to see two New York players racing down the ice, skates flashing, while a lone Vancouver player skated backward, trying to stop them.

One passed the puck to the other. That man stopped and took a shot. *No!* He got the puck again, passed it and his teammate picked it up neatly and shot it at the goalie all in one smooth motion.

It was in!

Louise stopped herself from cheering just as Ethel, Alice and Viola all shouted.

Louise thought that she would be very glad indeed

when this young man was gone and her peaceful life was back to normal.

Whatever normal was these days.

⌒

Two pans of interesting-looking brownies, a container of delicious chocolate chip cookies and a somewhat lopsided cake were cooling on the counter by the time Viola left.

Randall had gone upstairs, Ethel had gone home and Alice and Louise were alone in the kitchen.

"I never knew watching hockey could be so much fun," Alice said as she wiped down the counters.

"It is very rough," Louise sniffed as she cut up the pan of brownies.

Alice nudged her sister's elbow. "Oh, come on, Louise. I caught you watching a time or two."

"How could I not," Louise said with a wry smile. "It was permeating the atmosphere."

"So was your baking." Alice lifted the lid of the container and pulled out a cookie. She took a bite and smiled. "These are great, Louise."

"Thank you, but they are very ordinary. They are nothing like Jane would have done." Louise smoothed the icing on the lopsided cake. "I have to face the facts, Alice. I am no cook. I can barely bake, even with someone helping me."

"You do your best, Louise." Alice gave her sister a quick, one-armed hug.

"My best is not good enough to run an inn. I cannot hope to come anywhere near what Jane accomplishes in this kitchen." She washed the knife off and wiped it dry. "She has a gift that should be nurtured."

"And you think that Debbie is the one to do that? Not us?" Alice asked. Then she said in an unusually firm tone, "Until we can talk this out with her, I think we should assume that Jane is staying." Alice bit her lip. "She likes it here. She loves us."

"You sound like you are trying to convince yourself," Louise said.

"I am," Alice said. "I just wish I knew why Aunt Ethel is so enthusiastic about the idea of the show. Has Jane told her something she did not share with us?"

"Aunt Ethel usually knows a lot of things we don't know," Louise said. "That is why she pops by here so often, to share the wealth."

"I must talk to Jane, though I'm not sure when that is going to happen. I have to work tomorrow night, so I had to postpone the ANGELs meeting until Thursday. Then there is another church board meeting on Friday evening." Alice ran her hand through her hair. "I think we should invite Randall to the Coffee Shop tomorrow morning."

"And not have one of my lovely breakfasts?" Louise asked with mock disappointment.

"I wasn't trying to insult your cooking," Alice said.

"You don't have to worry about that. My cooking insults itself. I think Randall might enjoy the respite, if not our company."

"It's settled then, the Coffee Shop tomorrow," Alice said, taking Louise's arm. "You know, I think you're warming to Randall."

"It's time something was warm around here," Louise said. She looked out the front door just before she turned the light off and shook her head in dismay. "It's snowing again."

"That's a worry for tomorrow," Alice said. "Now we need to turn in."

Chapter Eleven

*J*ane rolled over in her bed. The red glow of her alarm clock was the only illumination in the darkness. Though it was midnight, for the first time in days she felt wide awake and rested. The only problem was that nobody else was up. Her stomach growled with hunger. She sat up, pleased that while she was still feeling a little shaky, her mind seemed to be clear. She swung her legs over the edge of her bed and slowly got up, holding onto the end table for support. *Not too bad*, she thought.

It took her about ten minutes, but she managed to make it downstairs to the kitchen. Once there, she immediately sank into a kitchen chair, the room spinning around her head. *My goodness*, she thought, *I feel as limp as cooked spaghetti*. She closed her eyes for a moment, then opened them and focused on the kitchen counter. Things were still a little off kilter. That cake seemed crooked.

She blinked and looked again.

No. That cake actually *was* crooked.

Jane groaned and got up to inspect it. Her heart sunk lower than the side of the cake. *Poor Louise.*

"I think it will taste better than it looks."

The man's voice brought Jane's heart into her throat. She spun around and clung to the counter as the room kept right on spinning.

"You scared me," she said, catching her breath.

"Then we're even. I thought you were a burglar." Randall showed Jane the heavy hammer he had in his hand. "How are you feeling?" he asked, putting down the hammer and shoving his hands into the pockets of his blue jeans. The green plaid shirt he wore over a white turtleneck sweater made him look like a lumberjack.

"I can handle the pain until it hurts," Jane said with a smile.

"Obviously a little better. Do you want something to drink?" he asked walking to the stove. He filled up the kettle. "Or eat?"

"I can get it myself," Jane said feebly. "You are a guest."

"Sort of," he said. "I had to do the dishes after supper."

Jane was dumbfounded. Surely her sisters wouldn't make a guest work.

"Don't look so shocked," Randall said as he took a couple of mugs out of the cupboard. "I was hanging around the kitchen anyway. I was bored."

"The other guests are gone, aren't they?"

Randall nodded and set the mugs on the counter. "Do you want coffee, tea or hot chocolate?"

"Tea, please. It's in . . ."

"I know where it is." He found the teas and held up a box of ginger and peach flavored black tea. Jane nodded her agreement with his choice. "Do you want some toast and soup?"

"Is that the soup Louise helped to make?" she asked.

"Okay, I guess no soup," Randall took out a loaf of bread and popped two slices into the toaster.

"You are very capable in the kitchen," Jane said.

"Survival. That and a mother who was determined that her boys were going to learn to cook just as well as her girls."

"Smart mother."

"No. Lousy cook," he said, giving her another grin. "She is a great mother though. She and Dad raised us right."

"Where does your family live?" Jane asked.

"Most of them stayed close to Mom and Dad in Stony Plain, Alberta. I'm the only one that left the country. I miss them sometimes." He laughed again. "Actually I miss them more and more lately. They've always been really supportive."

"Why did you leave?"

"The lure of the silver screen. I knew if I wanted to do anything with movies, I'd have to move to LA. Now, I don't know if it helped me at all."

The kettle started whistling and Randall poured the boiling water into the mugs.

The smell of the tea and toast set Jane's stomach growling again. When Randall set them in front of her, she had to stop herself from grabbing the toast and wolfing it down.

"I understand you and your crew are checking out Acorn Hill as a possible movie location," she said between bites of toast.

Randall shrugged, and it seemed as if he was pulling back into himself. Jane wanted to find out more, but sensed that she needed to take a roundabout route with him.

"So what made you pick our town?" she asked, moving the topic to safer ground.

"It's not far from Philly, which makes transportation easier."

"Is that the only reason?"

Randall took another sip and shook his head. "Acorn Hill is exactly what we're looking for. The downtown is mostly older buildings and hasn't been too modernized. There are whole sections of the town with homes of the style that fit in precisely with the period we want to re-create. That means we could shoot from all directions at all times of the day and not have to play with the tricky camera angles to cut out modern buildings. There are wonderful interiors, which means we wouldn't have to build a lot of sets, provided we could use them, of course. And most important to Trey, the town has a church just like the one that Trey had in mind. When he saw Grace Chapel, he knew that we had to shoot the picture here."

"Do you think it will happen?"

"A lot of it depends on whether we can get the church board to agree, as well as a number of the other townspeople."

"So why did you all split up?" Jane asked, disciplining herself to take small bites and small sips.

"Dan is in the hospital, Trey and Lynette had another job to do and I have to do some work for Trey here." Randall hunched over his cup, stirring it slowly.

"You don't sound very enthusiastic about the work you have to do."

Randall just shrugged. "It's a job."

"And it pays for your candy-apple-red Mustang." She took a slow sip of tea, almost closing her eyes in bliss. "This tastes really good, Randall."

"That's me," he said with a laugh. "The tea master. Maybe I could quit the movies and get a job at Time for Tea."

"Or you could write."

"You remember that, eh?" He laughed mirthlessly. "Speaking of writing, I hope you don't mind, but I took the liberty of ordering some parts to fix up your dad's fountain pens."

"You didn't need to do that."

"I wanted to. They should be here by the end of the week." As Randall leaned back in his chair, Wendell jumped up on his lap. "Hey, cat. Aren't you supposed to be sleeping?"

"Wendell is a company cat. If something is going on, he wants to be in the middle of it," Jane said.

Randall tickled Wendell's ears with his fingertip, smiling as the cat twitched his ears away. In spite of the minor annoyance, Wendell stayed on Randall's lap, tucking his paws neatly under his chest.

As Jane buttered her second slice of toast, she asked, "So what kind of writing do you do?"

"Just dabble, mostly."

"In what," Jane persisted.

"I've done an outline for a series of books about a group of boys who snowboard competitively." He sat a little straighter, and Jane heard an eager note in his voice. "I didn't read much when I was a young boy because I never found books I liked. So I decided that I was going to write the kind of stories that I would have wanted to read."

"That sounds really interesting." Jane finished her toast

and dabbed at her mouth with a napkin. "That really hit the spot. Thank you so much."

"You're welcome. It's good to see you eating again. Your sisters are worried about you. I think they were wondering if you would ever get better." Randall leaned his chair back, resting his ankle on his knee, a melancholy smile playing over his lips as he toyed with Wendell's fur. "You're lucky to have them."

"I'm blessed. They're my family and I love them," Jane said, cradling her mug in her hands. "I used to live in California too. I was head chef of a very well-known restaurant in San Francisco. I thought of myself as very successful and fulfilled."

"What made you come back here?"

"A number of events came together. I believe God wanted me back here with my family. My father died and I needed to reconnect with my past, with my faith."

Randall rocked his chair and Wendell jumped off his lap as if unsure of his perch. "I used to go to church," Randall said, his voice quiet, "with my mom, dad, brothers and sisters. We got all cleaned up the night before, polished the shoes and got our Sunday clothes ready."

"It meant something to you?" Jane asked. She sensed Randall's seeking heart and wanted to encourage him to open up about whatever spark of faith might still be alive.

"At one time," he said. He sighed. "Doesn't mean much now."

"Why not?"

Randall shrugged and took another sip of tea, as if forestalling an answer. Jane just waited, content in the silence, realizing that with someone like Randall, time was a friend. Long pauses in the conversation could bring out more than questions could.

"Got busy," he said. "One day after the next. Chasing the next step. Moving up. Currying favor. None of it made it easy to keep faith alive, particularly when everyone you met was a self-made person who scoffed at the notion of God being in control of his life. Or when many of the people you met insisted that faith was only for the weak and simple-minded, for those who couldn't think for themselves." Randall sighed, running his hand through his hair, dislodging the ponytail.

"What do you think?"

He shook his head slowly. "I don't have time to think. Lately life has been all about hurry, rush and push. Just when I was getting used to yesterday, along came today. This is the most relaxed I've been since I started working for Trey."

He pressed his lips together, as if he had said too much.

"What is working for Trey like?"

"It's a job."

Jane could see the indecisiveness in his eyes and she waited.

"Trey is the kind of guy who takes everything in stride by trampling anyone who gets in his way," Randall continued. "Like I told your sister Alice, Trey always has his hand out for more, but never to give, and he usually gets what he wants."

"How do you know?"

"I see it happen again and again. People are often seduced by the lure of fame and the empty promises it makes. Trey is very, very good at making the promise seem more real than it is."

"It doesn't sound like you enjoy what you do."

"Better living through denial," Randall retorted.

"I don't believe people are that easily enticed," she said.

Randall laughed. "You're a perfect example. You said you moved away from success. Now you're going to go on a television show." He dropped his chair with a thunk.

"What television show?"

He was about to answer when his cell phone rang. "At this hour it can only be Trey," he said. "Sorry." He got up and quickly left the kitchen.

Jane took their dishes to the sink where she rinsed and stacked them. She waited to see if the call would be a short one, but when Randall didn't come back, she walked toward the stairs. Randall waved good night to her as he continued his conversation with Trey.

Jane really wanted to learn what he meant by his last comment to her, which had been thrown out like an accusation, but she was too tired to wait for his call to end. She was worried about Randall. She saw unhappiness in his eyes. She knew how easy it was to be caught on the treadmill of a lifestyle that demanded a certain wage to maintain.

She prayed as she slowly climbed the stairs. *Help us to show him the freedom he can find in You. He knew You at one time in his life. Help us to lead him to You again.*

As she walked past the doors of her sisters' bedrooms, she wished Louise and Alice were awake so she could talk to them. Randall's comment about the television show had made her recall snatches of conversations with Ethel, Louise and Alice that she couldn't put together. Her sisters could help her decipher these memories. She had also had some strange dreams. The strangest one involved Florence writing a screenplay and reading it to her. Maybe tomorrow she could sort all this out.

$\backsim$

"Jane?" Alice set a breakfast tray on the table beside the bed and touched her sister's shoulder.

A faint snore issued from the bunched-up blankets. "Jane," she said, gently shaking her sister's shoulder. Jane was in a deep, deep slumber and did not respond. Alice laid her hand on her sister's head. She did not seem to have a fever, which was a relief.

Alice tidied up the table beside Jane's bed and picked up the bottle of cough syrup. Frowning, she held it up to the light. Through the brown glass, she could see the level was farther down than it should be.

Louise and Randall were waiting for her in the front hall when she came down the stairs. "Louise, how often have you given Jane that cough syrup that Dr. Bentley prescribed?" she asked, as they put on their coats.

"I'm sure only a few times. Though I have been busy, I might not have given it exactly when she should have had it."

"From the looks of the bottle, she has had much more than she should," Alice said as they left the inn and walked toward the Coffee Shop.

"What's in it?" Randall asked, his hands shoved in the pocket of his coat.

"Codeine."

"She told me she was going to take some of it before she went back to bed," Randall said. "So she wouldn't wake you up with her coughing."

Alice looked at Louise as realization dawned. "I wonder if she took more of it on her own at other times."

"That probably is why she is sleeping so much." Louise stopped, a horrified look on her face. "She couldn't get addicted, could she?"

Alice laughed. "Not likely. Still, I'm going to cut her off."

They entered the Coffee Shop, and as Louise, Alice and Randall settled into their booth, the main topic of conversation amongst the other patrons was still Fred's interview.

Pastor Ley stopped to greet them as he was on his way out. After he asked about Jane's health, he commented on the interview. "It's a-a shame what they d-did. J-just a shame," he said. "I hope F-Fred is okay."

"I spoke with Vera this morning," Alice told him. "She was very angry about the interview. Fred is still in Punxsutawney and hasn't seen it yet."

"Fred has a lot more knowledge of the weather than that reporter," Louise said, "or a rodent."

Pastor Ley nodded in agreement, then left.

"That stutter is a bit of a handicap for a preacher, isn't it?" Randall asked, lifting one eyebrow.

"Associate pastor," Alice said, understanding his puzzlement. "He was supposed to be our pastor after our father retired, but the poor man couldn't get through a sermon, so my father continued preaching almost until he passed away.

Pastor Ley preaches occasionally and when he does, somehow he manages to keep his stutter under control. It's quite a feat for him to do that."

Alice wanted to say more, but Hope Collins came by to take their order.

"So how are the plans for the movie coming?" Hope asked Randall. "When are you going to start?"

"We're still in the process," he said evasively, keeping his gaze on the menu.

"Are you going to be putting out a casting call soon?" Hope grinned at Louise and Alice's puzzlement. "I've been doing some research on this movie business. When they need people for a movie, they put out a casting call."

"Casting director does that," Randall said with an apologetic smile.

"I thought Trey was in charge of that," Hope said.

Randall lifted one shoulder in a negligent shrug. "Trey can only make suggestions."

Alice could see he was very uncomfortable with Hope's persistence. She glanced quickly at Louise, who looked as confused as she felt. Randall had not said much to any of the people who stopped by their table. If Randall was supposed to stay behind to woo the people of Acorn Hill, his clipped answers and evasiveness were not going to do the job.

"That poor Fred," Hope said, pouring Louise and

Randall a cup of coffee. "It makes me so mad about how they made him look silly." Hope glanced at Randall again as if to make sure that Randall got the message. "He's not like that, you know. He's really smart."

Randall just gave her a quick smile, then looked away.

While they waited for their order, Craig Tracy stopped at their table. "Happy Groundhog Day," he said with a grin. "And how are you all this lovely morning?" He glanced around the group and then frowned. "Jane is still not feeling well?"

"She has been battling this flu," Alice said, "but I think she is on the mend now. She's at home sleeping."

"My mother always says that sleep is the best cure," Craig said.

"Oh, she certainly is getting enough sleep," Louise said dryly.

"I heard she is going to be on a television show," Craig said. "I wonder why she didn't tell me."

Alice heard the faint hurt in Craig's voice. Jane and Craig were friends, and for Craig to learn this news via Acorn Hill's grapevine must have been upsetting.

"We don't have much information either," Alice said by way of consolation, tapping her fingers restlessly on the tabletop. "Jane was asked just before she became ill and we haven't had a chance to talk about it. I don't know how it got spread over town so quickly."

"I heard the news from Betty Dunkle. She came in for some flowers for a friend. Florence and Clara Horn were with her, and I confess, I listened in." He gave them a careful smile, then looked down at his watch. "I better run. I have lots of orders to catch up on."

As he left, Alice said, "I'd like to know who doesn't know about Jane and that television show."

Louise shook her head, then folded her hands and bowed her head, and Alice followed suit. They prayed quietly, and when Alice raised her head, it was to see Randall looking at them with a mixture of curiosity and humor.

"You're not embarrassed to pray in public?" he said, glancing around the Coffee Shop, as if everyone had noticed their moment of devotion.

Alice shook her head. "God has done so much for me, I simply cannot be embarrassed to thank Him."

"Interesting," was all he said, as he picked up a piece of pancake with his fork and started eating.

They finished their breakfast without any more interruptions. As they walked back to the inn, their breath turned into three plumes of frost in the brisk winter air.

Alice pulled her scarf closer around her neck, looking back at Randall, who sauntered along about three feet behind them, his coat open to the cold winter air. He had said little during the meal and nothing at all on their way back to the inn. In fact, he seemed troubled.

The sound of a vehicle slowing down as they went up the walk to the inn caused them to turn around. A silver sports car pulled up to the curb and came to a halt. The woman in the car did not get out immediately, but pulled down the visor and applied some lipstick.

"I wonder if she is a guest or just someone who lost her way," Louise said, hugging her coat close to her.

"No one made a reservation. You go inside. I'll see what she wants," Alice said.

As Louise and Randall entered the inn, the car door opened and the woman, swathed in a full-length black mink coat, got out of the car. "Good morning. Is this Grace Chapel Inn?"

"It is, and I'm Alice Howard, one of the innkeepers," said Alice, going back down the walk to greet their potential guest.

"Great." The woman pulled her mink coat close around her as she came around the car. "I talked to Ethel about staying here. I'm Debbie Mandrusiak."

⁓

"This is lovely," Debbie said, sweeping into the Sunset Room on a wave of musky perfume. "Absolutely lovely." She turned to Randall, who had volunteered to bring up her suitcases. "Thank you, young man," Debbie said, discreetly handing Randall a folded bill.

Rather than argue, Randall simply took it and winked at Louise, who had escorted Debbie to her room. Louise managed, just barely, to keep from smiling.

"I was hoping to see Jane right away," Debbie said, slipping off her fine leather gloves one finger at a time. "Where is she?"

"I'm afraid Jane has been quite ill with the flu," Louise said, folding her hands in front of her. "She is just now beginning to stir from her room."

"Well, as soon as I'm rested, I must speak to her," Debbie said. She laid her gloves on her briefcase and gave Louise a patronizing smile. "I don't have much time."

"I will let Jane know you are here. She can decide when she is able to see you." Then before Debbie could debate the issue further, Louise left.

Chapter Twelve

"Is Jane up?" Alice asked as Louise came into the kitchen. "I thought I heard the shower running."

"She's up. I knocked on her door and told her we would like to talk to her as soon as she is done."

"I just hope we can get to her before Debbie does," said Alice, pulling out a bowl. She was going to make some muffins before she had to go to work. If they turned out, maybe tomorrow they wouldn't have to go to the Coffee Shop for breakfast. "She must want to talk to Jane pretty badly if she came all the way to Acorn Hill. How did she even know where to come?"

"Jane spoke one evening about calling Debbie to talk to her about the job. Perhaps that's when the arrangements were made."

"This is truly puzzling," Alice said, "but right now, I want to try to make these muffins. Who knows, I might have to learn to do more cooking."

"I would like to help, but Tabitha is coming in a few minutes. I don't want to run late and make her tardy for school."

"I'm fine. Viola's no-fail recipe is just the ticket right now. Plain and easy to follow." Alice gave her sister a quick smile, thankful that Louise didn't press the matter.

The front doorbell sounded, and Louise glanced at her watch. "My goodness, Tabitha is here even earlier than usual. That girl's enthusiasm for her music lessons is boundless, but also inconvenient right now."

"I'll try to find a way to talk to Jane on my own then." Alice had hoped that she and Louise would approach Jane together.

"I'll be in the parlor if you need me," Louise said, giving Alice a quick smile. "It's probably not as bad as we think," she said.

"I hope not," Alice said, as she looked around the cozy kitchen. Alice was sure that Jane was happy here, but if that was true, then why had Jane invited Debbie here?

◦◦◦

Tabitha's fingers flew through the piece of music, the cheerful notes dancing in the room. When she was done, Louise clapped spontaneously.

"That was wonderful," Louise said, amazed at the girl's talent. "You have certainly been practicing hard."

"My mom was getting tired of this music," Tabitha said with a shrug. She half turned on the piano bench. "So I thought about what you said?" Tabitha said, her voice rising up on the end as if she were asking a question rather than making a statement. "About the ANGELs? I think I'd like to go. Maybe if I do, my mom won't bug me about being too focused on my piano lessons."

Louise smiled. "I am so glad to hear that. Miss Howard has a meeting organized for tomorrow evening. We can tell her when we are done here."

"My mom was happy when I told her I was going to go."

"You know that your mother is right. Life is not just about music."

Tabitha shrugged again, but in the casual movement, Louise read skepticism. Louise took a chance and sat down on the piano bench beside the girl. "Music isn't just about hitting the right notes, Tabitha," she said softly, praying for the right words. "It's more than simply being precise and having good technique and practicing regularly. It's also about heart and passion. Even though you are playing pieces written by somebody else, you can still put yourself into the music. Your feelings, your reactions, your emotions." Louise smiled at her, hoping Tabitha understood that Louise wasn't trying to lecture her but to help her. "You can only express emotions if you experience life, and the best way to do that is to spend time with other people, to open yourself to other experiences. I want you to think of the time you spend with the other girls as a way of filling up a well that you can draw from when you are playing."

Tabitha frowned, biting her lip, and Louise prayed that the girl understood what she had said.

"So you're saying if I don't do this, I won't be as good a player?"

Louise heard the faint hurt in the girl's voice. "You're already a very good pianist, an excellent one. What I'm trying to tell you is that by broadening your experiences and balancing your life, you will become even better."

Tabitha nodded slowly, her fingers automatically picking out the opening bars of "Für Elise."

Louise had to smile. Even while Tabitha was thinking, she was playing.

"I see what you're saying. I guess it makes sense." A smile spread over Tabitha's face as the notes tumbled out of the piano, echoing her changing mood.

"I'm glad to know that," Louise said, smiling herself. "Now, I don't want to waste your time, so let's move on to the next piece."

❧

"It's been an amazing adventure, Jane. You would not believe the people I've met and the places I've been." Debbie paced around the room, gesticulating as she spoke, her long fingernails flashing in scarlet arcs through the air.

For the past fifteen minutes Jane had listened to Debbie talking about her cooking show, her apartment in New York, her expensive car and anything else that Debbie seemed to think would impress. But Jane was not impressed with any of the things Debbie had to say.

"I'm in such a good place in my life." Debbie stopped and caught one of Jane's hands between hers, squeezing it earnestly. "I want to share that place with you. I want you to be a part of all this."

Jane ran her hand over her still damp hair. "But Debbie, I . . ."

"Now, don't play coy with me, Jane," Debbie said patting Jane on her cheek. "I know you. You have drive, ambition and talent, and they're just wasted here in this little town. You need to be with me on my show. I want you on my show. Now, the first thing we must do is decide on the best time for you to join me. Right now I am on a schedule that can't be changed, but in a month or two we will be setting out the spring line-up and we can put you on the program then."

Jane held her hand up. "Debbie, I don't know where you got the idea that I was going to be a part of your cooking show."

"Isn't that why I'm here?" She gaped at Jane. "We spoke about it on the phone. I even had my lawyers draw up a contract for you. I was that sure that you were coming. In fact, your secretary Ethel helped me make the arrangements. She told me you would be happy to be on the show. She invited me to come here so that we could decide on the final details."

"Ethel is my aunt, not my secretary. I can't understand why she would do that. She knows that I love living here and I love working with my sisters in this inn. I have no plans to move anywhere or do anything different."

"But Jane, my dear, you could do so much better."

Jane just smiled. "I'm sorry, Debbie," she said as gently as she could. "I don't think anything you might have to offer is better than what I have now."

"Oh c'mon, Jane. This place? This town? I know what you were able to do at the Blue Fish Grille. All you'll ever do here is make eggs for people who have no appreciation of the amazing things you can create." Debbie's surprise was tinged with mockery, and that didn't sit well with Jane.

"I get all the appreciation I need, Debbie. God has put me in this place not simply to cook, but to help make our inn a place of refuge and peace for our guests."

"You sound like a missionary," Debbie said slowly, as if only now the words of the welcome sign on the inn and Jane's e-mail were sinking in.

"I do believe that God put me here for a reason and I'm happy and content and fulfilled with what I'm doing here."

"You don't think God would change His mind on that?"

Jane laughed and linked her arm through her old friend's in a gesture of conciliation. "Now we aren't going to talk about this anymore. It's good to see you again and I want you to meet my sisters."

They left Jane's room and walked downstairs together, but Jane could sense that Debbie believed that she still could change Jane's mind. The old Debbie would have given up, but there was an edge to this new Debbie that simply underlined Jane's decision to say no.

Alice was just pulling a tray of muffins out of the oven as they entered the kitchen.

"Jane, how wonderful to see you up. Come and sit."

"If it's wonderful to see me up, why are you making me sit down?" Jane said with a grin.

"Because you shouldn't be up too long." Alice gave her sister a quick hug, then led her to the chair. "Do you ladies want some juice? Tea? Coffee?"

"Juice sounds good," said Jane.

"How are you feeling?"

"A little woozy, but I think I've finally turned the corner."

Alice smiled down at her, holding Jane's hands between her own. Jane suspected that if Debbie were not here, she would have hugged her again. "I'm so thankful you're feeling better. I was starting to get worried about you. I thought we might have to bring you to the hospital as well."

"How is Dan?"

"He's getting better. They hope to release him today, and he's going to join the rest of the crew in New York where they are doing some work on another project." Alice patted Jane on the shoulder and turned to Debbie. "May I get you anything?"

"If you're getting juice for Jane, I'll have a glass as well."

Alice returned to the table with two large glasses of orange juice.

"Is this freshly squeezed?" Debbie asked, taking a careful sip.

"Fresh from the carton," Alice said with a quick grin.

Debbie gave Alice a weak smile and tipped her head toward the counter. "Those muffins smell good. What are they?"

"Bran muffins," Alice said with a self-deprecating shrug as she took them one by one out of the pan and set them on a wire rack to cool.

"Those pans look seasoned enough, I'm sure you didn't need to use muffin papers," Debbie said.

"I'm a novice cook, so I don't always do things the way they should be done," Alice said, setting the pan aside. "Jane usually does our baking and cooking, but while she's been ill, Louise and I have been stumbling along doing the best we can."

"What happened to the lopsided cake I saw on the counter yesterday?" Jane asked suddenly.

"When did you see that?"

"I couldn't sleep last night so I came downstairs and had something to eat."

Alice's gaze darted past Jane to the parlor, then back to her sister. "Louise baked that," Alice whispered. "I put it in the freezer for now. I don't dare serve it to anybody."

Jane stifled a laugh. "Maybe we could make trifle out of it if it's halfway edible."

"Yoo-hoo. Anybody home?" Ethel slipped into the kitchen and rubbed the steam from her glasses. Her bright eyes danced from Alice to Jane and landed on Debbie. "Good morning," she said, giving Debbie a quick smile.

"Aunt Ethel, I would like you to meet Debbie Mandrusiak," Alice said to her aunt. "Debbie, this is Mrs. Buckley, our Aunt Ethel. She lives just behind us in the carriage house."

Ethel's eyes grew wide in surprise as Alice introduced her. Then she caught herself and her smile spread from round cheek to round cheek. "Debbie Mandrusiak? You came? You actually made the trip all the way out here. Oh, that's wonderful." Ethel reached out and caught Debbie's hand between hers, shaking it with enthusiasm. "It's an honor to have you. My goodness, our own television celebrity right here. Wait until Florence hears about that. She won't have as much to brag about, that's for sure."

Debbie looked a little dazed at Ethel's exuberance, but to her credit, she simply smiled graciously, waited a moment, then slowly reclaimed her hand. "Thank you, Ethel. It's lovely to be here."

Ethel scooted into a chair next to Debbie. "So, when is Jane going to be on your show?"

"I can't seem to convince her to come," Debbie said, taking a delicate sip of her orange juice. "Maybe you can help me."

"My goodness, yes, I surely can," Ethel said, leaning forward, her eyes snapping with excitement. "Jane, this is a chance of a lifetime. Of course you have to do this."

"What does she have to do?" Louise asked, entering the kitchen. Tabitha trailed along behind her, her eyes on the music book that she was carrying.

"Go on Debbie's show, of course," Ethel said, turning her head to look at Louise.

"There's not any 'of course' about it," Louise said with a touch of asperity.

"You shouldn't hold her back, Louise. It isn't fair to Jane."

"We can let Jane decide that," Debbie said, wiping her mouth with a napkin.

"Jane has been ill," Louise said. "While this choice is up to her, she isn't in any condition to be making quick decisions right now."

"Quick?" Debbie looked indignant. "I wrote her almost a week ago."

"And talked to her on the phone," Ethel put in.

Jane felt as if she was watching an erratic ping pong match with three vigorous participants. "Please, everybody," she begged, raising her hands to catch their attention. "Can we not talk about this right now?" She glanced at Tabitha, who stood behind Louise, and gave the puzzled-looking girl an encouraging smile. "Good morning. How was your lesson?"

"Good, thanks."

Louise frowned, then also turned to the girl behind her. "Alice, Tabitha wants to talk to you about your meeting with the ANGELs."

"Of course, Tabitha," Alice said. "Did you want to join us tomorrow after school?"

"Yes. I was wondering if I should bring anything and where you are going to meet."

Alice bit her lip, then shook her head. "I was hoping to do something special, but because of the weather we are just going to be meeting here. I thought we could play some games and have supper. Afterward we will do some baking if Jane is feeling well enough to help us."

"Of course I will," Jane said with more bravado than she felt. It was a good thing that Alice's girls were not meeting tonight. Even though she felt well enough to be up, spending an evening with eight or nine giddy girls was more than she could handle right now.

"Okay, I'll be here," Tabitha said. "Thanks again for the invitation."

Just then, the back door flew open and Randall burst into the kitchen, grinning as a blast of cold air came in with him.

"It's a great day out," he said, closing the door and pulling off his coat. "Just great."

Jane shivered as the cold swept across her feet. At the same time, she took a deep breath, reveling in the freshness of the air that still surrounded Randall.

"How was your skating expedition?" Alice asked.

"Not bad. Those skates need to be sharpened though. I think I can get that done at the hardware store."

"You were skating?" Jane asked, turning around. "Where?"

"On Fairy Pond. Your dad's skates are a little dull, but it was great fun."

"You can skate here?" Tabitha asked.

"You can now," Randall said, shrugging out of his coat. A bit of snow fell onto the floor. "Oops. Sorry about that," he said with an apologetic grin. "Can you please toss me some paper towels, Miss Howard?" he said to Alice.

She passed the towels to Randall and he wiped the melting snow off the floor.

"I have skates," Tabitha said.

Jane looked from her smiling face to Randall's red cheeks to Alice, who stood smiling at them both, and her fuzzy mind pulled together an idea.

"Alice, you were saying you want to take the girls on an outing outside? Why don't you take your ANGELs skating on the pond right after school? We could still do some baking afterward if you want."

Alice considered the suggestion.

"Hey, that would be a great idea," Randall said. "I've got some of the pond cleared off, and it's as smooth as glass under the snow. I could clear some more off today and make a rink big enough for the girls to skate on."

"They could go after school and come here afterward

for dinner," Jane said, catching Randall's enthusiasm. "Maybe we could go skating too, couldn't we? I'm sure there are some skates of ours stored away somewhere."

"I did see a few more pairs," Randall said, unwinding his scarf and laying it on top of the coat he had draped over the back of a chair. "I could bring them to get sharpened."

"I think that would be a wonderful idea," Alice said, tapping her finger on her chin. "I would have to phone the girls, though, to see if they all have skates, or at the least some they could borrow. We would have to make arrangements to pick them up after school."

"I have to go now," Tabitha said. "Thanks for the lesson, Mrs. Smith."

"You're welcome, Tabitha. We shall see you tomorrow," Louise called out behind the girl as she rushed out of the kitchen.

"I remember skating on that pond with Daniel, Madeleine and the children," Ethel said, resting her elbow on her chin, a faraway expression on her face. "But that was years ago when it would often get cold enough for the pond to freeze."

"Mother skated?" Jane asked.

"Oh my, yes," Ethel said. "Daniel and Madeleine were very good skaters. They would link arms and make the most graceful S figures, the two of them." She sighed, remembering other times.

"Maybe you could teach us, Aunt Ethel," Alice said.

"No, no," Ethel held her hands up, "but I would love to come and watch." Ethel glanced up at Louise. "You could teach them, Louise. I remember Madeleine showing you how to do it."

"I'm a bit too old for that kind of thing," Louise said.

"Do you want something to drink, Randall?" Alice asked.

"No. I'm fine, thanks."

"Come and sit down, Alice," Louise said, pulling out a chair. "We don't need to be served."

"I wouldn't mind a bit more juice," Debbie said, loudly, as if to establish her presence.

Jane felt a flush of guilt. In the memories and the chatter, they had forgotten about her.

"I'll get it for you," Randall said, forestalling Alice by laying a hand on her arm.

"What exactly do you do here?" Debbie asked Randall.

"I'm a guest," he said, pulling open the refrigerator door. "Orange or apple or peach nectarine or . . ."

"Just orange juice, please," Debbie said, her mouth set in prim lines as if remembering the tip she had given Randall. "Now Jane, about the show. I really believed that you were willing to come."

"Of course she's willing to come," Ethel said, her blue eyes flitting from Debbie to Jane. "It's a wonderful opportunity."

Jane frowned at her aunt's exuberance, trying to understand why Ethel was so excited about her leaving.

"Of course it is," Jane said. "I don't deny that." She was about to say more but Debbie cut her off.

"Then listen to me," Debbie said. "I know how hard you work, Jane. I know that you need a challenge." She laughed as she waved her hand indicating the kitchen.

"I get challenges . . ."

"This is very nice and cozy," Debbie continued, ignoring Jane's comment, "but let's face it, what can you do here? You only cook breakfast." She leaned forward, ignoring the other people sitting around the table. "Jane, this place is going to stifle you. I need you on my show. It's growing and changing and I want you on board."

Jane saw Alice and Louise exchange troubled glances while Debbie was talking.

"Don't let your sisters hold you back, Jane," Debbie was saying.

"They don't . . ."

"They do tend to do that, you know," Ethel chimed in, cutting her off.

"Aunt Ethel, you know that isn't true," Louise said.

"No, it isn't . . ." Jane said.

"Jane has come up with all kinds of wonderful ideas and you won't let her do any of them. I know you don't want her to be on Debbie's show either." Ethel sat back, folding her arms over her stomach.

"That is unfair, Aunt Ethel," Alice said, hurt by her aunt's implications. "We want what is best for Jane. It's a big decision to leave Acorn Hill to appear on a show . . ."

"Not that big. She won't be gone that long."

Alice frowned. "What do you mean?"

"How long would it take?" Ethel turned to Debbie. "She'd only be gone a week if she was going to be a guest on your show, wouldn't she?"

"A guest?" Debbie sat back, frowning. "She wouldn't be coming as a guest."

"What would she be then?" Ethel asked.

"I want her on the show full-time."

Ethel's eyes grew large as the information sank in. "All the time?" she whispered. "Not just for one show?"

"Of course not. I don't need a guest, I need a full-time assistant."

"But when I talked to you . . . when I read the letter . . ." Ethel's voice drifted off, her confusion obvious.

Suddenly Jane realized what had happened. Dear, confused, exuberant Ethel.

"I wouldn't go through all this, come all the way here

just for a guest on the show." Debbie turned to Jane, puzzled. "You knew what I was offering, didn't you?"

"Oh yes," Jane said, thankful to be finally participating in the conversation. "I knew it was a full-time position as, I'm sure, did my sisters." She glanced at Louise and Alice, who both nodded.

Ethel's mouth made a perfect O and she blinked once, twice. "Full-time," she repeated, as if to make sure she had heard it right.

"Of course," Debbie said, her voice gaining an edge. "When you invited me to come here, Ethel, you didn't know what I was proposing?"

Ethel shook her head, for one of the few times in her life at a loss for words.

"You silly woman," Debbie said.

"Hey, don't talk to her like that," Randall said. "She made an honest mistake."

Jane smiled at his defense of Ethel and at the surprised look on Debbie's face. "Folks," she said softly, "my head is still spinning a little, so I'm having a hard time keeping up with you all." She drew in a long, slow breath. "I want to thank you, Debbie, for the offer. I have to confess I was tempted, but only for a moment. I'm sorry that you made the trip all the way out here for nothing." She looked around the table at her dear sisters and her dear, misguided aunt. "But I'm going to be staying here at Grace Chapel Inn with my sisters and my aunt and all my friends for as long as I am needed and wanted. I can't think of any other place I would rather be."

Louise sank back in her chair, smiling her relief.

"Thank You, Lord," Alice said quietly, reaching out and stroking Jane's arm.

"So that's it?" Debbie said. "You're not going to consider my offer?"

Jane just shook her head.

"Well," Debbie said, getting up from the table. "I don't need to waste any more time here," she said. "I'm sorry to see you squandering your talents, Jane. I think you're making a mistake." She turned to Louise. "I'll be checking out."

"But you just got here," Ethel said. "Don't you want to stay a night and see Acorn Hill?"

"I saw it when I drove through it and I'll see it when I leave. There's nothing here I'm interested in." Debbie swept out of the room, her footsteps echoing in the sudden silence.

Randall clapped lightly, as if applauding. "An exit worthy of the diva-est of divas."

The tension created by Debbie's anger was swept away with Randall's comment.

"I'm so thankful you're staying, Jane," Louise said. "The

entire time you were ill, we were laboring under the impression that you were leaving, that you felt stifled here. We felt as if we were holding you back and we didn't want you to turn down this opportunity if it was what you wanted." She stopped, then ran her hand lightly over her hair, composing herself. "I'm just thankful that you're not going with her."

Alice gave Jane a quick hug. "I am too."

"She is certainly not as pleasant as she seems on her show," Ethel said with a hurt tone in her voice.

"Some stars are, some aren't," Randall said dryly. "She's definitely not."

"I am so sorry, " Ethel said quietly. She squirmed in her chair, obviously uncomfortable. "I made a big mistake. I didn't know she wanted Jane full-time on the show. I thought it would be just one show, like Florence's niece."

Alice smiled. "It's okay, Aunt Ethel. I'm just glad to find out that you don't want our Jane to leave."

"Oh no, not at all," Ethel looked shocked. "Though now I have to tell Florence that Jane isn't going to be on television after all. I dislike eating my words more than I do Louise's cooking."

They all laughed at that, even Louise.

Randall glanced at the clock. "Well, I better get going if I want to get that skating rink cleared off." He got up from the table and slipped his coat on.

"I should put those muffins away," Alice said, "and then get ready to go. I want to stop in on Vera on my way out."

Ethel reluctantly got up from her chair. "I suppose I should go too." She sighed dramatically and looked across the table at Jane.

"Wouldn't you consider doing even one show, Jane?" she asked plaintively.

Jane just smiled and shook her head.

"Florence wanted me to tell her when you were going to be on television. She didn't believe me. Now she's going to think I was fibbing to her."

"Don't worry, Aunt Ethel," Jane said with a placating tone in her voice. "I can tell Florence all about it the next time I see her."

"Well that might be pretty soon," said Ethel. "Florence said she wanted to come here and talk to you some more about her movie script."

Jane realized then that what she had thought was a hallucination had actually happened. She gave Alice an anguished look. "When Florence comes, can you please tell her I'm not well?"

"My goodness, Jane," Alice said, pretending innocence. "Wouldn't that be lying?"

"I know for a fact that if Florence comes to read her script again I *will* be ill. So it's more a matter of timing."

Chapter Thirteen

I am trying not to be angry about that interview," Vera said, crossing her arms over her chest as she and Alice walked around the school playground. Alice had stopped by the staff room to learn that Vera had volunteered to be the playground supervisor at noon. So she joined her outside. "Fred called last night, and I didn't have the heart to tell him how he came off."

"He will have to know sooner or later," Alice said gently, wishing she could do something for her friend.

"He wanted me to tape it, but now I just want to erase the tape." Vera shook her head. "I was going to show it to my class in school this afternoon, but needless to say, that isn't going to happen."

"How is Fred doing?"

"He seems to be enjoying himself. He was surprised how many people were in Punxsutawney just for this festival." Vera almost snorted. "Imagine, a groundhog gets more respect than my husband does."

"Fred is well respected in our community," Alice said,

putting an arm around her friend. "He doesn't need an interview on television to give him that."

"Thank goodness it was only a local station." Vera sighed, pulling her hat farther down over her ears. "Alice, I feel silly admitting this but I simply couldn't face my fellow teachers at noon today. That's why I volunteered to be playground supervisor. I was so proud of Fred and his moment of fame." She glanced sidelong at Alice. "I guess the Lord is teaching me humility."

"You don't need to learn humility," Alice said softly. "We were all proud of Fred and we still are. He has wisdom and knowledge that the people of Acorn Hill respect with or without a television interview."

Vera sighed. "The worst part is that Fred didn't want it to be a big deal and I was the one going around town telling people to turn on their televisions." She shook her head. "It's just that some people don't take his weather forecasting seriously. And it was those people I wanted to convince." Vera stopped. "Oh, that Charlie Matthews. He's a wild man. Look at him running around." Vera was about to blow the silver whistle she had around her neck when Alice stopped her.

"It's so cold out," she warned her friend, "your lips will freeze to the metal."

Vera looked down at the whistle as if unable to understand how something so simple could be dangerous. "Thanks for the warning," she said. "I hadn't thought of that."

Alice patted her friend on the arm.

"I'm glad you stopped by," Vera said. "I feel a little better about the interview. I guess I just have to swallow my pride and let it go."

"Fred is liked and appreciated in Acorn Hill for the kind and intelligent person he is," Alice said. "The audience who saw the interview was robbed of the opportunity to know him like we do."

Vera smiled and laughed. "Thank you for putting this into perspective. Now you better go to work, and I better make sure that Charlie doesn't hurt himself."

$\backsim$

"Alice won't be home until seven," Randall said, handing Louise the phone message that he had scribbled down.

"I suppose I'll have to see about making supper then," Louise said, frowning at the paper Randall had given her. Jane was resting in the living room with a book. Though she was feeling better, she was still weak. "Or we could all go to Zachary's for supper."

"Why don't you let me cook tonight?" Randall said. "I have one surefire, no-fail recipe."

"No. You are our guest." Though he had been unfailingly polite and considerate, she still didn't trust his presence in the kitchen. She couldn't help wondering if it was part of his assignment to win over the people of the town.

"I'm trying to bribe you," Randall said with a quick grin.

Louise's heart skipped at his words. *There, he's as good as admitted what he is up to.*

"If I make supper, then I can watch the hockey game," he continued.

Louise's confusion must have showed in her face.

"Like we did last night?" he prompted.

"Is there another game on?" Louise said, feeling guilty about jumping to a wrong conclusion.

"This time of the year there's a hockey game televised most every night."

"I suppose we could do that," Louise said carefully. She had heard enough remarks about her cooking to make her reluctant to try again.

"I'm a good cook, Mrs. Smith. Let me help you out."

"Oh, very well," Louise was tired and didn't have the energy to argue. Although discovering that Jane was staying had been a great relief, Louise felt as if the stress of the past few days had finally caught up to her.

"Great stuff." Randall rubbed his hands together in anticipation. "I already took the liberty of getting Miss

Howard to take some breakfast sausages out of the freezer for my recipe. If you feel too guilty about me working, I could get you to help."

"I would be comfortable with that," Louise said, pulling an apron out of the drawer. "Perhaps you should put a hair-net over your ponytail."

Randall gave her a skeptical grin as if wondering if she was joking. When he realized she wasn't, his smile faded away. "Does Jane wear one when she's cooking?" he asked.

"No." Louise thought this over. "I suppose that means you don't need to wear one either."

Randall drummed his fingers on the countertop. "I guess it might be better if I had one on. I think my hair is longer than Jane's. Why don't you tell me where they are?"

Louise was about to protest, when she recognized this as his way of making peace with her. She found one in the drawer and handed it to him. He slipped it on, winked at her and started setting out the ingredients for supper. "So how many people should we expect?"

"Someone is always stopping over, in addition to Aunt Ethel, that is." Louise shook her head. "I'm not sure."

"I'll make a big batch, just in case."

A few moments later the sausages were sputtering in the frying pan and Randall had the mixer going at high speed. He was surprisingly capable.

"All we need to do is cut the cooked sausages into small pieces, put them on the bottom of this greased casserole pan and pour this flour, egg and milk mixture over the top."

"That's all?"

He nodded.

He put the dish in the oven and then turned it on.

"Shouldn't you have preheated the oven?"

"Nope. This is how I need it for the recipe."

"I see," Louise said, though she really didn't.

"We can set the table and make a salad while we're waiting for it to cook," Randall said. "Or did you want vegetables with it?"

"We could make broccoli," Louise suggested.

"Maybe we'll just stick with a salad." Randall flashed another one of his beguiling grins. "I don't like broccoli."

"Hello," Viola came into the kitchen, shivering as she shed her coat. "Goodness it's nice and cozy in here."

"Good evening, Viola," Louise said, taking her friend's coat from her. "What brings you here?"

"I thought I would help you make supper," Viola said, angling her head down so she could look at Louise over her frosted glasses.

"Thanks to Randall, we have that under control."

"Do you want to join us?" Randall said.

"Well, I don't want to impose."

"You were going to help me make supper, Viola, so joining us would hardly be imposing. You can help me decide what to have for dessert."

"We could use that cake we made last night."

"I don't know where it is and Alice is gone. Perhaps she took it in for the nurses."

"How about I drive over to the Good Apple and buy a dessert? That can be my contribution," Viola offered.

"We have these cookies," Louise said, opening the Tupperware container full of chocolate chip cookies and sniffing uncertainly.

"Perfect," Viola said. Just then Florence came in through the back door, clutching a tote bag.

Louise resisted the urge to roll her eyes. What was Florence doing here this time of the day? Surely she had her own supper to make?

"I'm sorry to bother you right at this time of the evening," Florence, said, puffing as she struggled to catch her breath. "Ethel told me that Jane was up and about and I must talk to her for a moment." She glanced over her shoulder at Randall, who was standing by the open refrigerator, frowning at the contents. She came closer to Louise and said sotto voce, "It's very private."

"We will be eating in about three quarters of an hour," Louise warned her.

"I only need to talk to her for five minutes," Florence said quickly. She clutched her bag close as she eased past Louise. Did she think Louise was going to inspect it?

Jane had asked to keep Florence away, but now that Louise was confronted with the situation, she didn't feel right about fibbing to Florence.

Florence held up her hand, fingers spread. "Five minutes," she repeated. Then she lifted her head as she heard a cough. "Is that Jane?"

Louise sighed. "She's in the living room."

"Thank you," Florence said. "Randall, I will need to talk to you as well."

Randall gave her a sick smile as she bustled off, full of self-importance.

"Okay, we can use these," Randall said, taking some romaine lettuce, tomatoes and assorted other vegetables out of the refrigerator. They started to cut and chop, but just before the five minutes were up, Randall manufactured an excuse to leave the kitchen and was gone when Florence sailed through again. *If he is supposed to be buttering up members of the church board, he is failing as far as Florence is concerned,* Louise thought.

"I heard about Jane's decision not to appear on that television show," Florence said, pausing by the counter on her way out. "It's probably for the best. You and Alice wouldn't be able to manage without her."

Louise shook her head. *Why is it that the same comment from anybody else would be a compliment to Jane, but coming from Florence, it's an insult to Alice and me?*

"We're thankful that she's staying, to be sure," Louise said, keeping her eyes on the celery she was chopping.

Florence lingered a moment, fidgeting with the handles of her bag. "Where is Randall?"

"I have no idea," Louise said.

"I must talk to him. Could you tell him when you see him?"

"I will," promised Louise. She breathed a sigh of relief when Florence left. First Debbie. Now Florence. Two domineering personalities in the inn over a period of eight hours was more than enough for anyone.

"Is she gone?" Randall whispered.

Louise spun around, then laughed as she saw his face peeking around the swinging door between the dining room and the kitchen. "Where were you?"

"I ducked out and came around the front of the inn so she wouldn't see me," Randall said as he came back into the kitchen. "That was too close. Poor Jane."

"Well, she was here only five minutes."

"Long enough." He picked up his knife and resumed cutting and chopping.

"Yoo-hoo," Ethel called out as she came into the kitchen with Lloyd right behind her. "We're on our way to Zachary's. Does anyone want to come with us?"

"We decided to stay home with Jane tonight," Louise said, dropping the cut vegetables in the salad bowl. "Randall and I are making supper."

Ethel's puzzled glance darted from Louise to Randall, who was whisking together a salad dressing. "You are helping Louise?"

"Actually, it's the other way around, Aunt Ethel. I'm helping him."

"Well, isn't that amazing, Lloyd? Randall is a young man with many talents."

"So it seems." Lloyd fingered his bow tie and sniffed the air. "It smells very good. What are you making?"

"It's something I made up myself. I call it Sausages in Yorkshire Pudding. Basic, college-kid comfort food."

"Well, I am glad to know that Jane will be getting something nourishing to eat," Ethel said with a smile to offset her comment.

"You can join us if you wish," Louise said to Ethel and Lloyd, and the invitation was taken up with alacrity.

Jane came in at that moment and greeted Lloyd and Ethel. While they were chatting, Alice arrived and a few moments later, Viola returned with a pie for dessert.

The kitchen was abuzz with conversation, noise and busyness. A few times Louise caught Randall standing at the counter, looking around the assorted group of people, a bemused expression on his face. She realized that he had a perfect opportunity to push his agenda now, with Lloyd, Alice and Ethel all in one place. Surely this was an excellent opportunity for him to sell them on the movie.

To her surprise, Randall didn't bring up the subject, not during dinner nor afterward.

"That was an excellent supper," Lloyd said, dabbing his mouth with a napkin. "As you said, simple but satisfying."

"It was very good," Jane agreed. "If I had known about your talents, I would have recommended you to Debbie for her show."

"I'm basically a one-dish wonder," Randall said, "and I'm not very good in front of the camera."

"What do you actually do?" Lloyd asked. "Trey explained his job, but was a little vague about yours."

"When did you talk to Trey?" Ethel asked.

Lloyd cleared his throat but avoided looking at Ethel or anyone else. "He came by my office to, well, talk."

"What about?"

Lloyd held up his hand in a motion of regret. "I'm not at liberty to say. It was confidential, though he did make some very interesting points. He is quite a persuasive man." Lloyd smiled and smoothed down his hair.

That sounds very mysterious, thought Louise.

"So, young man, what is it that you do?" Lloyd continued.

Randall toyed with the crumbs of the peach pie on his plate. "I'm a location scout. I check out the buildings, the lighting, the acoustics and the possibility of using them on their own as opposed to making a mock-up on a sound stage. I also keep myself available during the filming process in case we suddenly need to find another place to film."

"I have not seen you around town much."

Randall avoided Lloyd's gaze, his full concentration on picking up the crumbs with his fork.

"I don't need to do any more looking around," he said, putting his fork down and crossing his arms over his chest in a defensive gesture.

"I understand you've been visiting with Cyril Overstreet, Pastor Ley and Florence Simpson."

Randall nodded and put on a forced smile. "Just doing some basic behind-the-scenes groundwork. Happens all the time when we're dealing with a number of people."

Louise realized, with a start, that the people Lloyd had mentioned were members of the church board. Was

Randall still trying to get the church board on his side? On the one hand, his actions seemed to suggest that, but at the same time, he did not seem to be very dedicated to the job Trey had given him.

Louise wished she could understand what Randall was up to. In spite of what she knew he was supposed to be doing, she had grown to like him. He was helpful, amiable and fun to have around.

Randall pushed away from the table. "I better get helping. I have to keep up my end of the bargain," he said, picking up the dessert dishes. "I was promised I could watch the hockey game afterward."

"Who is playing tonight?" Ethel asked.

"My team, the Edmonton Oilers, against the Philadelphia Flyers."

"That would be our team," Ethel said with a note of satisfaction as she turned to Lloyd to explain. "We were cheering for New York last night, but it is way more fun to cheer for a hometown team."

"You were watching a hockey game?" Lloyd asked, clearly puzzled. "I didn't think you enjoyed sports."

"It is more fun when you watch with other people," Ethel said.

The telephone rang, and Alice rose and walked across the room to answer it.

"It was Vera," Alice reported after she had hung up the receiver. "Let's turn on the television. They are broadcasting the second interview with Fred."

Louise picked up the remote and flicked on the television in time to see Fred's smiling face as he spoke.

"Meteorologists have a large number of tools at their disposal, but the ordinary person can do some weather predicting armed with basic knowledge available to anyone with a willingness to be observant as well as to keep records."

"And how could that happen?" the young lady asked him, her bright expression showing her interest.

Fred talked a bit about formal weather prediction and how it is conducted using information gathering and mathematical formulas.

"Now these were not available to people in earlier times, so observation and knowledge passed on through folklore became the method. People looked at cloud formations, geography and signs in nature and could come up with some accurate information. Some folk beliefs are sheer silliness, but others, combined with other knowledge, can work."

He went on to explain how a barometer can be an aid to the ordinary person and how cloud formations work.

"Could you explain what some of the different kinds of clouds are?" the interviewer asked.

"Well, today we have cumulus clouds," Fred said as the camera panned the blue sky dotted with clouds overhead. "They are associated with fair weather, but when they pile up high and become bunched, they can cause heavy showers in warm weather. My favorites are the cumulonimbus clouds. These are the towering storm clouds, often anvil-shaped on top. These bring extreme natural phenomena like sleet, hail and tornadoes."

"I've always been fascinated by lightning and I know it has to do with positive and negative charges but no one has ever been able to explain it to me. Maybe our viewers have the same problem. What can you tell us?"

Fred gave a gentle shrug and smile. "Trained meteorologists could explain better than I could, but I'll try. Think of the cloud as a collection of large air masses rising quickly into the atmosphere, forming the cumulonimbus clouds I was talking about. Those clouds look pretty peaceful and puffy from below, but inside there's a battle going on with severe air currents. Pilots avoid these clouds for good reason. These air currents cause water droplets and ice crystals to crash into one another, and this creates friction which creates static electricity in the cloud." Fred demonstrated with his hands. "The charges build up between the top and bottom of the cloud, and the bottom of the cloud and the earth. When these opposing charges become intense, a gigantic spark occurs that jumps the gap between the cloud and the earth." He clapped his hands and the woman interviewing him jumped. "And there's your lightning, and afterward the sound of that spark snapping is the thunder."

"Isn't that interesting," Alice murmured.

Fred answered more questions about folklore and a few minutes later the interview was over.

"So now when the forecaster is talking about fronts and air masses, I know I certainly have a better understanding of what they're saying. Hope you do too," the interviewer said, smiling into the camera. She signed off and the station cut to a commercial.

"I knew Fred was knowledgeable about weather," Lloyd Tynan put in, "but I had no idea he had such a wealth of information."

"Thank goodness this interview showed him to be very intelligent." Louise muted the sound on the television.

"I'm sure Vera will be pleased," Alice said feeling proud of Fred and happy for her friend. She got up and started gathering up the plates.

"No, Miss Howard, that's my job," Randall said holding up his hand to stop her. "You sit down and I'll get the dishes."

Alice was about to protest but Randall shook his head, glancing at Louise. "Mrs. Smith and I made a deal. I offered to do the cooking. I could not watch the hockey game in good conscience if I did not do the dishes, as well."

Louise held his gaze, as if hoping to find out what he was up to, but he simply smiled back at her, his expression guileless. "All right then," she conceded. "Though I hope I'm not expected to sit in on the game."

"You do whatever floats your boat," Randall said.

Alice poured coffee for those who wanted another cup and then sat down again at the table.

"I heard Florence stopped by again." Alice cradled her steaming cup of tea between her hands. "Are you two cooking up something together?" she asked, her eyes sparkling with mischief.

Jane rolled her eyes. "She has a movie script she's trying to pitch to Trey."

"So *that's* why she's in favor of the movie being filmed here," Alice said.

"She figures once Trey is done with this movie, then he can move right on into hers because it takes place in Acorn Hill," Jane said.

"What is this script about?" Louise asked.

Jane made a motion of locking up her lips and throwing away the key.

"Is it that secret?" Alice asked with a giggle.

"*Very* secret," Jane said.

"What could she possibly have to write about?" Alice asked.

"All kinds of surprising things that go on in Acorn Hill," Jane said in a dramatically hushed voice. "Mayhem, intrigue and deep, dark secrets. Some things happen right here in this inn."

Louise gave Jane a dry look, and Jane winked at her.

"When does the hockey game start?" Ethel asked, clearly having heard enough of Florence and her masterwork.

"In about ten minutes," Randall replied, stacking up the plates and gathering the utensils.

"We are going to stay, aren't we, Lloyd?" Ethel asked.

Her question was really more a statement and poor Lloyd looked confused.

"Join us," Alice encouraged him. "It's a lot of fun."

"Since when did we start watching television?" Jane asked.

"Since Randall started doing the dishes," Louise said.

Jane didn't look any more enlightened.

"It's a deal I made," Randall said as he turned on the taps to rinse the dishes. "I do the dishes, and I get to watch the game."

"You don't have to watch," Louise said to Jane, getting up from the table. Deal or no deal, she couldn't just sit and let Randall do all the work.

"I don't mind," Jane said. "We see so little television. It

would be a change of pace to watch something other than cooking shows."

"And we're not going to talk about that," Alice said, patting her sister on the shoulder.

"Do you need some help, Louise?" Viola asked.

"No. We have things under control here," Louise said, giving Randall a sidelong glance.

"As long as I have the remote, I would agree," Randall said.

A few minutes later, he put the last pot on the drying rack, wiped his hands and turned up the sound on the television. He got himself settled in a chair. Ethel, Lloyd, Alice, Viola and Jane were all ready for the game as well.

Louise wrung out a cloth and wiped down the counters, wondering if Viola was going to stay.

"Come and sit down, Louise," Ethel said. "You can't see very well from there."

"I can see what I need to see," Louise said, rinsing out the coffee pot. She would make a fresh pot and then go to the parlor to go over the songs she had hoped to play for Sunday's church service.

As she was filling the pot, she glanced up at the television just in time to see a Philadelphia player go shooting down the ice. She frowned, watching as he wove past the two players from the other team skating backward. The cheers from the people in the kitchen grew louder as he got closer. He lifted his stick while in motion, took a shot that looked impossible.

It went in.

The cold water flowed over her hands at the same time that a loud cheer went up from her sisters and their guests.

Even Lloyd added his voice to the noise.

Louise turned off the tap and gave in to the inevitable. She pulled up a chair and sat down beside Randall. *This is silly*, she thought, *but if you can't beat them, then join them.*

Chapter Fourteen

I think we have everything ready," Alice said the following afternoon, double-checking the supplies that she and Jane had laid out.

After skating, they were going to have the girls in for dinner and then they were going to bake. It made for a busy night, but the girls would enjoy it. Alice just hoped Jane was up to it. "Are you sure you're not too tired?" Alice asked Jane.

"I have been sitting around most of the day precisely so I could save up enough energy to help you now," Jane said. "If anything, you should be tired after working at the hospital."

"Thankfully things are slowing down there," Alice said. "And it was a short day."

"Where is Randall?" Jane asked, sorting the recipe cards that she had printed from the computer. She had suggested to Alice that they make something simple that the girls could take home with them. They had decided on basic cupcakes that they could decorate. Simple, but fun.

"He's clearing the rink one more time," Alice said. "We had a dusting of snow last night."

"How are you going to get everyone out there?"

"Ashley's mother is lending her van to Randall, who'll take most of the girls. The rest will come with me in my car. We are picking them up right after school."

"I am surprised he's willing to help you like this."

Alice glanced over her shoulder as if to make sure he was not around. "I am, too. According to what Louise overheard, he is supposed to be talking to people about this movie."

"What do you make of him?" Jane asked, taking out her cake decorator. "I've only spoken with him a couple of times, but he doesn't seem to like his job."

"Well, certainly he hasn't spent any time trying to convince me and he knows I'm against the film. Even though Florence is for it, he's been avoiding her."

Jane laughed. "Who can blame him?"

The back door opened and Randall entered the kitchen. "I think we're all set, Miss Howard," he said to Alice. "It's a beautiful day. The girls should have fun."

"So I'm hoping. They seemed excited about it all."

The phone rang and Jane went to pick it up. "I am calling for a Randall Marquette," a nasal voice on the other end of the phone said.

"It's for you, Randall. You can take it in the study," Jane suggested.

"Doesn't matter," he said with a shrug. He took the phone but turned away from Jane and Alice as he spoke.

"There has to be enough. That check was supposed to have been deposited two weeks ago." Randall tapped his fingers on the wall beside the phone. "Look, call this number. They'll take care of it." He pulled out his wallet and read off a number. It was not hard to hear the anger in his voice. "Okay, then, I'll do it."

He hung up the phone and then picked it up again and punched in a number. "Hey, Andy. Just want to let you know that there might be problems with the car payment. Starlight Productions didn't put my paycheck in the bank when they were supposed to." He sighed, spoke a bit longer, then hung up.

He turned to Jane with an apologetic smile. "I'll have to take you up on your offer of the study phone. I am going to be busy for a few minutes."

"We don't have to leave for a while yet," Alice said. "Don't rush."

He bit his lip, looking disgusted. "That Trey. He said he would take care of that check problem. This causes so much trouble for me." Randall gave a short laugh. "I wish I could afford to quit on him." He gave them an apologetic grin, but Jane could see that it was forced.

"Okay, girls, let's get those skates on," Randall said, clapping his hands to get the girls' attention. "There is a log on one side of the pond for you to use as a bench."

Randall had led the way from the road to the pond, and Alice and Jane trailed along behind him. Alice had encouraged Jane to stay home, but she said she was tired of being inside and the fresh air would do her good.

As Jane sat down beside the girls, Alice had to concede that Jane had been right. Her cheeks were rosy and her eyes bright. She looked like the old Jane again. Alice sent up a prayer of thanks. She hadn't wanted to alarm Louise, but had Jane not turned the corner when she did, Alice had thought they would have to admit their sister to the hospital.

"I can't tie my laces, my fingers are too cold," complained Ashley, rubbing her hands together.

Randall patiently bent over her skates and helped her lace them up. When Linda Farr complained, he helped her too.

"My mom says you work for a movie producer," Sarah said as she laced up her skates. "Do you live in California?"

"I do," Randall said, tying a bow on Linda's skates.

"Do you get to meet any movie stars?" Tabitha asked, slipping on her mittens.

"Yes. When I'm working on a movie."

"Have you ever met Josh Kerrigen?" Ashley asked.

Randall nodded. "I worked location for a couple of movies he did."

Complete and utter silence greeted his offhand remark.

Ashley was the first one to catch her breath, her hand on her chest as if she was trying to hold in her heart. "You talked to him? In person?"

"Oh yeah. A couple of times."

"What is he like?" Tabitha pushed herself off onto the ice and made a graceful figure eight.

Randall shrugged as he bent over to tie up his own skates. "A little too full of himself. A little too caught up in all the things that teen magazines write about him."

Sissy gave Ashley a teasing poke. "I guess you won't be marrying him after all."

"I don't care. I still think he's a nice guy. He's cute and he gave all that money away to that camp for kids with cancer."

"I heard he's very generous," Randall agreed. "I think he would like to be nicer than he is, but it's really hard when you're in the spotlight all the time."

"What is hard about being in the spotlight?" Alice prompted, sensing that she might be able to generate a lesson for the girls.

"When you're an actor working on a movie, two things

happen. One is that people are always all over you, treating you like you're a big deal. When they set up a scene, you've got people fussing with your hair, one with your makeup, another with your clothes." He tugged on the laces, his head down, but the girls hung on every word, obviously fascinated by his brush with the famous people of the world. "As soon as you're done, though, and the director says cut, everyone kind of drifts away. Then you realize you're not really an important person, you're just another part of the scenery for the movie."

He looked up at the girls, who were listening raptly. Alice could see that they had heard him but hadn't completely understood him.

"So you are saying that actors get treated like things?" she asked.

Randall nodded, his mouth pulled up in a wry grin. "Exactly. Important and fragile things, but things nonetheless. Just another part of the movie."

"All the time?"

"Not if you're a big star. Then you get treated like a person, but even then, you're often surrounded by people who want something from you. So in a way, you are still treated like a thing."

Tabitha skated closer to the other girls, who were now just starting to glide onto the pond. Her skates sang over the ice, the hiss of the blades bringing back memories for Alice.

"So you're saying that being famous is a bad thing?" she asked.

Alice could hear a faintly defensive note in her voice and she remembered what Louise had told her about Tabitha and her dreams.

"Not all the time. Some people can handle it. Older movie stars know the name of the game and don't get caught up in the stories that go around about them." Randall got up and picked up a hockey stick he had brought along and pulled a puck out of his pocket. "You just have to know what the rules of the game are. In the fame game, one of the rules is don't believe your own press releases."

"What's a press release?" Sarah asked, gingerly getting to her feet, holding her arms out to keep her balance.

"The movie studios and actors' agents and anyone else who wants the newspapers to print information send out press releases. They're full of information about upcoming movies, awards, new shows that stars will be featured in. Someone is paid to write them and to make them sound as good as they can." Randall dropped the puck on the ice and tapped it between his skates and his hockey stick while he waited for the rest of the girls to get ready.

"So is Hollywood really an evil place?" Jenny Snyder asked, still sitting on the bench.

"There are a lot of good people in Hollywood and in the movie industry. It's just a hard place to be famous and be yourself, that's all. You need to be strong." Randall tapped the puck and sent it spinning across the ice. "You need a good support network to keep you grounded. Friends, family and community. Lose that and you can get pulled into places you shouldn't be going." He skated up to the puck and gave it another hit. As he played the puck up and down the ice, Alice wondered if he was talking about himself.

Tabitha skated along behind him, lazily making S curves like those Alice remembered her mother making. "But you can be famous and still be a good person."

"Absolutely," Randall said. "In fact, there are a lot of people who do it, but it's hard. Like I said, you need other people to keep you grounded."

Tabitha only nodded and spun in a graceful circle. Alice had to smile at how effortlessly she talked and skated at the same time. The girl had many talents.

"Why are you asking me these questions anyhow?" Randall asked with a wink. "Don't tell me you want to be a famous movie actress?"

"Nope, I want to be a famous concert pianist," Tabitha said, swinging out her arms as she spun in place. "I want to play at Lincoln Center in New York City and the Royal Albert Hall in London and the Concertgebouw in Amsterdam." With each location she named, she spun faster, then extended her arms wider as if she wanted to encompass all the places she was talking about.

"You're aiming high," Randall said, "but it sounds to me like a different kind of fame. You'll be making music, giving people an experience, something they can take with them when they leave, and you'll be in charge."

Tabitha stopped spinning and looked from Randall to Alice, as if she was piecing together what the two of them had told her. "That is like a gift from God to me to other people."

Randall nodded. "That's a good way to put it."

Alice's heart was warmed by the interaction between the girl and the young man. People tended to be more open to young children talking about faith than they were to adults. She was glad Tabitha had said what she did.

"Aren't you coming skating, Miss Howard?" Linda Farr asked, slipping on her mittens. "You don't have your skates on."

"I think I will stay in my boots and help the girls who can't skate that well. I can do that better if I keep myself solidly on the ice instead of on skates."

"But you have to try. Please? And you brought your skates."

Linda's pleading face made Alice laugh. She started

taking off her boots. "I guess I could at least try. After all, Randall did all this work just for us."

"Great. I'll skate with you."

At that moment Ashley and Sarah went squealing past her. They were being chased by Jenny, who was throwing snowballs at them, and Linda was swept up in their fun.

Soon all the girls were ice skating around the pond, laughing and throwing snow. Jane got up from the bench and joined in, her laughter mingling with the others in the cold afternoon air. The sunshine glinted off the snow that dusted the trees and mantled the ground. It was a beautiful day, Alice thought, well pleased with what had come of her plans—actually, Randall's plans.

"Hey, girls," shouted Randall in a mock serious voice, "stop messing up my ice!"

This command only served to have them turn on him.

"Aren't you supposed to be a grown-up?" Sissy laughed, when Randall managed to throw some snow back at her.

"Why should I grow up? This is way more fun." Randall returned.

"My goodness, who is the child and who is the leader?" Alice heard behind her.

She turned in time to see Louise, bundled up in a scarf and a long winter coat. "They certainly look like they are enjoying themselves," Louise said, smiling.

"How did you get here?" Alice asked.

"The same way you did. I drove, then I walked."

Alice noticed the skates that Louise held in one hand. "Are you going skating?" Alice asked.

"I would like to try. Are you going to join me?"

"I brought my skates, but I'm a little fearful, I have to admit."

"Then let's try together."

Louise quickly put on her skates and Alice followed suit. When she was done, Alice stood up slowly, her feet sliding in two different directions. She waved her arms, hampered by the bulk of her winter coat, trying to keep her balance. Louise caught her by one arm, then, to her surprise, Jane caught her by the other. It took a few rounds, but she caught the rhythm and soon felt the bite of her skates in the ice, reveled in the cool air rushing past her face.

Jane left them and returned to the bench. Alice and Louise carried on.

"This is wonderful," Alice said, turning to Louise, who was also smiling. "I'm so glad you talked me into it."

"Let's try to skate the way Mother and Father always did." They came to a halt at the end of the pond and Louise looked over the group of giggling girls chasing Randall. "He has done a lot of work shoveling this off. I do believe that boy has done nothing else but work here." Louise bit her lip as she turned to

Alice. "I wish I could understand him. I know Trey wanted him to stay around and convince people to sign onto the movie, but he doesn't seem to be doing that. Yet I hear reports of him talking to people around town."

"I know I learned a lesson with Jane," Alice said, tucking her arm more firmly in her sister's. "Instead of indulging in conjecture, we need to sit down and speak with him. We could try tonight."

Louise nodded, then laughed. "But what if there is a hockey game on tonight?"

"Then we shall have to do it after the game." Alice tugged on Louise's arm. "Now, let's show these young things how to skate." They pushed off and glided in one direction; both on one foot with their other legs out behind them, then as they slowed down, their free legs came to the side. They transferred their weight to those legs and repeated the process in the other direction, making graceful S turns.

The girls stopped their giggly play and watched. Louise could see that they were surprised two older women could actually do something besides be older women.

"Neato," one cried out. "Can you teach us how to do that?"

It took a few minutes of directions and misdirections and girls falling down and pulling other girls down, but after a while, they caught the rhythm. Soon all of them were weaving across the rink, being urged on by Randall, who skated around and beside them, playing with his puck and hockey stick all the while.

⟡

"I had a lot of fun today, Miss Howard," Tabitha said to Alice, setting the cupcakes she had iced carefully into one of the boxes Jane had provided for all the girls. "Thank you so much for letting me come."

"I'm so glad you could join us," Alice said, placing a bowl that had held bright blue icing into the sink. The girls had helped with the dishes after dinner. She would do the dishes from making the cupcakes later on.

The girls had mixed their own colors to ice the cupcakes with results in shades that ranged from pastel to neon.

Tabitha licked some icing off her finger and glanced at Louise. "My mom wants to talk to you before my lesson next week," she said softly, as if she didn't want the other girls to overhear.

Louise felt a touch of dread. "Do you mind telling me what she wants to talk about? Just so I have an idea what to say to her."

Tabitha moved a little closer, blushing lightly. "It's about paying for the lessons."

Louise smiled at the girl. "I'm sure we can come to some sort of arrangement for that," she said. Tabitha smiled up at her and Louise wiped a dot of blue icing from her cheek. "I'm very glad you came. You looked as if you were having a good time."

"The girls are really nice," Tabitha said.

"My sister has always encouraged them to welcome new people and to treat them with respect."

Ashley and Sarah had cornered Randall and were still peppering him with questions about the movie industry and stars he had met. From the grin on his face, Louise could see that he did not seem to mind.

"Okay, girls, your parents are going to be coming soon," Alice said, clapping her hands to get the giggling girls' attention. "Put your cupcakes in the boxes and clean up the area where you were working."

Louise glanced around the once-tidy kitchen. Bowls of icing were scattered over the counter, icing sugar dusted the girls and the floor, and cake crumbs were everywhere.

In spite of Alice's directions for the girls to clean up, she knew that she and Alice were going to be busy for a while getting the kitchen back to its usual immaculate state. Thinking about the work ahead, she had a sudden inspiration of how Mrs. Harke could help to pay for Tabitha's piano lessons. With Jane still not feeling one hundred percent, and with Trey and Lynette coming back in a few days, Louise and Alice were hard pressed to keep up with the cleaning. If Mrs. Harke would agree, then it could work out well for all concerned.

Chapter Fifteen

One hour later, the kitchen was tidy again, and Randall, Jane, Alice and Louise were sitting at the table resting.

"Those girls have a lot of energy," Randall said with a sigh, tipping his chair back on two legs.

Louise frowned at him.

He gave her a crooked grin and lowered the chair. "Sorry, Mrs. Smith," he said. "Bad bachelor habit."

"All is forgiven, Randall," she said.

"Do you do this every week?" Randall asked Alice.

"I try to spend one meeting a month with them doing something fun." She took a sip of her tea and smiled at him. "I don't know if I thanked you properly for all you did for the girls and for me. The skating party turned out very well. The girls really enjoyed themselves."

"They certainly were full of high spirits," Louise said. She glanced at Jane, who sat quietly at the table. "Are you feeling well, Jane?" Louise asked her. "You seem tired."

"I am tired, but in a nice way. It felt so good to be out-side again. I enjoyed watching my sisters show those young things how to skate. Where did you learn to do that glidey thing?"

"Father and Mother used to do it with a long line of people," Louise said. "I forget what it was called. They taught me."

"It looked really graceful," Jane leaned back in her chair and looked around her kitchen. "It's good to be back in here. I can hardly wait to get to work."

"Surely it's too soon," Louise protested.

"Now, Louie, don't tell me we are going to have a territorial dispute. You know this is my place in the inn." Jane's voice was serious, but her eyes danced with mischief.

"No, we are going to have a discussion about how well you are and whether you want a relapse." Louise cradled the earthenware mug in her hands. "By the way, what do you two think of having Tabitha Harke's mother help out in the inn for the next couple of weeks? I believe that they are having some financial difficulties and Tabitha is afraid she might have to quit her lessons."

"That would be fine," Alice said. "What do you think, Jane?"

"Until I'm feeling one hundred percent again, we could probably use the extra help."

"Okay, that's settled then."

They sat in silence, each lost in thought.

"Do you always get along this well?" Randall asked

finally, his surprised gaze flickering from one sister to the other. "Don't you ever disagree?"

Jane tipped her head to one side as if considering what he was asking. "We disagree, but we try to talk things out." She gave her sisters a mischievous smile. "We do have the occasional communication breakdown."

"Your being ill created unusual circumstances," Louise said in her own defense.

"My ears and mouth still worked," Jane said.

"Not that well. You could hardly utter a coherent sentence."

"You see, Randall," Alice put in with a quick laugh, "we do disagree from time to time."

"If you want to call that disagreeing," he said. "Trey's version of disagreeing has a lot more pyrotechnics."

Louise glanced at him. "You mention Trey often but never in complimentary terms. Do you respect him?"

Randall looked taken aback at her bluntness but recovered quickly. "Actually, I don't."

"Why not?" Alice prompted.

"Like I told you a few days ago, Trey is a taker."

"I remember your saying that, Randall, but I guess we would like you to explain," Alice said. She prayed for wisdom, sensing that Randall wanted to talk, but that he didn't dare speak his mind quite yet. At the same time, she knew that he had information that the church board needed to make a proper decision . . . information that would not be beneficial to Trey. "When you say he is a taker, I'm thinking that has implications for Grace Chapel and Acorn Hill."

Randall folded his hands and looked down at them.

"I was also wondering if you would be willing to talk to our church board on your own," Alice continued, trying not to push too hard. "I think you could give us a more specific idea of what will happen to Grace Chapel if Trey wants to use it in his movie."

Randall shook his head. "Sorry. Trey is the spokesman of the group. I'm just the gofer." He gave Alice an apologetic smile, but he didn't meet her eyes. "I've got my job to think about. Going to talk to the church board to convince them not to take Trey's offer is not what I'd call a smart career move."

"But you know what is going on, don't you?" Alice asked, pushing just a little harder.

"We know what you were supposed to be doing, Randall," Louise put in softly, her voice encouraging. "I have to confess I overheard Trey talking to you about staying behind and convincing the church board and anyone else you could to agree to filming here in Acorn Hill."

"That was what he wanted me to do all right," Randall said, his eyes still focused on his hands.

"If I may be blunt, you haven't been spending a lot of time doing that, which doesn't show a lot of commitment to the project, does it?"

Randall only shook his head, like a child caught with his hand in the cookie jar.

"Why aren't you committed?" Jane asked.

Randall blew out his breath and laughed shortly. "The truth? I don't want to see the movie made here. Not by Trey. I figured that there were enough people opposed to it that if I could just bide my time, when he came back, the whole project would be turned down by the people of the town."

"I don't understand," Jane said.

Randall tapped his fingers restlessly on the table. "Thing is, if I convince people to have the movie made, I won't be able to live with myself. I'll have to come back here during the filming and watch what happens. If I don't say anything and things go the way they seem to be going, then I can't say I was involved in the decision at all." He shrugged lightly. "That way I can keep my job and my integrity."

"But what if it goes the other way?" Alice asked. "There are enough people who want to see this go through. Florence is a force to be reckoned with. June and Hope both are in favor, and they have a lot of people coming through the Coffee Shop that they might convince. I know there are other people in this town that like the idea of the publicity that a film would bring Acorn Hill."

"Then they get what they want and it's not my problem." Randall got up from the table and for a moment Louise thought he was going to leave. At the same time, she sensed his restlessness and a desire to let something off his chest. She took a chance.

"You don't like your job, do you?"

Randall came to a stop by the counter and turned toward her, his ponytail hanging over one shoulder. "I like parts of it. I can travel. I meet interesting people. I have a chance to move up into other parts of the movie industry that I'm more interested in."

"Like what?"

"Just other things. Until I can be where I want to in this industry, it's a paycheck . . ." His voice trailed off as if he was running out of words to convince himself.

"When the check goes through," Alice put in.

Randall laughed shortly.

"And what about your writing?" Jane asked.

Randall shot her a look. "What about it?"

"Don't you want to spend more time on that? You're young and single and other than your candy-apple-red Mustang, you don't have any obligations," Jane said. "Why spend your time on something that doesn't satisfy you?"

Randall sighed and toyed with his hair.

Louise had to smile at the mannerism. Only a week ago, the gesture would have annoyed her, but in the past few days, he had let his guard down and had shown them a far more pleasant and engaging side of his nature. It was a side, she suspected, that he didn't show much around his boss.

"Because writing doesn't pay for the things I want," Randall said, with a defensive edge in his voice. "It's the direction I want to go in, but for now that's a dream out of reach. This is just a way to get there, that's all."

"And it keeps you doing the things you don't want to do," Jane replied.

"You have youth on your side, Randall," Alice said. "Time. Don't waste it on work that doesn't satisfy. On building up treasures that will rot and rust."

"That sounds like something out of the Good Book," Randall replied with a wry grin.

"It is," Louise said. She left the room and returned with her Bible. She flipped through the pages, easily finding the passage. "This is from Matthew 6. 'Do not store up for yourselves treasures on earth, where moth and rust destroy, and where thieves break in and steal. But store up for yourselves treasures in heaven, where moth and rust do not destroy, and where thieves do not break in and steal. For where your treasure is, there your heart will be also.'"

"So what's the deal with that? What kind of treasure?"

"I think the clue is in the last line," Louise said, placing her finger on the text. "'Where your treasure is, there your heart will be also.' What Jesus is saying is that your heart follows your treasure, what you think of as most important, what you value and esteem. And if you put all your happiness in things that are going to decay and lose value, then your happiness must lose its value as well."

"That's deep," he said.

"It's not that complicated," Louise said. "Right now you are working for things that will disappear. In fifteen years, where will your car be? The things you want so badly now?"

"Replaced," Randall said.

"With something else that will break down."

Randall sighed and sat back down. "I know what you are saying, Mrs. Smith. I've heard it before. It's just that I don't dare change my life. I feel like I've gone too far down this path and I don't know anymore how to turn around. How to get off."

"Do you want to get off?" Jane asked.

Randall ran his hands over his face and sighed once again. "I do, but I need the money this job gives me."

"What could be the worst thing that could happen if you quit?" Alice prompted.

"I would lose my car." Randall bit his lip, thinking. "I would have to give up my apartment."

"Would it be hard to find a cheaper place to live?" Alice asked.

Randall squeezed the bridge of his nose and closed his eyes, as if imagining the possibilities he had just mentioned. "Actually, not that hard at all."

"So why don't you do it?" Jane asked. "Why don't you break the vicious circle, sell your car, do what you want to do?"

"You mean quit working for Trey?"

"Why not?" Alice suggested. "You said yourself you don't care to work for him."

"I could work for someone else," Randall mused. "Or I could work for myself. I've always wanted to write a script."

"Florence could give you some pointers," Jane said with a grin.

Louise bit back her own smile. Jane had a sharp sense of humor but there were times when she didn't want to encourage her. Right now she wanted to focus on Randall and his needs.

"If that's what you want, then I think you should take the time to do it," Louise encouraged him. "You have no other obligations. You have the freedom to make choices."

"Except for the car," he reminded her.

"Which you can sell," Alice said, leaning forward. "It sounds like it is a burden to you anyway."

Randall accepted her comment with a shrug. "Only when the payments come out of my bank account—or can't come out because my check hasn't been deposited."

"So sell it," encouraged Alice.

"I still need wheels," Randall said.

"Buy cheaper ones," Jane said. "A car is just transportation. As soon as you turn it into a status symbol, you get caught in a race you can't hope to win. There is always going to be a nicer, newer, fancier, more expensive one somewhere on the road."

"The rat race," Randall said.

"Exactly," Jane said. "A race that only the rats win!"

"Think about the passage that we read," Louise urged, sensing the young man's hesitation. It was hard to see him struggle and she wanted to encourage him. "Watch where your heart is leading you. We want you to know that Jesus wants us to focus on Him, because only when we do that, when we give Him the heart that we so easily give over to things, will we find anything that lasts and has substance in our lives."

"The come-to-Jesus stuff I used to hear at revivals?" Randall said.

Louise refused to be baited. Sometimes, when feeling cornered, people push back in a negative way. Behind his bravado, she heard a faint note of fear. "Jesus calls us through all kinds of circumstances and in all kinds of ways. Maybe there was a reason you had to stay behind. Jesus knows what is in your heart and He knows what you want even before you do. Maybe this week here, without your boss around, was a chance for you to rest, to reevaluate your life."

"Maybe," Randall said as he pushed himself away from the counter. "You ladies have given me lots to think about. Thanks for taking the time to talk to me."

"You're welcome, Randall," Alice said. "Thank you for all you did for the girls. I know they had a great time and it made my job a lot easier."

Randall looked a little embarrassed. "I had a lot of fun too." He hesitated, as if he wanted to say more, then turned and left.

The three women said nothing until they heard the door of his room close.

"I don't know about you, but I think he needs a lot of prayer," Jane said, folding her hands on the table in front of her. "I'm not sure he really is convinced to change his life right now."

"He's afraid. Many people are afraid of change. It means you have to make a decision, a choice," Louise said.

"Why don't we pray for him right now," Alice said. She reached out a hand to Louise and to Jane, and then they all bowed their heads. "Dear Lord," Alice prayed, her gentle voice drawing along her sisters in her prayer, "tonight we want to lift Randall up to You in prayer. We ask You to help him in the decisions he has to make. Guide him and show him that he needs to trust in You and to help the people of this town to make the right decision about this movie. Whatever happens, Lord, we know if we give it over to You, You can use it for Your glory and honor. Amen."

Louise looked down at the table a moment, as the words of Alice's prayer sank in. "Thank you, Alice," she said softly. "It is a good thing to realize that if people want this movie to be filmed in Acorn Hill, then we can find a way to use it for good."

"We could," Jane said with a sigh, "but I sure hope we will not be put to that test. I don't know if I care for having all that busyness in our small town."

"We don't truly know what kind of disruption it would cause," Alice said. "It might not be that bad after all."

"It might not," Louise said, "but I'm still not in favor of it."

"We have to meet with the church board tomorrow night to discuss Trey's proposal once again," Alice said. "If the board votes in favor of his plan, then it sounds like many of the people in the town would go along with it as well."

"We shall just have to pray and let go," Louise replied getting up.

"Are you going to bed already?" Jane asked, glancing from Alice to Louise.

"I thought you were tired," Louise said.

"I am, but I've spent so much time in that bed that I am heartily sick of it."

"But what are you going to do, dear?" Alice asked.

Jane caught her lip between her teeth, thinking. "I could read a book, but I don't feel like doing that either." She snapped her fingers. "I know. I'm going to see if there's a hockey game on tonight."

Louise looked at her over her glasses. "Really, Jane. Not you too?"

"Hey, it was a lot of fun," Jane retorted.

"I am going to bed," Louise said, stifling a yawn. "Good night, Jane. Don't stay up too late."

"I won't, Mama Louise."

"All done," Randall said, putting a box on the small marble-topped table.

Jane, curled up on the burgundy sofa, looked up from the magazine she was flipping through. It was early Friday afternoon and she was resting. That morning she had insisted on making breakfast and had basked in the compliments from her sisters and Randall, but even that simple job had tired her out.

"What are you talking about?" she asked Randall, puzzled as she laid the magazine down and picked up the box.

"Open it up," he said, dropping unceremoniously onto the matching overstuffed chair. He leaned back, frowned, then hitched to one side and pulled a pillow from behind his back. "Do people seriously use these things?" he asked, setting the pillow on the floor.

"And sometimes unseriously," Jane said.

No sooner had Randall gotten comfortable in the chair than Wendell jumped onto his lap, settled himself and began to purr.

"If he's a nuisance, you can make him go away," Jane said, opening the box.

"I don't mind him at all." Randall absently stroked the cat's head. "He makes me feel as welcome as you ladies do."

"Oh wow," Jane said as she glanced inside the box, then drew out one of the fountain pens that lay inside. "My goodness, did you fix up all of these?"

"Only the ones I could get parts for. I had to special-order a few but thankfully they came right away. The others I just cleaned up so they look their best."

Jane put the one pen back and picked up the next. It shone lustrously. "This is amazing. I am impressed, Randall Marquette. Impressed and pleased. What a lovely thing to do."

Randall shrugged, running his finger over the tips of Wendell's ears. "I enjoyed doing it. There's something kind of neat about working with pens that I know other people have used. I sometimes wonder what they used them for and what was going through their heads when they used them."

"That could make an interesting story," Jane mused, turning one pen over in her hands, watching the colors change in the light. "Follow the life of a pen from owner to owner."

Randall sat up suddenly, startling Wendell, who jumped off his lap and trotted away. "You know, that's an excellent idea. Some of these older pens have changed hands a number of times. People buy and sell them." He leaned forward, his eyes wide with excitement. "You could follow the stories of the people's lives and at the same time intersperse it with some of the things they wrote." He slapped his hand on his knee. "That's a great idea."

"Tell you what you can do, Randall," Jane said, closing the box. "I'll give you the ideas, you write the story and we split the proceeds fifty-fifty."

The surprised look on Randall's face made Jane laugh out loud.

"I was kidding, Randall," she said.

"Lots of people who suggest exactly the same thing aren't," he replied. "People think that half of the work of writing is coming up with the idea."

"I know. We've had a couple of writers staying here and they said the same thing. And then there's poor Florence Simpson, who is convinced that spies are waiting around every corner to steal her idea."

Randall sighed heavily. "I have never met someone with so much persistence and so little talent."

Jane put her finger over her lips, looking past him.

Randall spun around, ready to make a hasty exit, when he realized there was no one behind him. He turned to Jane, his hand on his heart. "I thought for a moment Florence was here."

"Don't worry," Jane said, giggling as she got up from the couch. "I would have been out the door and down the walk before you would have had a whiff of her perfume."

"You have a twisted sense of humor," he said, also standing up.

"What's on your agenda the rest of the day?" Jane asked as she walked to the kitchen. Because she had not cooked for so long, she was itching to make something extra special for her sisters and Randall. Randall followed along behind her and sat down at the table.

"I need to do a bit of out-of-town location scouting. Some of the scenes are shot in a farmyard and I still haven't found the perfect location."

"What do you look for when you hunt out a location?"

Jane said, taking out her worn recipe book and laying it on the countertop. Randall did not seem in a hurry to leave, so she thought this would be a good opportunity to ask him a few questions.

"I start with the script. I have fairly detailed descriptions of what the director wants in each scene, so I go out and look for it. If it needs a house with a hill in the background, or a copse of trees with a brook running through it, it's seek and ye shall find."

"But it's winter now. How will you know what to look for?"

"The script takes place in winter, which makes things doubly difficult. We can shoot some things in season, but many times we have to manufacture the weather and the lighting. But I still need to look for settings they can use for the various shoots."

"What if the weather doesn't cooperate and it gets too warm?"

"We make fake snow." Randall grinned at the puzzled look on Jane's face. "Seriously. We have machines that blow out a form of Styrofoam that turns into flakes and coats whatever surface we want to look snow-covered."

"Sounds to me like a lot of work and awfully messy." Jane stopped at a recipe and scanned the ingredients. "What do you think of hamburger roll-ups?" she asked absently.

"Sounds like a lot of work and awfully messy," Randall shot back with a laugh.

Jane grinned.

"Do you need any help?"

"Why, is there a hockey game on tonight?" Jane replied.

Randall laughed. "There is, but it's on late." He glanced at his watch. "I should get going."

"To do your job?" Jane asked, archly. As soon as she said the words, she regretted them and how they sounded. She had hoped to have him open up to her, but after that little comment, she doubted that he would.

Oh, for the steady grace and wisdom of my sister Alice, she thought, biting her lip as if she could stop the words from reaching Randall.

"Yeah. I guess I better. Don't want the bank to be hounding me again," he said. "I suppose I should make an appointment with Rev. Thompson if I need to talk to him, shouldn't I?"

Jane shook her head, feeling humbled. "Ken is always available. You can talk to him any time."

"Great. I mean, if he's the head honcho, I suppose I should make sure to get on his good side," Randall said. He slipped on his coat and strode out of the kitchen, his hands in his pockets. He did not look back.

Chapter Sixteen

I'm going to need some finishing nails as well," Alice said to José, checking the list she had scribbled on the back of an envelope on her way to the hardware store. "I noticed a casing coming loose in the upstairs hallway."

"Do you want me to come and fix it?" José asked with a smile as he carefully wrote the bin number of the nails on the plastic bag and then slipped in the nails. It didn't seem to matter what José did, it was all done with a positive attitude.

Alice was about to refuse, then thought about the broken dishwasher. "José, that would be wonderful if you could. More importantly, do you think that you could fix our dishwasher when you come?"

"I can take a look at it. I'm pretty good with machinery," José said. "I will come this afternoon."

"That would be wonderful," Alice said.

"Good afternoon, Alice," Fred said, coming out of his office behind the till. "I feel like I haven't seen you for weeks instead of a few days."

Alice grinned at Fred. "Well, we've seen lots of you. Our local celebrity."

Fred just laughed as he tucked a pencil behind his ear. "Hardly a celebrity. Goofy weather forecaster one day and prognosticator the next. Keeps a man humble, that's for sure."

"I definitely liked the second interview more."

"I did too."

"I don't understand how the first one ended up so different."

Fred shrugged. "She asked me a lot of questions, but kept going back to the folklore stuff, so I indulged her. Guess that was all she wanted to hear." Fred turned to José. "Mrs. Holzmann called and was asking if we had any more of that varnish stripper she uses. Would you check for me and call her back if we do?"

José nodded and ambled off, hidden by the shelves of materials that lined the aisles of the stores.

"Don't forget about the church board meeting I called for tonight," Fred said, tapping his finger on his chin as he turned to Alice. "I want to talk about the movie crew's proposal."

"I'll be there." Alice tucked the bag of nails into her carryall and looked up at Fred, frowning. "What is your personal feeling about the film crew shooting a movie in Grace Chapel?"

"I don't like it," Fred said, shaking his head. "My

extensive television experience clearly shows me that what you see is not always what you get." He said the latter with a self-deprecating grin, but it triggered something in Alice.

"We have one of the members of the movie crew still staying with us, Randall. I was hoping he could come to the meeting and tell us precisely what we would be getting into," Alice mused. "I'm not sure Trey Atkinson would give us all the facts we need to make an informed decision."

"Randall stopped by here early this afternoon," Fred said. "He asked me point-blank if I was in favor of making the movie in the church. I told him I wasn't. Yes, it is a building, but it is more than that. Grace Chapel is where people come to worship. I also said that I'm sure no matter how careful they are, there will be disruptions to our worship services."

"What did he say to that?"

"Not much." Fred straightened a display of key chains. "I got the feeling that he didn't seem to care much one way or the other."

"I wish I knew how to help him," Alice said sadly. "He seems so confused."

The buzzer sounded, announcing another customer, and Fred straightened, pulling the pencil from behind his ear. He smiled as Dee Butorac, one of the high school teachers, came up to the counter.

"Good afternoon, Dee. What can I get for you today?"

"Good afternoon, Fred." Dee inclined her head to Alice as she pulled off her mittens. "Hello, Alice. How are you and Louise managing? I heard Jane was going to be leaving to star on a television cooking show."

Alice shook her head. "Dee, that was misinformation spread by the grapevine. It's not true."

Dee smiled, looking relieved. "I'm glad about that. I've heard about the high tea you put on occasionally and I would love to come next time you do one."

"We'll put your name on the list," Alice said, opening her purse. "I'll make a note of it."

Dee turned to Fred while Alice finished writing down her name. "Fred, I caught your interview on the television and I must say I was impressed with how accessible you made the information."

"The information about the turkey breastbone or dogs lifting their legs higher when a change in the weather is coming?" Fred said with a laugh.

"Did you talk about that in your interview?" Dee sounded puzzled, and Alice guessed she hadn't seen the first interview. "I don't remember that, but I do remember your talking about how lightning occurs and it finally made sense to me. I mentioned the interview to our science teacher, Mr. Williams. He watched it, too, and was impressed with your knowledge. Because my daughter is in Vera's class, I offered to ask if you would be willing to come to talk to the high school students about weather prediction."

Fred blushed. "Well, now, I don't know if I am that knowledgeable. I only know what I'm interested in."

"That is just the point. If you are enthusiastic about something, the students pick that up and in turn become enthusiastic themselves," Dee said, sounding excited herself about the idea of Fred's coming. "It means more to the students if they find out that you have gathered all this information on your own, that you weren't forced to do it."

"I'm sometimes forced not to do it," Fred laughed. "Vera thinks I spend too much time listening to weather reports from different parts of the world and going on the Internet researching."

"Would you be willing, though?" Dee asked. "Having people come in to talk to the kids makes my job as a teacher much easier."

Fred pursed his lips, thinking. "Vera says the same thing," he said finally. "I'll do it, but don't expect anything too much in depth."

"If it's anything like that interview, then that will be just fine, I'm sure," Dee said. "I'm so glad you're willing. I know Mr. Williams will be so pleased. I'll let him know and he will be in touch with you about a date."

"I found the varnish stripper, Mr. Humbert," José said, bringing two cans to the counter. "I just don't know which one the Holzmanns bought before."

"I'll let you get back to your work," Dee said, slipping her mittens back on and flipping the hood of her coat over her head. "Though I wouldn't mind if you could tell me when we are going to get warmer weather."

"Give this cold snap a week or so. From what I see there's going to be some warmer air coming up from the Gulf, pushing out that Canadian cold front that has been hanging over us."

"Wonderful news," Dee said, zipping up her down parka. "Have a great day and I look forward to seeing you at school." She left and Alice turned to Fred with a smile.

"Now isn't that interesting, Fred. Goes to show you never know what will come from an interview."

"Goes to show you never know what is going to come from life, even in a place as peaceful as Acorn Hill," Fred added, picking up one of the cans of stripper José had set on the counter. "I think they will want this one, José," Fred said.

"I better go," Alice said, gathering up her purchases. "Please tell Vera that I expect her to be up bright and early tomorrow morning. She promised me a walk, and now that my workload has eased at the hospital I'm going to hold her to that promise."

Fred said he would, and when Alice stepped out of the warmth of the hardware store, she shivered. The cold weather had made for a wonderful afternoon with her girls, but she would not mind some warmer weather for a change.

"The warm weather will come," she promised herself, looking up at the steel gray sky. "Fred said so."

Alice caught a whiff of pastry baking at the Coffee Shop across the road. She had some time to spare, so she crossed the street, looking forward to some company and some hot tea.

A few moments later she was settled in her usual booth, cradling a mug of steaming Earl Grey.

"Here's your turnover," Hope Collins said, setting the flaky pastry in front of her. "I'm glad you came by, Alice. I hear you've been busy."

"The hospital work has been keeping me hopping, I'm afraid," Alice said. She took a welcome sip of her tea and glanced up at Hope. "You changed your hair again?"

Hope smoothed back a tendril of soft, brown hair and sighed. "I thought the blond look would appeal to those movie people, but they haven't paid attention yet. Neither has that young man that has been hanging around town. Do you know if they are still going to make that movie here or not?"

"It's not entirely up to them, you know," Alice said. "If the people of this town don't want it to happen, then the movie company can't film here."

Hope frowned, folding her arms over her stomach. "Who doesn't want the movie to be filmed here?"

Alice shrugged, sensing Hope's opposition to her comment. "A number of people. I know I'm not very keen on it."

"Why not? It would mean a lot of business for your inn," Hope said. "And it would mean business for the town. I don't have to tell you that keeping a business going in this town is not always that easy."

"It isn't always that hard either," Alice said with a smile. "You have a lot of people coming in here regularly, a loyal clientele."

"That's true," Hope said, her fingers tapping her arm. "But don't you think it would be exciting to try something else for a change? I do."

"Not if that change isn't good for us in the long run," said Alice, thinking about the last couple of weeks.

"It would be so much fun to be in a movie." Hope sighed dramatically as if already practicing for a role.

"Aren't you happy here in Acorn Hill?" Alice asked. "Would you want to become a movie star?"

Hope shrugged. "I like watching the extras in movies and I'm sure I could handle being the secretary at the next desk, the passerby holding the umbrella, the waitress no one listens to." Hope laughed. "That role I can play with one hand tied behind my back."

"That would be a challenge for a waitress."

Hope laughed. "I guess."

"Do you really think it would be fun?" Alice asked. She didn't want to be negative, but she felt uneasy with Trey's assessment of the impact the movie would have on the town.

"It would," Hope said with a grin. "People coming and going. A chance to meet some movie stars. I think it could be very exciting."

Alice sighed. She was beginning to wonder how many people in the town felt the same way. Maybe she was worrying too much. Maybe the moviemaking would turn out just fine.

Maybe.

She wished that she could convince Randall to come to the board meeting. He knew more than he was letting on and maybe, if prodded, he would tell the truth about what would happen if the board agreed. Alice simply couldn't get rid of the idea that having a movie made in Acorn Hill would end up being more of a problem than an adventure.

"I'm wondering if we get goodies at this meeting," Fred said with a wry smile as he sat down beside Alice at the table.

"My guess is that no movie director equals no goodies," Alice said quietly, pulling her chair closer to the table.

"I'd like to know why we are having this meeting," Florence asked from her seat across the table.

She didn't have her binder with her. Either she had given up on the screenplay or she didn't think it worth her while to bring it to a meeting when Trey Atkinson was not present.

"I called it because the decision that lies before the church board is important, one that merits serious discussion," Fred said quietly. "When Mr. Atkinson returns, we must give him a definite answer."

"I see." Florence wouldn't look at Alice, as if she sensed opposition.

The door opened and Sylvia Songer slipped in, looking a little flustered. "Sorry I'm late," she said. "My car wouldn't start."

"You're fine. We haven't started yet," Fred said. "We are still waiting for other members."

Sylvia sat in an empty chair next to Alice and smiled at her. "How is Jane doing?"

"She is just fine. She misses seeing you."

"I haven't been feeling too well myself." Sylvia unbuttoned her green wool coat but kept it on. Then she unwound a scarf from around her neck, untangling it from her strawberry blond hair. She laid the scarf on her lap, then began folding and unfolding it. She took a breath, as if she was about to say something to Alice, then looked down at her busy hands, her dark eyes clouded with concern.

"Is something wrong?" Alice asked quietly, keeping her voice low so the others could not hear.

Sylvia glanced around the room, then back at Alice, looking agitated. "I heard that Jane was going to be on a cooking show, that she was leaving Acorn Hill."

Alice stifled a sigh. The story Ethel had spread was still floating around Acorn Hill like ashes after a fire. "No, Sylvia, Jane is not going anywhere. That rumor is totally untrue."

Sylvia sank back in her chair, obviously relieved. "Thank goodness. I was wondering if I had made Jane angry, since she didn't say anything about her plans to me." Sylvia laid her hand on Alice's arm. "Not that I want to come across as high maintenance, you know, but I consider Jane my dearest friend and to not know what was going on in her life . . ."

"Trust me, Sylvia, Jane would let you know if she had a hangnail that was bothering her."

"I did hear she was sick, though."

"And so were you. Are you feeling better?" For a moment Alice felt a tinge of guilt. In spite of their busyness, Jane had her and Louise to watch over her. Sylvia had very little family.

"My mother came from Potterston. She helped to run the shop for a while, though business is not really her strong point. And the chicken soup you brought was delicious." Sylvia ducked her head, as if uncomfortable with the extra attention.

"Well, you must come to the inn tomorrow night for supper. I'm sure Jane would love to have you."

Sylvia beamed, her dark eyes sparkling now. "I'd like that a lot. Thanks for the invitation. It will be relaxing to be with you and away from all the visitors that I've had at the shop since I've been back to work."

"Visitors?"

Sylvia sighed and shook her head. "People from the town wanting to know where I stand on the movie. As if I have the power to decide whether it will be made or not."

"Who has been coming?"

"Your Aunt Ethel. Florence Simpson has come a couple of times, Clara Horn, Craig Tracy, Betty Dunkle and a number of other people, some who are for and some who are against. Why do they care what I think?" She fluttered her hands in a nervous gesture.

"Because you're on the church board. Trey told us that if he doesn't get church board approval, he might not make the movie in Acorn Hill. Some people want it to happen, so they are campaigning for it."

"I actually think a movie made here would be kind of fun." Sylvia smiled and Alice felt her own smile fade.

The door of the room opened and Ethel and Lloyd hurried in, deep in a discussion with June Carter and Cyril Overstreet, which stopped as soon as Lloyd noticed that people were watching them. He left the two women and sat beside Fred. His bow tie was askew and he didn't look happy, which made Alice wonder what they had been discussing before they came to the meeting.

Cyril sat down beside Florence, a frown creasing his forehead.

Henry and Patsy Ley were the last to arrive. Pastor Ley opened the meeting with a Bible reading and a prayer. When he was done, Fred called the meeting to order.

"Trey Atkinson has made it clear that he needs our approval in order to proceed. I know there has been a lot of talk going through the town about the pros and cons of having this happen. Whether we like it or not, as a church board, we have a lot of control over what will happen in the town."

"Don't I know it," Cyril Overstreet put in, shaking his head. "I've never had so much attention from . . . " he paused, glancing quickly at Florence, then cleared his throat and said, ". . . other people before."

Alice saw Fred bite back a smile and had to control one herself. Florence was making herself felt all over town, it seemed.

"What I have proposed is that I lay out the facts for this church board this evening and we make a decision. Mayor Tynan has called a town meeting to explain our stand one way or the other. If we vote down the proposal, then we can explain why. If we vote for it, then we can give the rest of the people of the town a chance to make their own decision. Trey Atkinson and his crew will also be present at the town meeting to give us all some more information.

"What I want to hear now is any information you might have and also your opinions. We'll discuss this for a short while, then we'll put Grace Chapel's participation in the movie to a vote."

Alice felt anxious, as if they were moving inexorably to a point of no return. She glanced around the room, wondering where people stood. She knew Florence was for, Fred was against and she was against. The rest?

After Sylvia's surprise comment, she wasn't sure anymore.

"If I may begin?" Mayor Tynan asked.

Fred nodded.

"The one thing that comes to me again and again is the temporary nature of this intrusion," Lloyd said, slowly getting to his feet. "We are not looking at a long-term situation, but something short-term. The disruption could be less than we think. I have looked into various shooting schedules of other movies and from what I have learned, four to six months is not unusual. Of that time, I believe not all was spent in the actual location. The way I see it, Acorn Hill can benefit from such a project, while facing very little change to our lifestyle over the long run."

Alice felt her heart sink. Lloyd was another for, and where Lloyd went, Ethel would more than likely follow.

Cyril stroked his chin thoughtfully. "There's some sense to that," he said quietly.

"I know the Coffee Shop would do some good business," June said. "As would the bakery and Zachary's."

"Yes, that's right. You *would* do a lot of good business. That certainly is something to think about," Florence put in, slapping her hand on the table for emphasis.

"We have to think of the good of the town," Mayor Tynan said. "I have received a number of phone calls from other business people in town who would like to see this movie be made here. I was assured by Trey Atkinson that the impact on the church would be minimal. Also, I think it quite a blessing that Hollywood is willing to make a movie that is based in a church and in a church community. We all like to complain about the quality of movies coming out of Hollywood, and here is a chance to show support for one that could be good."

"*Could* be good," Alice put in quietly. "We don't know exactly what the movie is about. We were told it will be humorous. Will the church be portrayed in a humorous light? That may be fine, if it is gentle humor. But what if it isn't?" Alice glanced over at Fred. "What if the movie is like the first television interviewer who spoke to Fred? What if they want to show a group of Christians as silly or closed-minded? I am sure Fred talked about more than breastbones of turkeys and high-stepping dogs with the first interviewer."

"Alice has a good point," Fred said. "Both interviewers asked me a lot of questions, but out of the questions came two completely different interviews. One made me look foolish, the other, thankfully, not as foolish."

"That was terrible what that first lady did to you," Florence put in.

"The same thing could happen to our church or to our town," Alice said.

"We could ask to see the script," Florence said. "I am sure it wouldn't hurt if someone else looked at it anyway."

Someone like you? Alice wondered.

The discussion went around and around and as Alice listened, she felt her heart sinking. Yes, some of the points in favor were valid. She knew that any business in a small town could use extra income.

"How long would they be here?" June asked.

Fred looked down at his notes. "Trey said he figured

about three months at the most. They would be filming next January, February and March."

"Our slowest time of the year," Sylvia put in.

"That is true," June added.

"It doesn't sound like a very long time," Lloyd said, nodding.

Alice glanced around the room and sensed where people were going. She remembered what she and her sisters had talked about and she knew she had to let go. If this was what the church board wanted, if this was what the town wanted, who was she to push people in another direction?

"I was hoping we could vote this evening." Fred looked at Lloyd. "I would like to have everything in place before the town meeting you have scheduled for Monday. I want to be able to explain our position and give Trey our answer as soon as possible."

"I don't think we should vote with a show of hands," Cyril said.

"I agree. I made up some ballots." Fred pulled some pieces of paper out of an envelope. "I would prefer this to be a blind vote. I don't want people feeling influenced by others."

Fred passed the ballots around. Everyone registered his or her vote, and a few moments later, Fred came around with the envelope again to gather up the ballots.

"I thought that I would simply count the ballots right now in public," he said, "unless someone has any strong objections to that."

A general murmur of assent filled the room, and Fred shook the envelope and slid the ballots out on the table.

"I need someone to move that we take the highest number of votes as either a yes or no."

Cyril so moved, and Florence seconded.

Fred began the count, and Alice found her heart speeding up as he unfolded the ballots and sorted them. It was silly, really. She had prayed about it and was willing to let go. She watched as Fred counted. He seemed to move in slow motion. One on this side. One on the other. Back and forth, one in the middle, and then Fred raised his head, looking puzzled.

"Four in favor, four against and one abstention—a tie vote."

"I would like to move that we vote again," Cyril said, clearly troubled by the outcome.

Fred glanced around the room. Alice could see he also was troubled.

"A re-vote in the case of a tie should have been decided before the voting process," Lloyd said, fingering his bow tie in a nervous gesture. "The vote has been cast and tallied."

Cyril sank back against his chair.

"What is our next step?" Florence asked, glancing around the room as if she could find out who had voted how.

"We shall inform the people at the town meeting on Monday of the outcome of our vote," Fred said. "There will be more discussion there and another vote will be taken on the town's position."

"Is this tied vote classified as a decision?" Alice asked.

"In light of our tied vote, I think we shall have to agree that we will go along with the decision of the town," Fred said.

It was not difficult to see that he was not happy with the outcome either.

She wished that Randall had come to the meeting. She was convinced that if he told the people what he knew, they would have had better information to use in making a decision. Trey had made it very clear that if the church board voted against the filming, he was not going to film in Acorn Hill at all. Now it was up to the town. If people on the board were in favor, how many people in the town were?

Fred glanced around the room. "This was the only item on the agenda, so I would like to call for a motion to adjourn the meeting."

Cyril obliged, his motion was seconded and the meeting was declared over.

Chapter Seventeen

A few minutes after the church board meeting adjourned, Alice let herself into the kitchen of the inn. Louise, Jane and Randall were sitting at the table, and when she came in they looked up, their expressions hopeful.

Her disappointment must have shown on her face.

"I'm guessing from the frown that the ayes had it?" Jane asked.

"The ayes had as many as the nays." Alice sighed as she walked over to the table to sit down. "It was a tie vote with one person abstaining."

"Really?" Randall spun around, the surprise on his face evident.

"Really," Alice returned, holding his gaze a moment. "I was hoping you would come."

"I couldn't make up my mind," he said with a forced smile. "You know me. On the one hand I'm indecisive and on the other hand I'm not."

"Would you like some hot chocolate?" Louise asked.

"Do I look that despondent?" Alice asked with a gentle smile.

"How about some lemon meringue pie?" Jane asked, getting up as well. "Maybe that will turn your frown upside down."

"I'm sorry I didn't come," Randall said softly. "I didn't want to influence the decision."

"Trey wanted you to stay so you could influence the decision for him. That didn't seem to bother you."

"Trey is my boss," Randall mumbled, looking away, a faint blush staining his neck. "If he found out I went the other way . . ." He let the sentence hang, then added, "I didn't think the board would pass it."

"Well, they neither passed it nor turned it down," Alice said. "And because we didn't make a decision, the board agreed to go along with whatever the town decides."

"Here you go." Jane set the pie in front of her sister. The glistening meringue with its browned swirls atop the bright lemon filling gave her heart a tiny lift.

"Looks divine," Alice said.

"And hot chocolate," Louise added, setting the cup beside the plate with a faint grimace. "A most interesting combination."

Alice had to smile.

"Perhaps we should go around town tomorrow,"

Louise said. "I would like to get a feel for what people want."

"Do you think it will help?" Jane asked.

"Other people must have already been doing precisely that," Louise said. "Otherwise, how could the church board have voted the way they did?"

"I tried to say my piece at the church board meeting, but it didn't make a difference," Alice said. "I don't believe campaigning in town would either."

"I suppose you're right," Louise said, "though I hate to feel that I'm sitting back and letting this happen."

"If it's what the people want," Jane added, "how can we say it shouldn't happen?"

"Aunt Ethel must have voted in favor," Alice said, feeling a little more despondent. "When Lloyd spoke I got the feeling he thought having the movie crew come into town was a good idea. I am sure Ethel voted the same way he did."

"And we know how Florence voted. That makes three. Who could have been the fourth? Or the abstainer?" Jane wondered.

"Not Fred nor I. I'm sure Pastor Ley was against it," Alice said. "Cyril seemed quite upset about the outcome, so I doubt he voted in favor."

"So that would leave June and Sylvia for the abstention and the 'for' vote. Though I can't imagine why Sylvia would vote in favor," Jane said. "Of course I haven't spoken to her for a while, so I wouldn't know how she feels."

"Well, she sounded as if she might vote for the movie, though I can't be positive about that. By the way, I invited her to come for supper tomorrow," Alice said.

"That will be great." Jane said.

The phone rang and Alice got up to answer it.

"Alice, this is Cyril Overstreet. I had to talk to someone about the vote. We have to do it again."

"Why?"

"Because I made a mistake. I'm sure that I put my vote on the wrong line."

Alice felt her heart sink. "I don't know if there's anything we can do about it now. We have recorded the numbers and Mayor Tynan will be reporting that to the town council and to the meeting."

"I'm sure that I made a terrible mistake. I don't want that movie made here. I like Acorn Hill just as it is."

"As do I."

"I was kind of in favor until I heard what you said about Fred's interview. I realized then how things can change. I started thinking about what could happen and I changed my mind. I think that's what confused me when I voted."

"It doesn't matter. What will happen will happen. Maybe people in the town will be against it as well."

Cyril sighed. "Well, I found out why Lloyd Tynan was in favor. That movie man offered Lloyd a part."

In spite of the turmoil of her emotions, Alice had to chuckle. *Oh, the lure of fame.* "Don't worry," she said. "We shall deal with things as they come."

As she hung up the phone, she wished she felt as confident as she had made herself sound.

"Who was that?" Jane asked when Alice returned to the table.

"Cyril Overstreet. He feels that he made a mistake when he marked his ballot. I wondered why he was so upset after the vote and why he asked for another vote. Now I know why." Alice giggled.

"What is so funny?" Louise asked.

"According to Cyril, Trey has offered Lloyd a part in the movie," she said. "If that's true, we can be fairly sure that he voted in favor."

"It doesn't really matter who voted which way," Jane said. "The decision has been made. Now we shall simply have to work around it."

Louise gave Jane a wry look. "Looks like you'll have your wish for more business this time of year if they film here next winter."

"Hurray," Jane said without any enthusiasm.

Alice smiled at her sisters. Since they had started the inn

they had weathered the settling in that comes with three different personalities living and working together. They had dealt with a wide variety of guests, demanding and undemanding, helping people whenever they could. If the movie was going to be made in this town, they would weather that change too. They had their home, they had each other and, more importantly, they had their faith in God.

⌒

Saturday was a quiet day at Grace Chapel Inn. Jane and Alice, with the help of Tabitha Harke's mother, cleaned the inn while Louise caught up on the bookkeeping.

Randall had left early in the morning and didn't return until late in the evening, when he slipped into the house and went straight to his room.

Ethel stayed away, which made the sisters wonder if she was feeling guilty about her decision. Of course, which way she voted was only a guess.

Saturday evening, Sylvia phoned and begged off coming for supper. She still was not feeling well. Jane was clearly disappointed.

The sisters spent a quiet evening reading and listening to the radio. Later on they caught part of a hockey game, but it was not as much fun to watch without Randall's commentary.

At bedtime, Alice again spent time in prayer for Randall. He seemed so confused. She tried not to feel as if their chances with him were running out, though he was going to be leaving on Tuesday. Alice reminded herself to trust that God would work His way in Randall. It was not up to her or her sisters.

Sunday morning Louise left early for church. She wanted to practice her music on the organ before the service began. Randall had joined them for breakfast, but when they invited him to church, he mumbled something about having some work to do.

Alice and Jane walked to the chapel and sat in their customary pew.

Pastor Ken made a few announcements, and then they started singing the first hymn. A gentle peace came over Alice. Halfway through the song, she caught a movement out of the corner of her eye as Randall slid into the pew beside them. He gave Alice a grin.

Kenneth based his sermon on Isaiah 55:12 and 13. Randall leaned forward, his hands loosely clasped between his knees, his eyes on Kenneth.

The pastor spoke of the signs God laid out for His people, how they were a reminder of God's renown and how God required their praise and attention. The people had to learn again and again to trust in the Lord, to put their faith in Him.

Kenneth's words held Randall's complete attention. Alice noticed the difference between today's and last week's service when Randall looked very uninterested.

Alice turned her attention back to the sermon. Yes, she had to learn to trust. Having the movie made in Acorn Hill was a small thing. It could turn out to be a good thing. It didn't matter in the long run. God was in control.

◦

"Do you want a brochure?" On Monday evening, Lynette stood in the foyer of the gymnasium handing out colorful leaflets. On the front was the title of the movie and underneath that the name of the production company, Starlight Productions.

Trey was on the other side of the doorway glad-handing people, smiling and keeping up a steady stream of conversation.

"Thanks, Lynette, but I'll pass," Jane said. "How is Dan doing?"

"Much better." Lynette said. "In New York now." She was already looking beyond Jane to the crowd behind, holding out flyers. Jane sighed.

Although Lynette and Trey had come into Acorn Hill that morning and were booked to stay at the inn for the

night, Jane had not seen either of them until now. She had
heard about what they were doing, though. It seemed that
nearly every one of the businesses in town had received a
personal visit from Lynette, Trey or Randall concerning the
movie. Jane was glad that she and her sisters had decided
not to do the same. It would be too much like a political
campaign.

She looked around the gym for a place to sit.

Alice and Louise had left for the meeting earlier than
she had, and Jane could see Louise with Viola and Alice
with the Humberts.

"I love your outfit," Lynette said, her glance flicking up
and down Jane's loose flowing top. "Very artistic."

"Thank you," said Jane, giving Lynette a quick smile as
she fiddled with a chunky wooden necklace she had put on
at the last minute.

She had found the gauzy yellow shirt in Potterston at a
vintage clothing store, and she and Sylvia had refurbished it
by stamping it with olive green and bright orange leaves.
She wore it over a marigold-colored turtleneck with flowing black pants.

"So things are looking pretty good for the movie being
shot here," Lynette said with a smile, tugging her navy blue
blazer straight. "I guess that once the church came on
board, the rest of the town followed."

"The church board was split fifty-fifty," Jane reminded Lynette. "The town might go the same way."

"We'll see," Lynette said with an arch smile.

"Where's Randall?" Jane asked.

"I don't know. He said he didn't think it was necessary that he come tonight."

Jane's heart fell. Though he hadn't responded to Alice's invitation to come to the church board meeting to explain more about the movie, she had hoped that he might make a stand here. But how could he? Trey was here tonight. At least at the church board meeting there had been a chance for anonymity.

Jane glanced around again, looking for Sylvia. She spotted her, moved past the milling groups of people and slipped into an empty chair beside her friend. Sylvia was looking at the brochure with a dismal expression on her face.

"What's the matter?" Jane said, leaning close to her friend.

Sylvia jumped, pressing the paper to her chest. "You scared me," she said, then lowered the paper and fussed with it, keeping her eyes on the print.

"I'm sorry," Jane said, glancing again at her friend. "You missed a good dinner on Saturday. I made roast beef, potato cakes, spiced beans and glazed baby carrots."

Sylvia gave her a quick smile. "Why are you torturing me like this?"

"I have no mercy," Jane said. "And I will continue until I find out why you avoided coming." Sylvia was a good friend, but a bit shy. Jane had found that the best way to talk to her was a combination of teasing and pushing.

Sylvia sighed and fanned herself with the paper. "I want to apologize for not coming on Saturday. It's just that I felt so bad . . ." she let the sentence trail off as she bit her lip.

"About what?"

"What happened at the church meeting. I just, well, I just got flustered when Mayor Tynan spoke," Sylvia's hands fluttered around, accentuating her speech. "He sounded like he wanted the movie crew to come and I was thinking about my business. You know, I lost some money when I was sick and I thought this would help, though that's clearly silly, it's a whole year away . . ."

Jane caught her friend's hand and squeezed. "Don't worry about it, Sylvia. You make your own decisions for your own business. If they make the movie here it will be good for our business too."

But the thought did not appeal to her at all. She remembered her big push to keep the inn busy over January and she had to smile. Being sick had set her back on her heels and she realized the value of a quiet time. Much as she hated to admit it, Louise had been right. "It doesn't matter, Sylvia. You are still my dear friend."

Sylvia smiled at her and Jane saw the tension that hunched her friend's shoulders loosen.

The buzz of conversation grew louder as more and more people came in and sat down. Jane heard girlish squeals and turned to see what the fuss was. Trey was handing out pictures to some of Alice's group of ANGELs. From their excited voices, Jane guessed the pictures were of the actor the girls had talked about during the skating party. Trey knew what he was doing, she conceded.

Just as she was about to turn around, she saw Florence sweep into the foyer of the gym followed by Clara Horn. She saw Trey slip on a pair of sunglasses, shove the rest of his brochures at Lynette and beat a hasty retreat. Florence just missed him and ended up talking to Lynette, her expression puzzled.

"I was so sure I saw him here," Jane heard Florence say with a peeved note in her voice. She was carrying her binder again. She turned to Clara. "We'll just have to talk to him afterward." Florence's gaze swept the gym. Jane quickly lowered her head.

"What's the matter?" Sylvia asked, glancing back to see what Jane had seen.

"Don't turn around," Jane hissed, grabbing her friend's shoulder. "It's Florence and she's got her binder with her."

"What are you talking about?" Sylvia whispered.

"We need to keep a low profile." Jane took her friend's brochure out of her hand and held it up, pretending to be engrossed in it. Thankfully Florence sailed on past and found a place nearer to the front.

Jane breathed a sigh of relief.

A few minutes later, Mayor Tynan stepped up to a podium that was set up on the gymnasium stage. Trey had reappeared and he and Lynette made their way to the front of the gym and sat down in the front row where there were still a few empty chairs.

Randall was right behind them.

"I'm sure I don't need to talk too much about why the town council called this meeting," Mayor Tynan said, his gaze flicking over the audience. He adjusted his bow tie, cleared his throat and licked his lips.

He looked nervous.

"As you all know by now, Starlight Productions is considering filming a movie here. Their decision hinges on the Grace Chapel board's agreeing to permit filming at the church. The board's vote was split down the middle, so it agreed to allow the vote to fall to the town. Now, before we decide on this matter, I want Trey Atkinson and his associates, Lynette Teskey and Randall Marquette, to talk to us about the movie."

Lloyd nodded at Trey, who was already bounding up the stairs. Lynette and Randall came up behind him. Randall had his hands in the pockets of his coat, his pony-tail hanging over one shoulder. He looked as ill at ease as Trey looked comfortable.

Trey drew the people's attention to the brochures. He talked a bit about the movie and what they were going to be doing, how long shooting was going to take and the advantages to the community. He sounded perky and upbeat and made it sound as if having a movie filmed in their town was the smartest thing that they could do.

Lynette explained a few things about the potential for local businesses. She listed some statistics relating to other towns where movies had been made and the likely income benefits for the town. It sounded too good to be true, Jane thought.

Randall just stood to one side, fidgeting.

Mayor Tynan opened the floor to questions. People asked about the movie's story, and Trey said there was a possibility for a sequel.

Wilhelm Wood asked how much purchasing the company would do locally and how much outside of the town.

"I own a tea shop that would be pleased to supply your needs," he said.

"Purchasing locally is our first priority, unless of course a local business can't supply us with what we need," Trey said with a quick smile.

Jane saw Randall roll his eyes and wondered what he was thinking.

"Let's take the Holzmanns and their antique store as an example," Lynette said. "I can see us working with them to either purchase or rent furniture. Because the movie is a period piece, we would require specific pieces."

"Will we get a chance to be in the movie?" Bobby Dawson called out from the audience.

"We often use locals as extras," Trey said with a wink. "Sometimes we'll give out small speaking parts. This might be your chance to be seen in movie theaters all over the country." A rumble of excited conversation followed this remark and Jane couldn't help but look at Lloyd Tynan, who was smiling at Trey.

After a few more questions and answers, Kenneth Thompson raised his hand. "Trey, you spoke about the economic benefits for the community. Are there any negatives?"

Trey laughed a little too loudly. "Having a movie made here is a great thing for the community. Isn't that right,

Randall? Tell the people here about what happens when a movie gets made in a town."

Randall bit his lip and glanced from Rev. Thompson to his boss. He looked down, as if thinking. Then, with a shrug he stepped to the microphone.

"There are a lot of things that happen, that's for sure," he said quietly. "I've worked on a number of projects with Trey and sometimes things get a little hectic." He bit his lip and toyed with his ponytail in a nervous gesture. "There might be more traffic than Acorn Hill is used to, more people walking around town. I've talked to some of you about this movie, about the reasons for making it." He paused, slipped his hands in the back pockets of his blue jeans. He straightened as he looked out over the audience.

"I understand that if the movie is filmed in the church, the church will be compensated," Rev. Thompson continued.

"That's true. I know the church is a little short of money. You will get paid quite a bit on top of the renovations. There will be . . ." Randall hesitated, ". . . other expenses, though, that are hard to pin down."

"Like what?" Kenneth pressed.

"Electrical bills for one thing. You need to keep an eye on them."

"I don't understand what you are saying."

"Neither does Randall," Trey said, inching closer to the

microphone, as if trying to push Randall away. "Any extra incurred costs will be discussed with the parties that are involved."

This sounded suspiciously evasive. Jane stood up. "Randall, can you explain in ordinary language what is at stake for our town and for Grace Chapel if a movie were to be filmed here?"

He gave her a careful smile and glanced sidelong at Trey, who was glowering at him. He looked over the audience, and Jane could see when his eyes met Louise's, then Alice's. He straightened his shoulders as if making a decision, then nudged Trey aside and took over the microphone. Jane's heart skipped a beat as she realized what he was about to do. *Please, Lord, give him the strength and the right words*, she prayed.

"I think it's only fair to let you know exactly what you will be getting yourselves into if you go ahead with this project," Randall said, rocking back on his heels. "For starters, what Trey didn't tell you was that he wants to knock out the wall between the vestibule and the main part of Grace Chapel."

A general murmur followed this comment.

Pastor Ley stood up. "Why w-would he do that?" he asked.

"The space now is too cramped to get the right camera

angles. It will be replaced, mind you, but in the meantime the people of Grace Chapel would be worshiping in a building minus a wall. He also wants to shorten the bell tower. What he would really like to do, but thankfully can't, is move the church across the street."

The murmurs increased.

"That's ridiculous," someone called out.

"That's show business," Randall said, ignoring Trey, whose face was growing redder by the second.

Lloyd stood up and Randall acknowledged him. "Surely a contract would protect us?"

"The contract is drawn up by lawyers that have far more experience in the movie business than any lawyer from any town or city in Pennsylvania would have."

Jane could see that Randall was warming to the subject.

"In these contracts, the movie companies give themselves a lot of wiggle room."

"What other disruptions would we be looking at?" Lloyd asked.

"This town is going to be inundated with people and traffic, and I don't think you'll get as much business as you were led to believe. A movie production company comes with on-set caterers, trailers set up for the cast and crew. Many, many things that the movie company needs are bought in bulk and brought in because small local businesses can't handle the volume." Randall clenched his hands as he spoke and Jane could see him slowly getting more and more agitated. "I made mention of the power bill. If you've ever been on a movie set or on location, you've seen the number of power cables and lights and the amount of electrical equipment needed for filming. What is never made clear is who is going to pay for all of that. I can tell you right now, not the movie company. The people of the town are. Grace Chapel will.

I know your church board is having a hard enough time making the budget as it is. The electrical bill, if they shoot in the church, will bankrupt Grace Chapel in spite of any money it might get for having the movie made there."

Trey closed his eyes and took a slow breath. Jane hoped he was counting to ten, because if he wasn't, it looked as if he was going to throttle Randall.

"We could put that in the contract," Florence piped up. "The movie company pays for electricity."

"Remember what I said about contracts and lawyers?" Randall said. "Remember what I said about wiggle room? There are production companies in Hollywood who are notorious within the business for taking as much as they can and giving as little back as possible. And it isn't just electricity. Who pays for the water? Who is going to make sure the people of this town don't get inconvenienced because of this movie? Not this production company."

"What about the parts in the movie?" Bobby called out.

"What you need to know is that for every day of filming, you end up with about three minutes of usable material. You could wind up being filmed and later, in the editing process," he waved his hand in a slicing motion, "out goes your part. So it's very easy to promise that you will be in the movie. The cutting and editing is done by someone else, so it's their fault your part got cut out. You know when people say something sounds too good to be true? If this movie is made here by this director, you will find out the real meaning of those words."

Randall stood back from the microphone, his words echoing in the heavy silence that followed his comments.

Jane glanced around the room, relieved to see uncertain frowns on people's faces. Slowly some people started murmuring. Trey leaned over and whispered something to Randall. He was smiling, but Jane could see that it was a forced smile.

Then Trey and Lynette left, but Randall stayed on the stage.

He answered a few more questions and from the tone of the queries, Jane could see that people were having second and third thoughts.

She sat back, proud of Randall and of what he had done. He had probably lost his job, but she could tell from the smile on his face that he had found himself.

Chapter Eighteen

"Y ou, my dear Randall, are a star," Alice said, giving him a hug.

People were still milling around talking about the movie after the town meeting. Alice heard a few disappointed comments, but overall people seemed glad the decision went against filming.

"Trey didn't seem pleased with what you had to say," Louise said, lowering her glasses. "Indeed, he seemed almost apoplectic."

Randall frowned.

"Upset," Jane translated.

"I'm glad I couldn't see him from where I stood," Randall said. "I might have lost my nerve." He grinned at the sisters. "But I could see you three smiling up at me. And that helped me stick to my guns."

"You shot a bull's-eye," Jane said. "What you said really turned the meeting around. Trey was making it sound so wonderful. I'm glad you showed us another aspect of it all." She shook her head in disbelief. "Though I never thought it could be that bad."

"It could be worse," Randall said, rocking back again on his heels.

"Well, I am very proud of you, Randall," Alice said. She tucked her arm in his and, giving in to an impulse, squeezed it lightly. "You sacrificed a lot for our town."

Randall smiled down at her. "Spending a week here with you made me see what a good place this is. I'd hate to see it overrun and taken advantage of."

Alice felt him pull away and straighten. She glanced behind her and saw Trey come storming past a few clusters of people, pushing chairs aside in his haste to reach Randall, calling out his name.

"Marquette, you're fired. Dead in the water. Over. Career is finished," Trey called out before he even reached the young man. He yanked his sunglasses off and waved them in Randall's face. Because Trey was shorter than Randall, the effect was like a terrier barking at a Labrador. "I'll make sure you never get a job in Hollywood again. Ever." He made a slashing motion across his throat. "I'll never look at that script you've been working on. I'll make sure no one else does."

Randall just smiled. "You haven't done anything with that script in spite of promising to look at it for years. I just realized that you probably never would. As for my job, well, I haven't liked my job for a while now so you aren't taking anything away from me. As for never working in Hollywood again," he shrugged, "all I need for that is a hot concept and a must-see premise and my transgressions this afternoon will all be forgiven and forgotten."

"Never. You're over, Randall. You're toast," Trey shouted.

Randall glanced past Trey to Lynette, who stood to one side, fidgeting with a clipboard, obviously embarrassed by her boss's public display.

"You don't have to put up with this, Lynette," Randall said with an encouraging smile.

She looked down and avoided his gaze.

"We're out of here," Trey said, his angry gaze flicking over Alice, Louise and Jane. "And as for you, you three musketeers, I don't know what you told this kid that made him do something so incredibly dumb, but you lost him his job."

"I believe Randall made that decision all by himself," Alice said quietly. "The only thing we did was pray for him."

"See! You did have something to do with it." Trey stabbed the air with his finger, then spun around. He stopped as if he had just remembered something and turned back.

"Lynette and I will be checked out when you come back to the inn," Trey said loudly, and then, after taking care of this last bit of business, he stormed out of the auditorium.

People from the town watched him go and then looked

at each other as if relieved they had not let this madman take over Acorn Hill.

"Do you think he's going to stiff us for the bill?" Jane asked.

"I guess we'll find out," Alice said.

"I would like to go back to the inn right away anyhow," Louise said. "I invited Viola, Vera, Fred and a few others for a minicelebration." She gave Randall an apologetic smile. "Though losing your job is not really what I would call a cause for celebration."

Randall laughed. "You know, I think it is."

"Thank goodness I baked," Jane said.

"And if we don't have enough, I found the cake that I made when you were sick. It was in the freezer," Louise added.

Jane glanced at Alice, who shook her head imperceptibly. As soon as they got home, they would have to find a way to secretly get rid of that cake.

⁓

The next morning, Randall spent most of his time on the telephone. He put his car up for sale, cancelled the lease on his furnished apartment and stopped his newspaper subscription.

"Never read it anyway," he said to Jane as he hung up and scratched another item off his list. "I managed to find an apartment in Edmonton. Mom and Dad have some old furniture they can lend me, and my brother said he'd help me move it with his truck."

Jane leaned her elbows on the kitchen counter and grinned. "Sounds like you are well on your way to a new life."

"A new start anyhow. I'm still the same person so we'll have to see how I transplant into a different life."

"I think you'll do just fine."

The timer rang. Jane jumped and went to the oven, carefully drawing out a tray of cookies. "There, these just have to cool and we can have some with coffee."

Randall glanced at the clock.

Louise strode into the kitchen, glancing at the clock as she did. "Jane, where did you put . . ." she paused, then smiled at Randall.

"We're having some cookies and coffee," Jane said.

"You didn't need to make cookies," Louise said, walking to the refrigerator. "I defrosted that cake." Louise pulled a plate out of the refrigerator.

"That's great, Louise," Jane said with a feeble smile, taking another look at the lopsided cake. The icing had melted while the cake defrosted, leaving glistening puddles of frosting around the cake.

"My goodness, it's melting," Louise said.

"I'm sure it will be fine," Jane replied.

Louise took a knife and started slicing. Jane gave in to the inevitable and arranged the pieces on a platter as nicely as she could, hoping that the presentation would make up for taste. She added a few of her cookies and set the platter on the table.

As she did so, Jane heard a knock on the door and when no one came in, she went to the door. She was surprised to see Ethel standing in the doorway, fiddling with her gloves.

"I would like to come in if I may," she said quietly.

"Of course. You're just in time. We are having cookies," Jane paused, glancing over her shoulder as she stepped aside for Ethel, "and cake."

Ethel slipped through the door and stood in the warm kitchen, wiping the fog off her glasses. Jane felt confused. What had happened to their usually exuberant aunt?

"I came to apologize," she said quietly. "I feel bad about the church board vote."

Jane almost laughed. "Why should you?" she said. "You voted the way you thought you should. There wasn't a right or a wrong vote."

"I didn't think that Trey would want to knock walls out of the church," she said, a trace of the old Ethel returning. She shook her head, her red hair flashing with indignation. "I was a fool to be blinded by the idea of Acorn Hill and Grace Chapel becoming famous. I thought that I had learned my lesson with the television show and Debbie, but it turns out I didn't." She sighed as she walked over to the table. She looked from Louise to Jane. "Will my very wise nieces forgive me?"

Louise lifted one eyebrow at her sister and then laughed. "There is nothing to forgive," Louise said. "Now, sit down. Alice will be down in a minute and we'll have a cup of coffee with Randall before he goes. Alice is driving him to the airport and he is flying back to Canada."

Alice joined them at that moment, and soon they were all sitting around the table.

Ethel took a piece of Louise's cake, ate a bite, then frowned. "Jane, what is in this cake?"

Jane held her hands up in a gesture of surrender. "I didn't make it. Louise did."

Ethel took another bite and licked her lips. "It is very tasty. It has a most unusual flavor. What did you put in it, Louise?"

Louise looked at the cake, then at Ethel, and shrugged. "You know, I have no idea. I was making brownies and cookies at the same time and we were watching hockey . . ." Her voice trailed off as if she was trying to remember. "I mixed up the ingredients. I think that's why it turned out lopsided."

Curious, Jane took a piece and tasted it. Ethel was right.

It was tasty. It had a soft texture and an interesting flavor of almonds and coconut. "You are sure you don't remember? It's delicious."

Louise shook her head, baffled. Then she laughed. "Is that not poetic justice? My one culinary triumph and I cannot remember how I did it."

"Maybe you should always watch a hockey game when you bake," Randall said with a laugh.

"Maybe I will just rest on my laurels," Louise said, shaking her head as she took a piece of cake herself. "I'm not so sure I want to spend a lot more time baking or cooking. I will leave that up to Jane, who is much more capable than I am."

"Well, I must say, Louise, this is very good," Alice said as she finished the last of her tea.

"Will the ice on Fairy Pond still be good enough to skate on?" Jane asked Randall. "I really want to have a go at it again now that I'm feeling better."

"The ice will hold for a while yet," Randall said. "Unless you get a really warm spell, you should be able to skate on it for a couple of weeks."

"Hey, Aunt Ethel, you and I can go out there together and make like the Ice Capades."

"More like escapades," Louise said.

Jane clapped her hands. "Alice, Aunt Ethel, we need to

mark this moment. Louise has made a joke." Jane grinned at her sister and sat back feeling well pleased with herself. Then she snapped her fingers, remembering something. "I'll be right back," she said as she left the kitchen.

She returned a few moments later with a wrapped box in her hand. She set it down beside Randall's empty plate.

"We don't usually do this with guests," she said with a grin, "so don't spread the word around, but we wanted to give you a little going-away present."

Randall looked down at the brightly wrapped box and a smile teased the corner of his mouth. "I . . . I don't know what to say."

"We're not looking for eloquence," Jane said, "just action. Open it."

Randall unwrapped the box and pulled out a fountain pen.

"It's one of the ones you admired," Jane said, "and fixed up. We wanted to give it to you as a memento of your stay with us and a reminder to you to follow your writing dreams."

Randall shook his head in surprise. "You gave me the Parker 51. This pen has helped make history." Randall turned the pen over in his hands, still grinning. "Did you know that General Eisenhower used his Parker 51 to sign the surrender that ended World War II?"

"See, as I said, every pen has a story," Jane said with a

wink at Randall. "I'll be expecting to see my cut on that joint project we were talking about. My people will talk to your people, okay?"

"What on earth are you talking about?" Louise said.

"Inside joke." Jane laughed.

Randall put the pen back in the box and carefully replaced the lid. He looked at the women gathered around the table. "I want to thank you for all you've done for me." He shook his head, running his thumbnail along the edge of the box with a bittersweet smile on his face. "I certainly didn't think I'd end up losing my job when I came here. Nor did I think I would end up rediscovering community and family." He stopped, overcome with emotion. "Thank you for helping me find my way back. I know I haven't been living my life the way I should and I've been running after the wrong dreams and plans. I hope, with God's help, to follow better dreams."

"We will be praying for you," Alice said quietly, placing her hand on his.

"That means more than you can know," Randall said with a smile.

He stood, and they all got up reluctantly. They stood for a moment. Then Ethel went up to the young man and gave him a quick hug.

He laughed and hugged her back. Then Jane, Alice and Louise all took a turn.

They walked him to the door and stood on the front porch as Randall got into his car. He waved until the car disappeared from sight.

$\backsim$

That evening, Jane, Alice and Louise sat in the living room. The lamplight cast a gentle glow over the room. Louise was knitting a sweater for Cynthia, and Alice was doing a crossword puzzle.

Jane had been reading, but put her book down and smiled at the sight of her sisters each cozy in her chair.

"We have a blessed life, don't we?" she said suddenly.

Louise looked up from her knitting and smiled. "We do, indeed."

"I'm glad that we're not going to have a movie crew traipsing all over Acorn Hill and Grace Chapel next year," Jane added.

"Do you mean you are willing to have a few quiet weeks?" Alice asked.

"Actually, I am glad because I have this great plan . . ."

"No," Alice and Louise said in unison.

"Not even for . . ."

"No," they repeated.

Jane laughed and sat back. "Just testing your reflexes," she said with a grin.

"Good thing," Louise said. "Of course, if you get too rambunctious, we could simply dose you with cough syrup."

Alice laughed aloud and Jane demanded to be in on the joke. When they explained it to her, she said, "No wonder I was sleeping so much. I was guzzling down that stuff all the time."

"It might have helped your recovery, though," Alice said. "A body does most of its healing during sleep."

"I don't need to do any more sleeping. I think I am learning to appreciate the ebbs and flows of the seasons," Jane said, smiling at Louise and Alice. "And I'm learning to be thankful all the more for my dearest sisters."

Alice smiled. "Amen to that."

Tales from Grace Chapel Inn®

We Have This Moment
by Diann Hunt

Ready to Wed
by Melody Carlson

Hidden History
by Melody Carlson

Back Home Again
by Melody Carlson

Recipes & Wooden Spoons
by Judy Baer

Once you visit the charming village of Acorn Hill, you'll never want to leave. Here, the three Howard sisters reunite after their father's death and turn the family home into a bed-and-breakfast. They rekindle old memories, rediscover the bonds of sisterhood, revel in the blessings of friendship and meet many fascinating guests along the way.

Carolyne Aarsen is the author of more than twenty books, including The Only Best Place *and* All in One Place. *She and her husband have raised four children and numerous foster children, and live on a farm in Alberta, Canada.*